Dedication

To all those who have travelled with me, shaping and reshaping the journey.

Acknowledgements

Many thanks to Emily Scally for venturing through, offering a valuable perspective.

To all those who read earlier works that never made it quite this far
To those Jobs that gave me more time and less work to do.

To the one who loses me to the words and worlds, love you.

Cover art: The author's original work. Prints available, please enquire via @hargest_ap_cymru on Instagram

So, we shouldn't listen to you then?

Did I say that?

Well?

At what point did I say, don't listen to narrators, story teller and alike?

The first bit?

Really?

Hmm

Try recalling what I actually said

No need to be so uptight

No need to be so ignorant

Alright so I wasn't really listening, you get that tone going and I just zone out

What tone?

The…my opinion is the central outlook and everyone else is wrong by degrees.

I do not

Hmm, okay before you erupt in your usual bloated defence and because I've heard this before…trust

Yes…trust…

Don't sulk

I'm not

Right

'Please press reset, malfunction has occurred, data stream corrupted…re-routing'.

The sun was not going to rise today, unrelenting and solid clouds cast aspersions of dystopia; beyond the clouds the sun was rising, it was the limited perspective of those under the mass of moisture that felt an oppressive countenance weighing on them. Well they would have, if this was not a regular occurrence. Familiarity was reputed to breed contempt; the people of the city of Pevnost had moved through contempt, bitter ignominy, disgust and had finally arrived at resignation. Of course, like any community inflicted by consistently dour climatic conditions, there were those who formed an optimistic view- the *could be worse crowd*. They looked at the limited information given to them from around the wider community of the planet they frequented and decided that persistent precipitation was something to be marvelled at or at least greeted with some sense of abandon. In some ways the perspective was not initially delusional, for the consistent level of rainfall, mild temperature and gentle humidity was a significant contributing factor in the rise of Pevnost's partner states into becoming a considerable economic, military and cultural realm in the planetary system they resided. Pevnost in and of itself was not a major player at the rise of the Gereza conglomerate, in fact the *tribes* surrounding Pevnost resisted violently for a significant period, but succumbed in the end to self-interest, military power and the sheer force of will that the Gereza conglomerate had during the period. With the *tribes* subdued, Pevnost's geographical resources were exploited and the city was the largest exporter of the fuel resources that propped up the Gereza for three hundred cycles. However, with new fuel sources and political pressure being applied, Pevnost was jetisoned into the wilderness.

Nevertheless, due to the structural investment and the savage disconnection of the surrounding industrial communities, a new city was arising from the gloom; well, the economic and political gloom. The climate was not so concerned about the comings and goings of men and their structures of power. Pevnost itself had been through many cycles of change and growth, but was now struggling to re-define itself in the dramatic changes that were affecting the Gereza conglomerate and the wider planetry systems. How mighty had fallen, the Gereza conglomerate...

Irrelvant Data stream, adjusting parameters of search, please wait...

The voice was generic, the voices were always generic; decisions had been made. It was considered bad form to establish computerised technology with an overly standard vocal pronouncement, because a line had to be drawn, particularly after the scandal of the Anurian presidency. The Liveka were not fans of being mimicked and to be impersonated by something they had created was barbarous, though the Liveka were widely acknowledged to have no particular sense of humour and to be overly sensitive towards parody. So, it came to be that any voice produced by an electronic device, from a humble handheld device to the utterance of the [near] AI's, which the Liveka used; was sterile, safe and non-Liveka. Malkus was old enough to remember when multiple lines of code inserted themselves into computer relays to express a myriad of different voices. Tones, intonation and accents expressing something more than the cold, non-specific, mundane speech that rattled forth from all the devices. However, Malkus, even a generation after, still understood the draconian regulations that held sway. After all, Anurian did turn out to be a robot.

'Reset complete, immersion in...' The voice without life broke into Malkus' reality and Malkus dropped in.

Pevnost, a city that wasn't a city; disguised by the rains that fell from within a space that intersected with sections of a different reality. Varses N'on let the rains of the divided realities carress his skin, cold, energising, irrelevant dust. Who would plead mercy from the storms?

Just because you could see the foremost threat, did not mean that you had the required compassion to prevent it. In fact, neutrality was an interesting position to take when *world-storms* collided. They were frightful events, cataclysms that had changed the course of civilisations and rendered destruction on planet wide scales. However, they were irreverently inconsistent, not in the sense that the storm petered out before arrival; no, instead the nature of the destruction varied wildly. Varses had witnessed a tree falling in a forest being the extent of the devastation. While in the meantime, part of the same storm cut a planet in half. It wasn't as if warning the unwitting populous of the city would change anything, at least not so Varses understood and he was not a being who sought to waste energy. A minimal use of muscle, sinew and fluids, were not so much an art form perfected but an inheritance and lifestyle. His current choice of lifestyle was coherent with his ancestral history, but delving back into the stories of generations was not an efficient thing to be doing, particularly with the assignment approaching.

Being the death of a person was an intimate experience, details of the person's life were recorded, observed and analysed. Patterns of behaviour extrapolated, effective points of execution surveyed, considered and finally decided. Tobias Enderlock, humanoid, non-'Caucasian', just under two metres in height, a healthy eighty-four kilos, maintained through study and practise of physical combat. Facially he was defined by large green eyes, which were overhung by a prominent brow and split by a ridge of a nose. Toby had enhanced his physical inheritance by perfecting a particular scowl that had intimidated a number of allies and enemies alike. Not that he was given to scowling, he just found it effective when in the employ of his benefactors. His few friends knew him for the mischievous smile, a warm personality and genial manner; his enemies despised him as a cold-hearted bully. Working for a global initiative fund required a mild form of split personality, a mechanism to cope with the sheer sadomasochism of managing the resources of the sphere of minerals which Tobias' people called home. Well in some quarters it would be considered a mild split, in reality Tobias had to entertain a very strict regime of exercise to excrete the toxins that built up through his work time. Tonight, was no different as he cut through the Lakeland Park. The lake and the surrounding park were one of the many Greenfield areas in the city of Pevnost, saved from the ravages of the industrial era by those who were financially benefiting from the massive exploitation of mineral resources in the surrounding area. In that sense Tobias was continuing a long-held tradition of using rHath Park as a site to expel the physical build-up of the stress involved in managing an economy where minerals and people were both commodities.

rHath was a manmade lake, which was bordered by stately houses, surrounded by a tram system and marshalled by the local fawner. A pathway encircled the water and it was on this trail that Tobias jogged, his frame covered in sweat and rain, his exercise clothes drenched by the combination. Tobias was not one to be put off by a little extra moisture when exercising; he always felt that, psychologically, it helped to 'wash away the day', as his body pushed the toxins of such caustic decision making out onto his skin. Though it did require extra effort to transport the weight of his clothes and keep traction on the slippery surface of the path. Such was the extra exertion that Tobias changed the route markers slightly and his second stretch point was by a copse of trees that had grown over from the small island on the northwest shore of the lake. Also, his right calf muscle was sending signals of minor distress and so coming to a stop was a relief, hopefully one of the regimented stretches would release the muscle and the signals would stop or at least allow him to manage the pain so that he could finish his run. Halfway through his second set of stretches, the calf muscle no better, he sensed the presence behind him. It was a mild surprise; Pevnostians maintained a certain level of mobility when it came to days of persistent precipitation, they usually stayed indoors, few exercised and less still at nearing midnight. To add to this, Tobias had been completely unaware of the person until that moment. Smoothly moving from his stretching to greet the person who was now in close proximity, Tobias' vision blurred ever so slightly as he returned to his full height and for an instant, he thought he saw himself standing right behind him. Then he blacked out.

Waking up from a faint is a varying experience. Tobias had passed out twice before; once due to illness and the other due to taking a mistimed strike from a sparring partner. Both times he had returned to consciousness with medical staff in attendance. Tonight, only the shadows of the trees greeted him, and the persistent rain acknowledged that he had returned from the land of faint. Checking that his fall had not caused any damaged, he could only feel the background pain in his right calf muscle and a non-significant drop in his body temperature. From this information Tobias decided that the faint had been minor and that he had only been unconscious for the shortest of times, after all the dangers of losing consciousness were exponential and for all his superficial checks, he decided that there was no lasting damage. Slowly he regained his feet, finding a pain in his elbow and side where he must have slumped to the ground. Gingerly starting back to his home, at a walking pace, he decided he would see the medic in his office in the morning.

"Still having trouble engaging Malkus?"

The voice rattled Malkus from the information stream, did they not understand his methods by now. Yes, there was a time constraint, but his record surely gave him some kind of anonymity to work as he saw fit?

"The consensus is that this is an irrelevant data stream, we know what happens; how Tobias was replaced by the shape shifter and the consequences of that. It has been reviewed to the Elders satisfaction. What we have is a *live* situation and we need you to focus on that…we should not have to repeat *what* is at stake." This was not in any way a metallic voice; the harsh demanding tones came from the amassed paranoia of his handler- Ki-Regus. Malkus had never seen Ki-Regus in person, every personal detail about the handler was kept from the DRAs for their own protection. Massive complications could abound if the DRA stumbled across the handlers while moving through a data stream, having such pertinent information reversed the roles and lead to significant disruptions. Nevertheless, Malkus did not need information on Ki-Regus to establish a different power structure. Be it an intentional oversight or a game being played on Ki-Regus, Malkus and Ki had spent far too much time together. It was not a positive relationship, but strapped into the machine, Malkus still managed to manipulate Ki.

'Handler Regus, I *understand* the nature of the surrounding circumstances and recognise the resources being drawn to facilitate a solution to the impending crisis, however would it not be remiss of me to revise my calibrations in regard to the accents involved? After all, how would it look to the Elders for us to have *missed* a crucial piece of information because the compilations of the data stream are accented in a particular manner…" In many ways Malkus found it all too easy and slightly disappointing at how simple Ki-Regus fell for this little manoeuvre, the handler's fear of the Elders' enforcers obscuring her to the game.

"The situation..."

"Is *delicate*, as much as it is pressing, handler. Varses is a known convergence point for data streams regarding the crisis and if I can narrow down the nature of this information then we will have a base line with which to traverse." Malkus could almost hear Ki-Regus' thoughts about how to counter this argument, but Ki's position was distinctly untenable. Even now this would be seen as an unnecessary breach of discipline and a distraction of an asset from interacting with the data stream. "After all, as impending and obvious as the crisis is, if we come upon a vital piece of information, then you will be *heralded*."

"Stop playing to my vanity Malkus." This was a surprising turn of events; clearly the impending doom of the *world storm* was drawing the handler to some sobering conclusions.

"Fine Ki, explain to me how following the Elder council search parameters has worked out for us thus far?"

"Malkus, this pause is seen as an unnecessary delay as it is...do not make it an infraction." Ki warned, but Malkus knew his freedom, awaiting an answer to his question. "The council's parameters have been put in place by the most learned of our Elders..." Ki responded, but Malkus let the silence continue to ask the same nagging question.

"Malkus, *please*?" It was a hollow victory, Ki wasn't even trying; perhaps if she had been subjected to the sheer scales of brutality, destruction and death, which was normally viewed and processed by the DRAs, then her view on annihilation may have been less dramatic.

"Trust me Ki." And Malkus let the silence play again.

"Okay, okay...Malkus, is there any way you can do a split search, focusing on the main parameters?" What Malkus would never reveal was the glee that he felt, he had been split search for many, many cycles and still the handlers knew nothing of it.

"It's possible,"

"Then do it..."

"It may be costly..."

"Let it be Malkus, you've won; now find us all a solution." Ki sulked just a little and without further hindrance Malkus returned to the Data Streams.

<u>Varses, Third Rock from Energy Source, 4.56 data stream</u>

Varses had learnt early in his business life that assassination never suffered from a diminishing return. Death begat death, from the natural to the darker arts; there was something organic about death and on numerous occasions he had exploited the repercussions of a completed assignment. The Tobias Enderlock affair had actually been a particularly fruitful assassination: executing the board of the Heymore corporation had a catastrophic effect on the global and inter-global markets, which in turn saw the internal governmental structure fragment and unleash a wave of panic. Emotions, in the tense situation of inter-global markets, were a devastating weapon. The right use of tone, casual inference and suitable ear, would guarantee a suitably explosive reaction. For which some existed. For instance, resource markets devoured the carnage, the despair and the drama. Regulated or unregulated, they were not about benefiting society, it was exploitation of the moment; gaining, grasping and acquiring as much as possible. It was about consumption, not the miniscule concerns of business, corporation and multi-global enterprises. Varses was always impressed by the sheer *savagery* of the market and those who begged its gods for succour by sacrificing others in the process. What seemed unapparent to those who served at the temple called the market, was the utter destruction that their emotion unleashed upon the world around them. Occasionally there were up risings, political movements that attempted to balance the avarice of the market, but in the end the temple overpowered any redress and continued to consume.

The wave of panic, instigated by the death and summary execution of (patsy) Tobias Enderlock, was spurred on by the market and its tentacles of consumption. Enveloping the governing forces of several global infrastructures, the wave unleashed a resource attainment conflict. Surprisingly, mass conflict was not a particularly affluent arena for an assassin; governments tended to be unapologetic in wartime; using special forces, agents and all manner of assorted options to kill the opposition targets, meaning that specialist expenses and the need to keep up appearances went by the wayside. However, there were always those playing the long game; some seeking to exacerbate proceedings, steer the conflict in other directions or occasionally bring a halt. Yet the biggest payers, in Varses experience, were those taking an opportunity to express personal vengeance. Varses had become less fussy about who he worked for, he was not seeking to form a reputation and so varied his employer and assignments to manage his profile. Not everyone took to assassins and only the vain sought to be pursued by law enforcement, bounty hunters, other assassins and vigilantes. Of course, being able to mimic other assassins was useful when misdirecting any who did pick up his trail, but that was not something he was overly fond of doing. Though at one point, he'd explored the edge of his vanity by creating a celebrity assassin on a small world. After a generation of killing as *'The Cobra'*, a body pertaining to be *that* assassin had washed up dead with a suitable number of wounds to his body. No one really investigated the death; they were just happy that killings had stopped and someone was dead. Sometimes, between assignments, Varses toyed with the idea of reincarnating the *Cobra* on another world; but today was not the day, today he was killing a banker.

Elmore Desachi, twenty-eight solar cycles, born into the Desachi family of the Enic tribal line, educated in a private college and taking up a post at one of the largest global financial institutions, he had thrived. However, thriving in that volatile and all-consuming environment of the market meant that you made enemies. It was considered a requirement if you were to *be* someone of status, but there were times when the enemy was too big, utterly ruthless or completely unexpected- or all three. Clearly by the lax security and the cliché playboy attitude that young Elmore displayed, the latter type of enemy had called in the services of Varses. Nevertheless, Varses remained professional: he tracked the man's movements, correlated what passed for Elmore's routine and established the ideal point for interception and execution. Desachi worked in the centralised financial area of the central conurbation of the Gereza conglomerate. He had three forms of accommodation in the area, a family flat that was available to all members of his family, a place to entertain clients and his concubines' residence. Elmore had inherited a significant portfolio of residences outside of the central conurbation, but they were exclusively for his young family and he only visited on weekends. Varses had entertained a transportation accident, as Desachi had travelled to his family's abode, but the financier's prime female companion retrieved him from the conurbation and relayed him to their home. One of the few stipulations of the assignment was that there could be no collateral damage; it was a stipulation that Varses happily agreed to, more out of a personal sense of professionalism, than a concern for the wellbeing of those surrounding a target.

So, the regular journey to the concubine became the interception and execution point, a journey of just over twenty minutes by foot or public transport. Personal transport was consistently indeterminable; as the volume of transport versus the distance of commute was an equation that the conurbation had failed to solve. Elmore was more efficient; adjusting the journey to his concubine's residence into a stress management exercise. Removing the perquisite fashion of his employment, Elmore jogged at least three times a week to the concubine's residence, following a similar route; which, at first purveyance, rodents would have passed up as unnecessarily complicated. Varses admired the elegance however, because at no point was the route, he jogged invisible to the internal security of the conurbation or any attached family security services. It was a precaution and a subtle acknowledgement of the water in which the financier swam, though for Varses it was a minor complication. The execution would have to be timed correctly aiding Varses' departure from the scene and assuring that no medical assistance could arrive to complicate the financier's death. Therefore, on a wet night, the jogging financier paused, as he had a hundred times before, to stretch his calf muscles. Varses, wearing a wide brimmed hat and a long dark summer coat, stepped from the few shadows cast by the street-lamps and moved in on his target. His weapon of choice was a high calibre handgun from a planet thousands of light years away; to cushion the sound the muzzle was encased in a small plastic bottle filled with gas. The target did not notice his approach, due to the rain's insistence and the sound of the passing night. Varses was five paces away, as the financier straightened up to acknowledge the presence of another person on a cold, wet, lonely night.

In moments like this, Varses understood the myths that surrounded death; its appearance as an arbitrary force, with unyielding insistence on extinguishing what was regarded as life and replacing that with itself. Varses stood as a reaper, it mattered not the perceptions of others and the reaction to what was about to happen; in this moment he was *death* personified, in lapses he wondered if virus', germs and other diseases had the capacity to understand the stead in which they stood. Varses did not however, lapse at the moment of execution; one smooth action lifted the handgun to the height of the banker's chest and he double tapped the trigger. In the instant of the financier's confusion, three hollow point projectiles alighted from the handgun, slash through the plastic of the bottle and accelerated over the short distance to carve their way through skin, flesh, bone and then explode through the back. The financier's biological system barely had time to register what had happened, as two of the three hollow points had collected large amounts of the heart and sprayed them over the pavement behind him. Instantaneous signals attempted to react, but the horror of the injuries overloaded the brain and the late Elmore Desachi slumped to the floor, blood gushing to mingle with the rainwater.

Varses, with the dignity of a funeral director, moved to the side of a rapidly bleeding out assignment and fired another bullet in the skull, which finished its journey by burying itself in the pavement. He then dropped the weapon and moved away from the scene: the optimistic response time would be eight and a half minutes, as the execution point fell between the scope of two different surveillance devices, and so clarifying what was being broadcast would be more difficult.

Nevertheless, Varses respected the security of Gereza and was working to a six-minute time frame. Walking at a brisk pace, Varses cut into the next street, unbuttoning the coat as he went. Shortly after he moved under another of the surveillance devices and rolling the coat into a ball, he launched it over the device, ten metres from the ground. Preplanning was the mark of a safe departure from the scene of an assassination; Varses had discretely hidden a change of outfit in a bag behind a low wall, adjacent to yet another surveillance camera. A quick glance in all directions, ensuring solitude, and he retrieved another rain coat, a different style of hat and slip on shoes. In addition, he picked a bottle of specialised cleaning fluid from the bag and washed his hands; the handgun was untraceable, but the residue of the explosives used to project the bullet was not. He washed his hands, forearms and face before placing the coat, hat and shoes on.

Retrieving the discarded items and placing them in the bag, he returned it to the original hiding spot and set off towards a public transport stop. Only two actions remained, first he turned his skin from a shade of brown to a light shade of pink- the local security were known for focusing on skin and ethnicity- and then turning back onto a through road he pressed a button in his new jacket. Behind him the bag and the coat began to dissolve as a chemical was released. Still no obvious response from the conurbation's security, Varses continued to move at a relaxed pace; running would only attract observers to notice his movements, though the conurbations populace were not given to noticing much of their surrounds. As previously stated, preparation was key to a clean departure and earlier that day Varses had used his current disguise in the area, the hope being that any observer would draw simple conclusions about his presence in the area. Two thirds of his way to the public transport stops, not the most immediate to the execution spot, the sirens of local security could be heard approaching at high speed. seven minutes and three seconds, Varses was impressed. A minute later, a single person medical bubble vehicle, accelerated past him as he waited to cross the road, thirty seconds after that a more militarised looking vehicle headed in the same direction. Shortly after Varses used a credit paid card to move onto a public transport vehicle and was whisked away into the city, from which he would leave the planet and the star system. The world storm was at hand.

All you really need to know is that a really well worked conspiracy is never discovered, unless those who considered it, *intended* for its discovery. Of course, there is a tension in the use of the word intent, but a conspiracy's revelation suits the purposes of those who are working the angles. In cultural mythology, it is all too often portrayed that an individual, through certain characteristics, could expose an organisation. *This* however is an idealised perception to give hope to the masses and lead them *away* from asking the questions that would undermine such conspiracies. Anytime a conspiracy is uncovered by a hero, it is because a member or members of the conspiracy are engaging an agenda of their own. Sometimes those agendas will be to undermine or *expose* others within the conspiracy. Even potentially execute a conspiracy within a conspiracy, but often it is the nature of *conscience* that disrupts the fluid movement of a disguised power play. Of course, this does not mean that those involved in the conspiracy are openly aware that their conscience has decided to betray the best laid plans. No, often it is the conscience that has been long ignored that slips through the cracks in a conspirator's personality and unravels the machinery. The art of self-sabotage can never be underestimated, be it the lethargy of pride, the confession of morality or a simple act of *forgetting*, the conscience will finally have its way. It has been known for conspirators to be *relieved* at their discovery, a perverse pleasure in the 'weight' being lifted from their shoulders. We have mixed emotions towards these 'fallen' conspirators, for mostly their release leads them into bondage of some kind and it could be argued that all they have done is exchanged the responsibility of power for a *different* type of power. For within the revelation of the conspiracy and the punishment of those involved, a community must come to terms with the knowledge that such an act of conspiring has been *born* and *perpetuated* in their ranks. Suddenly the conspirators have turned the light on those conspired against, they can present themselves as victims, but on some level, they were complicit in the conspiracy, even if it was through ignorance. The most pitiful, above any other, conspirator, is the one who has intentionally exposed the conspiracy, for the good of the people, only to find that the people are comfortable in their complicity. (The conspiracy of silence is perhaps the most powerful and completely terrifying of all conspiracies.)

For instance, once upon a time, a government was revealed to be using illegitimate forms of surveillance to gain information upon their rivals. A man within the conspiracy released this information to a public forum; at a superficial level it caused massive changes within the leadership of the offending party. Now in the opinion of some, the people of this democracy *should* have realised that this activity was not just the act of a rouge group within their government; instead it was the symptom of a *disease* running throughout the whole system. The disease, being a military industrial state that had become all powerful, was obliviously ignored by the 'people', who continued to bleat of reform but comply with the machinery of state oppression. The truly necessary part of any conspiracy is complicity; it is the covering under…

Malkus. Hub Actual

Malkus knew he shouldn't have been there, but the lecture was particularly interesting, due to the magnitude of data strands that intersected with the speech. It was beautiful to see such a montage of energy: intersecting, collaborating, concluding, colliding and continuing along the paths of intention. In the past he would have spent hours drifting unnoticed along the streams, a leaf in the wind or a cloud in the sky, to quote someone he'd once listened to. However, those were the times when the *world-storm* didn't impinge on his reality, now, his every move, thought and flicker was scrutinised. Time was a religion that communicated no obvious rules and regulations but expected, nay demanded, you to obey. Even when you knew it was a construction, a reality within a reality, it still had a way of imposing itself. Malkus remembered a time when the religion of *time* hadn't been so forceful upon him, when he'd a freedom to express all his talents without them being noticed or conformed to the authority's regime. The *world-storm* had changed that- it was still changing that. He had been a *stream rider*, gatherer or a 'data retrieval agent', for thirty standard years and had actually heard of the World Storm in passing. Mostly it was termed an apocalypse or the end of days, but it was one of those filed pieces of information that was of little or no value when travelling the stream. It became significantly more pertinent when one of your fellow stream riders 'accidently' crashed into his own data stream and discovered, before perishing violently, a *world-storm* in the future of Malkus' people.

It was even more significant when you weren't sure when the 'Storm' would be arriving. As stated, Malkus' colleague's mind fractured, devoured itself and his body exploded before he could say anything more than- 'A World Storm'.

The first storm to directly unleash itself was not upon the world around Malkus, but within the leadership of the data retrieval agency. Panic, fear, accusations; after all, it was questionable that an experienced stream rider would 'accidently' run into his own data stream. Eventually, a plan was formed; the remaining data retrieval agents would attempt to use a wide-ranging search to isolate any reference to world storms, in the hope that they would find the string of information that would give them a solution to the *now* impending apocalypse. This seemed a particularly roundabout way of getting to the information, but a more direct attempt to uncover the information would leave the data retrieval agent vulnerable to crossing his or her own line and being obliterated while getting nowhere near the information. Malkus and, he assumed, other stream riders believed: if the supply of data retrieval agents was not so limited, then the council would happily bombard the timeline with agents- using them like cannon fodder. However, the retrieval agents were a rare product of a failed experiment: a genetic, cultural and scientific anomaly that Malkus' people had lost and rediscovered. In the recent past, the Elders of the Liveka had authorised an experiment into the nature of human consciousness and particle explosions, there was rumour that an unstable Elder had pushed through the experiment by investing their own funds. In addition, the site of the experiment was a small moon orbiting a gas giant of little relevance in an obscure system on the edge of known space, so if anything went particularly badly there was massive distances before a catastrophe could affect those who *mattered*. (Not that they were expecting one of course.) Nevertheless, the experiment appeared to be a complete write off, no results or data of any great value were returned to the Council of Elders in any of the first forty cycles. Not until the grandson of the original sponsoring Elder discovered his grandfather's documents did anyone investigate what had happened on Moon A. What they discovered was a project gone horribly wrong, death, destruction and carnage that had split the moon in half. However, in optical orbit of the moon was an auxiliary laboratory which had survived the carnage intact, the details of what was found inside remained off limits to all but the Elders of the era. Currently only certain Elders were privy to a redacted version.

The only real clarity could be found in that shortly after the discovery of the laboratory- the *data retrieval agency* was created. Formed out of a select group of genetically 'special' individuals, who were conscripted to work alongside a handpicked group of analysts, the data retrieval agency used the mysterious technology of the laboratory to travel data streams of multiple dimensions. Effectively, they used the breakthroughs of the Moon A Labs to gain insights into advancements found in other dimensions. The advances had been *immense*, across the board: medical, energy, military, health, philosophy. The impact of the advancements was almost immeasurable, it wasn't as if Malkus' people were cave dwellers. However, the details of the advancements had secured the long-term future of the people. Ironically though, throughout the seventy-five or so years of the agency, the stream had not revealed a way to create or multiply the numbers of DRAs. Malkus and his colleagues were unique individuals with chemical, genetic and 'other' markers, which appeared to only recur in a select group in a generation. The Liveka had covered a minor area of a solar system in citizens; Malkus' generation was over two hundred and fifty billion beings alone- the total population of the Liveka was ten trillion. They had only found six DRA's in the twenty years of his generation, currently there was only thirty-two active, fourteen in training and fifty in preservation, retirement or healing. Simply put, the *stream riders* were the pinnacle of his people, the foundation of their current golden age and rapidly becoming the only source of redemption- Malkus was *priceless*. He knew it. Not because the statistics were readily available or even that well known to Malkus; no, it was because of the way, even the Elders treated him with respect. He who had been born defective in the eyes of his parents, who would have been killed at birth in times gone by, the classic genetic mistake, was honoured by those who in turn were honoured by the majority of ten trillion members of his civilisation.

Such a position would normally have given to a mentality of pride and hubris, but it was the nature of stream riding that cut down the potential catastrophe of a rouge personality. The sheer *häftighet* of the data streams, the realities within realities, the beginning and end of universes, time being played out as a poem, song and an orchestral extravagance. It was terrifying as well, to see the violent birth and death of life, the abundant existence and swift retraction. The responsibility of such opportunity weighed heavy, not so much on the need to find information, but managing the knowledge, the visual experience and the recognition that as much as a stream rider viewed the streams, they themselves were part of the stream. Most of those DRA's in healing were there to recover from psychological disruption. Malkus himself had been into rehab on two separate occasions for minor issues, a case of transference to a heroic figure and over empathising with a disabled person in another data stream. They were dark times, when Malkus lost track of his core reality, which left his health to suffer and threatened his long-term mental stability. Retirement, even of one as young as he, was never out of the question and given his inherent inability to conduct any form of life outside of the agency, it was effectively a death sentence- at least in his own mind. The counsellor suggested otherwise, but Malkus was not given to that train of thought, he was not willing to sacrifice such a unique life. In his opinion, this motivation made him one of the best wave riders in the team; because it was his life, he had no plan 'B', he lived on the edge of one reality, viewing millions more. He also considered this quirk of thinking to be one of the reasons that he was so calm in the face of the storm, he had been facing a version of this storm all his life. So, Malkus ignored the panic, obeyed his masters' better suggestions and pursued Varses.

Varses. Planet A63921F, 2.31 Data Stream. Data translation required.

"Are you even aware of the beauty of the setting suns?" It was a rhetorical question; one would have to lock themselves away in a dark place to be unaware of the beauty of the triplicate setting of the suns of Creeus. A myriad of merging colours soaked every surface and shadow, spectrums of colour which satisfied the inner most places of those who surveyed them. Subtle differentiation of light painted in the slow decline of the orbit, golden strains of purple mixed across a pallet of orange that drew from the canvas of darkening reds. How golden the moment, as Creeus' triumphant beacons slipped for a rest from their vigil over the moon of Neelon. If you extracted Neelon from its orbit of the Dwarf planet Elsionthen, it would have been recognised as a planet in its own right, according to standard measurements. Made up of twelve continents, the planet was populated by around 12 billion humanoids, most of who lived in the southern continents where the climate was more conducive to the survival and increase of the population. The inhabitants of the moon-planet had suffered some catastrophic setbacks since Neelon had been terra-formed, including starvation, poisoning, flooding, earthquakes and in-fighting. Having lost the original conurbation to an earthquake and flood; early in attempts to invest themselves on the planet, the peoples of Neelon, roughly one million people at that time, had dispersed and effectively started again. Though for most, starting again was choosing to forget their extra-terrestrial inheritance completely, and digressing from the space-faring civilisation to tribal communities. Now, fifteen thousand cycles after the disappearance of the original conurbation, the peoples had a small number of spaceships capable of limited interstellar travel, six orbiting space stations and certain high-tech inventions that their progenitors would consider basic. Some on the planet continued to struggle with simple sanitation and written language, but on the whole Neelon would be considered to be basically civilised.

On a standard Neelon day, even as one sun would be setting, another would be rising. One would rest their eyes in the colour of the sunset and open them to see another sun rising only four hours later. However, in the night of peace, one whole day would pass before the horizon would whisper with the light of Creeus' blessings. For Duncan Eaves, there was no peace. His heart and mind were in turmoil, the setting suns were a marker of his diminishing options and the shadows of dusk were the encroaching boarders of his reckoning. All his life, he'd been able to outmanoeuvre, out-think and generally outsmart anyone and everyone. Yet in the increasing gloom of the abandoned ship-yard, Duncan found that his abilities were failing him. There was an old saying, 'step gently on another's toe and you won't break your own'. (It was a caution that in the act of living your life you would undoubtedly cross others, but the way you did that would have consequences). As it stood, Duncan had all his toes intact, but behind his dark eyes, the mind was *stalled* and fracturing in the sanctum of a derelict ship-yard. The area had the feel of an abandoned religious building; there were markers of long-term desertion, collapsed structures, discarded machinery and a thin cover of detritus on every surface. Even in the short time that he'd been there it felt as if the detritus was covering his thick brown hair, rigid face and drying peach pale skin. Any memories of the ship-yards community, which had thrived morning, noon and night, were gone. Replaced by animals who had claimed some of the empty buildings, leaving tracks, scents and even blood to mark their territory. Flora grew wild and had begun a long campaign of reclaiming the network of concrete and steel; undermining foundations, cracking concrete and forging new fields on the roads that once shuttled cargo. It may have been a refuge for birds and animals, for Duncan it was the edge of oblivion.

Standing alone, listening to the choir of wind haunt the corroded cavernous warehouses, he could find no inspiration or hope. The look of hurt, confusion and fear in his favourite wife's eyes froze most of his higher thinking functions; Duncan's chief of security had effectively manhandled her onto the boat. Their two boys wailing as the motor had revved into life, he'd been unable to watch them off, unable to wish them goodbye. He had refused to say it, because at that point he still believed that by dawn he *would* have a solution. Yet the more he considered the plight that his family found themselves in, the less he seemed able to link one thought to the next. Perhaps sending his entire family away had been a mistake, over the last few weeks he'd come to trust their perception, particularly when escaping his father in law. That had been a tense stand-off: Duncan, his family and servants- not on his Father in laws payroll- had left in the middle of the second setting sun and not looked back. However, a day and a half later, on the hills outside of the Asharan city, the White family caught up with them. They'd been leaving the Mandalay Scenic Hotel, a significantly dower establishment that only took tokens and had an odious smell of decaying standards. It was not a place Duncan would have considered boarding in any other circumstances, but he had young children to shelter and knew that going to any of the more significant hotels would have meant instant discovery. Mister White was connected; part legitimate businessman and part gangster; his sources would have been alerted by any electronic reservation and it would have alerted the family to Duncan's attempts to abscond. Nevertheless, even though Duncan had set up decoy families and attempted to leave little or no trail, his heart had sunk when his Father-in-Law stepped into the foyer of the hotel.

"There you are boy!"

Tall, dark, weather beaten skin, the *once* thick dark hair of Mr White was cut short and speckled with grey. He was handsome; a near symmetrical face, with large almond shaped green eyes, prominent cheek bones and a ridged jaw-line. Duncan wanted to hate that face, but whenever he looked at it, he was reminded of the face of his love. A woman of exquisite beauty, *the* woman he had worked, fought and lived for; *his* wife and mother to two of his children. Duncan had however managed to find something to *hate*, his Father-in-Laws nose. Genetic fortune had endowed his wife Eugenia with the slim nose of her mother, where as Mister White had a bulbous protrusion that had seen surgery but still marked him. It was a monstrosity and in Duncan's eyes was the true representation of the man.

Duncan's family had gasped with surprise, disappointment and fear as first they saw Mister White's arrival and then the entrance of his sons. They had hoped to avoid this conflict, for all had contravened the rules. It would have been one thing for Duncan to have abducted his family, but the reality was that Mr White's daughters had been *fully* aware of their actions. Duncan had tried to convince them to stage their departure, so if things came to this point, they could plead innocence, but they had refused, firmly, and Duncan had too much on his plate to try and convince them otherwise. If this meeting went badly then it would be painful for all of them, very badly and they would be severely punished, and Duncan would most likely be dead. After all it wasn't just Mister White's children and grandchildren that he'd absconded with; there was a fortune in the carry cases that his family and servants conveyed. It may have been earned by Duncan, but that didn't instantly mean that Mr White would see it that way. In many ways this day had been coming; from the moment that Mr White had agreed to Duncan's proposal to marry Eugenia. Now it was being played out in a third-rate hotel foyer; where the wood veneers on the reception counter were faded and cracked, the furniture in the waiting area was warn to the barest fabric, and the surly receptionist was slipping out of view. Ben, a babe in arms, began to whimper as the tension rose rapidly.
"You have some explaining to do!" As ever Mister White tried to take control of the situation, but Duncan knew him very well, over the last

two decades he'd observed every aspect of Mr White and behind the controlled fury was something Duncan had only seen once before, a glimmer of doubt. Duncan moved to meet his Father-in-Law, when he was a younger man, Duncan had considered Mr White to be physically imposing, but over the years Duncan had filled out and learned to stand at his full height. At two paces they stopped.

"What were you thinking, disappearing like that? They are *my* daughters and grandchildren, what possessed *you* to act this way, fleeing as if you'd committed a crime?" And there it was again. With the usual flair and exaggeration of movement Mister White communicated, but Duncan could see clearly the flickering doubt in Mister White's eyes. Maybe Mister White had finally listened to his sons, who had come to realise that Duncan had not so much committed a crime but had in fact brought restitution for the crimes committed against him. "If you'd wanted to return to your Father's house, well...well, I'd have given *you* a proper send off, we'd have rocked this town, it would have been talked of for years to come, instead *you* slung off like a criminal?" Mister White was genuinely hurt, and actual emotion was blending in with his usual parade of subterfuge.

"And to add injury to insult, *you* stole my wife's diamond!" Duncan had tried to remain composed, to keep his green eyes locked with his Father-in-Laws and show he wasn't intimidated,

"*What*?!" Duncan considered allaying his surprise, but any sign of deviousness could ignite the situation.

"The Imposia Diamond, for the sacred rituals is gone..."

"Look, Mister White, I accept that this wasn't my finest hour; but we both know who *you* are and how things work in this city. I'd heard rumour that *you* were moving against me and if I told you my plans,

well…" Duncan looked to his wives, "you'd have taken your daughters away from me."
"Rumours, what rumours, who told you this?"
"I'd rather not say, but I can *guarantee* that no one has your wife's Imposia diamond, if they do, well they're life is forfeit…"
"So, we can search your belongings?" It was not a request that could be turned down, even if it was nonsense.
"Go ahead," Duncan turned to his family "We have nothing to hide, don't interfere." Duncan looked particularly at his third wife Kartina, who was fiercely protective of the entire family, and his eldest son Ruel was of an age where he believed that he needed to prove himself. The Chief of security, Eli, noted this look and with a gesture two of his men moved closer to the possible places of conflict.
"Lucian." Mister White's youngest son and overall head of family security stepped forward. Whereas Mister White masked his hostility with a gregarious bravado, Lucian was forthright and *glaring* with intent. It had been an overheard conversation between Lucian and Mister White's third son Mayer, about Duncan's 'suspicious' success, which had been the final inspiration for Duncan eloping with his family. In addition, it was a point of server embarrassment for Lucian to have lost track of Duncan, four wives, twelve children and the entourage, if only for a day or so.

"I tell you what *boy*, if your benefactor hadn't visited me last night, this would all be *very* different." Mister White whispered the statement over the short distance between the two men, Duncan doing his best to maintain his composure on hearing of the *benefactor*, focusing instead on Lucian and two of his lackeys producing small handheld scanning devices. Duncan himself had used the device when they were securing a delivery from one of the central belt cities. It used a resonance field to scan packaged items; it was generally used on bulkier items, like crates, to give an overall picture of what was contained within, but if you programmed the resonance of a particular object then it could home in instantaneously. The search would be mercifully quick and hopefully Duncan and his family could finally be free of the lying, thieving, manipulator and his family of bulling collaborators. As for Mister White's whispered jibes, it gave hint to the source of doubt that Duncan had observed, but it was yet another confusing factor for Duncan, he had no friends in the city and no favours with anyone who would have so obviously staid Mister White's hand. He wasn't sure that the 'benefactor' was real or part of a fevered dream.

"He said not to speak ill or harm you…so I'm keeping my end of the bargain…" Lucian turned around, having scanned every person and bag, and shook his head with bitter disappointment.

"Bargain…bargain, you speak about *bargains*…" Something cracked in Duncan "I've been with you for *two* decades and here *you* are hunting me, *accusing* me of stealing, me…when Jerome's company ripped us off, didn't *I* foot the bill?" Duncan had swung round to unleash what he already knew would be a verbal assault; it had been coming for a long, long time. "None of *your* companies have failed to breakeven, even Trimec and when these companies took hits, *I* found the money…not *you*, *not your sons* or your daughters. I worked through endless nights and you, *you* thought it right and fair to change my wages, to *strip* me of bonuses, move me from company to company so that I'd *never* be calling the shots, just covering your son's fuck ups!" Mister White was caught; the conflict between wanting to defend himself and knowing that to respond was to draw down the *wrath* of Duncan's benefactor. Instead the older man clenched and unclenched his fists, the place was at boiling point and Duncan was pressing home his fury. Mister White's sons bristled, inching forward, waiting for a single sign from their Father to silence Duncan, once and for all, taking back everything they believed he'd stolen.

"I *earned* my wives; you *made* me pay every penny and when I asked them to come with me, guess what...they did not hesitate."

"Enough!" Regardless of what Duncan's benefactor had or hadn't said, clearly there was a line to which Mister White would accept no more abuse. "*Everything* behind you is *mine*; they are *my* daughters, *my* grandchildren, they are *my* companies, *I* gave you your security detail! When you arrived at my doorstep, you were *nothing*..." The slur was obvious, it took everything in Duncan not to strike out, "But...what can I do, these daughters and grandchildren are with you and not me..." In an instant the tone in Mister White's declaration took the air out of the explosive atmosphere, the way his body slumped at the shoulders knocked his sons back more effectively than any grenade. Duncan and his family were stunned,

"So here it is *boy*, we're going to sign a contract...you *love* these things," With a simple hand gesture Mister White's personal lawyer, Hampton, appeared from amongst the sons.

Duncan liked Hampton; he was unlike most of his profession, both in appearance and character. Barely two metres tall, he was rotund, balding, with a swarthy complexion and a collection of unkind genetics that had given him a large nose, mouth and ears. It was all too easy to for people to assume that his appearance correlated to his level of intellect, as was the culture amongst the legal profession and those who used them, but Hampton was a genius. Even if his clothing was tawdry, he had consistently made fools of those with far greater reputations. The reality was that he should have been a legal expert for one of the great houses of Neelon, but he had two great faults, brutal honesty and an unswerving stubbornness. His presence here meant that whatever document was about to be presented would be legally perfect and initially binding, Mister White had other legal representation for those parts of the business that Hampton refused to have any involvement in. Hampton came to Mister White's side and retrieving a legal pad he gave a single nod of acknowledgment to his client and then handed the pad to Duncan.

"Good morning Mister Eaves, you've looked better…"There was mischief in Hampton's small steel grey eyes, "you'll find that this agreement has three main clauses, *firstly* you are bound to my client's daughters, you agree not to marry any other women, to take no mistresses and to treat my client's daughters with the *upmost* respect and honour. *If* evidence is found of mistreatment of my client's daughters then my client reserves the right to *exact* vengeance upon your person and remove these, *his* daughters from your care." Duncan nodded his understanding; Hampton relaxed a little and continued, "The second clause is a confidentiality and competition clause, you are *bound* to silence in regard to Mister White's personal and public activities. You are hereby *forbidden* from communicating any proprietary or secondary knowledge in regard to my client, to your Father's house, media outlets, governmental or financial organisations. *My* client, on breach of this clause will *exact* vengeance upon your person by retrieval of all assets currently upon said person." Duncan, having gotten over the shock of not having a violent conflict with his Father-in-law, was not surprised by this particular clause. Duncan knew enough to bury Mister White; in fact, he probably knew enough to get Mister White killed.

"In addition, Mister Eaves, you and your Sons will not in the future take up or start financial or business interests that are in direct competition with my client's interests, in turn my client and his sons will not pursue interests in any locality you and yours set up residence." Hampton was beginning to flag; but the tension was dissipating out of the room, it was clear that whatever Duncan's benefactor had said, Mr White was making a clean break, Duncan knew what the next clause would be.
"Finally, Mister Eaves, you can never return to this city, *if* you are found within the limits of the city then your life is *forfeit*. In turn my Client will not pursue any course of action against you for the crimes you *have* committed and will restrict himself to the said limits. If my client is found to have breached this limit and crossed over, then my client will be at *your* mercy." The fury in the sons was now directed not at Duncan, but at their Father, murmurs and growls of discontent had been met by every clause. For the first time Mister White turned his back on Duncan and with one look the discontent was met and silenced. Graymore, Mister White's eldest son, acknowledged the rebuke and was first to lead his brothers and the security team out of the hotel.
"*Mister* Eaves, if you agree with the contract please respond appropriately to the legal pad." The legal pad was one of the cornerstones of the Neelon civilisation, as well as displaying the contract in the twenty-two major languages of Neelon, they also recorded vocal assent and took biometric data. Duncan took the pad, there were two or three points he would have sought to clarify under different circumstances, but this was a one-off deal from Mr White and Duncan was willing to sign.
"I Duncan Eaves, *willingly* accept the clauses of this contract and recognise them as binding according to the statutes of Neelon law." The pad was a thin tablet of electronics with a display screen, some were

holographic, but Mister White preferred the more basic model. Along with the display screen there was a small thumb patch, Duncan pressed down, it scanned his print and then a small needle punctured his thumb, drew blood and transferred it into a small internal canister. Duncan then handed back to Hampton, who stored the data and set it up to record Mister White's agreement. Hampton handed it over and Mister White hesitated, he looked to Hampton who *sagely* shook his head and with an exhale of defeat Mister White spoke,
"I Keefe Lucian Graymore White, accept the stated clauses of this contract and recognise them as binding, according to *the* statutes of Neelon law." Mister White didn't look up again; instead he pressed his finger, shoved the pad into Hampton's hand and with no other acknowledgement left the building, taking any final tension with him.

"Well that went better than expected young *sir*; your benefactor certainly is a person of great influence. I have rarely seen Mr White so rattled, nevertheless life takes us in separate directions, *I wish you and your family all the best...*" Unsurprisingly, Hampton was ever the professional, but there was genuine warmth in the hand shake exchanged and something of concerned disappointment in his eyes. The goodbye should have been longer, they would never see each other again, but Hampton had his place and so did Duncan. Far from the city. With a curt nod to Eli, Hampton was gone; and shortly after, the Eaves family and entourage departed the vile hotel for the abandoned shipyard in which Duncan stood alone.

In many ways the outcome of the 'meeting' between Mister White and himself should have cleared his lonely thoughts; after all there was no going back, Asharan city's boundaries were such that there was no way to traverse them by ground or air, once they had set off for the shipyard. However, what waited on the other side of the river was almost certain death. Duncan's past coming like a freight train and he was tied to the tracks. He had already attempted to allay the destruction of his entire family by splitting them up, which had been met with fury from his wives, but he could find no way of extricating himself. Even clichés were evaporating; his brother's revenge would be swift and brutal.

"Excuse me." *At last*, his mind was playing tricks with him, "Excuse me!" Actually, the voice wasn't some trick of the stress and desperation that Duncan was mired in, twenty paces away stood a *man*. He was roughly the same height as Duncan, two metres and somewhere between broad and slim. Due to the rapidly deepening dusk it was hard to make any more detail and Duncan had to shake off the fugue that had engulfed him, he'd completely failed to notice the man's approach.

"Are you *Mister* Duncan Eaves?" The man's accent was unfamiliar and his tone mostly passive, it was not anyone that Duncan recognised from Mister White's organisation and family.

"So, Mister White has reneged on his deal then?"

"I do not know a *Mister* White," There was a certain lightness to the stranger's response, which perhaps meant his brother was going to keep his hands clean or secure him before he could escape. "But I take it that this question is an acknowledgement that you are *Mister* Duncan Eaves and that *Mister* White, and you had some *kind of* agreement?"

"I thought my brother would meet me face to face?" Duncan awaited an acknowledgement and then he would run.

"*Mister* Eaves, I do not know *Mister* White, *your* brother or you. However it is *time*!"

"Sorry?" Duncan was now confused.

"*It is time*!" With that, the motionless figure in one swift movement; retrieved a hand gun from behind his back and fired. Everything was instantaneous, the sound, the flash, the shock, the confusion, the fear and the relief. There was no impact on flesh, the stranger had missed. "That *Mister* Eaves was your only warning…*run*!" Duncan's body took the command with all its might, he sprinted into the darkness of the shipyard.

As long as Duncan could remember, his life had been marked by conflict. His family seemed to cause and attract it; his grandfather was renowned in the region for leading a personal army against the overlords of Neblec and defeating them. His great uncle had survived the volcanic destruction of the cities of Edwards and Lehamann. His Father, as well as being an extraordinarily successful businessman, had been exiled from Revalia for social improprieties. And then there was his brother. Duncan could not remember a moment of his life when he wasn't at war with his older brother, apparently the spark of conception had instigated a conflagration for dominance. The struggle had eventually divided his father's house; his Father favouring his older brother and Duncan's mother taking his side of the affair. In hindsight, Duncan had come to realise that there were issues between his parents from before he and his brother were born, but at the time Duncan was pleased to have any parental affections at all. However, when you had one parents undying affections the reality was that you wanted the other ones as well, and anything keeping you from that was your mortal enemy. At least that was how Duncan and his brother looked upon it, there was no direct communication between the two siblings to confirm this, just a continuing campaign to embarrass, usurp and undermine. The first incident that came to mind was at the age of six; Duncan's brother had stolen his favourite paints and decided to 're-work' one of the family's priceless landscape painting. Duncan had instantly been a suspect; his brother had managed to come up with a twofold alibi: firstly, he had no access to paints. Unlike Duncan, his older brother had shown utterly no interest in pursuing artistic endeavours and thus had rejected any offer of art materials. And secondly, he convinced the jury of their parents that he had been elsewhere when the crime had been committed. Their Father had flown off the handle, though his mother had managed to deflect enough of the rage, for Duncan's punishment to be downgraded. He'd been grounded, which wasn't a particular punishment because Duncan preferred to be indoors anyway, but the second part of the punishment, losing access to his paints, was almost unbearable and completely unforgiveable. His brother's wink as he left the room drew furious accusations of innocence and a complete desire for revenge. Three months later, Duncan's mother had restored his access to paints and canvas, under supervision, but there was no restoration for his brother's crossbow. It was found bent and broken in one of the garages, once again the true culprit, Duncan, was never apprehended, but each brother *knew* the truth.

Sibling rivalry and petty childhood revenge was one thing, ordering an assassin to eliminate your brother was another. Regardless of the assassin's ignorance, about who had put a contract on his life, Duncan's conclusion was simple; his brother was not waiting for a face to face show down. Duncan understood why, as a bullet whizzed by him, plausible deniability. Though his brother would be un-impressed with the competency of the would-be assassin; the unknown figure had, as yet, failed to kill or wound him, and let him get to the cover of some empty buildings. Then again given the vicious threats that his brother had uttered before Duncan's exile, it would not have surprised him if this chase was part of the contract. Duncan swivelled away from his intended direction, slipped through a gap in the wall and into the building he had been skirting. His eyes had adjusted to the darkness outside, but he had to pause so his vision could find itself in the enclosed space, it was the *night of peace* after all. Some part of him had hoped that he had entered a space which would give him somewhere to hide, recover and think, but instead he found himself in one of the cavernous factories. It been stripped bare of every last piece of equipment. Quickly and quietly he started moving down the wall towards an open space that was a door. Adrenaline roared through his body and filled his ears; he desired to sprint but knew that with the lessened light he needed to be cautious. Though the place had been exercised of its equipment, it did not mean that the removal men had been clinical, and he couldn't afford to injure himself. Not that he was sure what he could afford; the chase was not freeing him from the mental block that had sabotaged him in the first place and should have ended his life. Though in a moment of clarity he realised the saboteur of this unending reality, which he'd fought every day, was *guilt*. It was more than a narrative; it was part of the substance of his being and he had a lot to be guilty for. Taking revenge on his brother 's cross bow was one thing, but Duncan had surpassed that with two calculated acts.

Firstly, though his brother had been the pride of his Father's house, in physical stature and martial skill, even he had one or two dirty little secrets. His brother was a drug addict, worse he had a genetic mutation that required him to have a strict diet. It was yet another of the family secrets that was protected by fire, but Duncan was an observant child and had soon picked up on his brother's flaw. However, knowing someone's vulnerability and exploiting it were two different things. An effective exploitation was about using the information at the ideal time, for something of value. On a night twenty years ago, not dissimilar to the one he was attempting to survive; his brother returned to their parents' villa, hours after the sun had gone down, exhausted. He'd been hunting for three days on their grandfather's Ussad reserve, which rolled out from the back of their parent's palatial villa, situated on the outskirts of Desma city. The hunting trip had been a disaster. On his first full day on the plain, Duncan's brother had managed to get lost, lose his pack and his weapon. It was a testament to his brother's skills that he'd made it back at all. However, his mistakes would still be extremely costly. He burst into the kitchen famished, thirsty, delirious and very much in need of his drugs. Duncan was cooking, both because he enjoyed the art and the main core of servants had gone to temple, with the parents, to celebrate the religious festival of Ta'l.

"Food…now!" In public, his brother was charming, urbane and witty, the darling of Desma city; in private he was a monosyllabic, *ingrate*.

Duncan had only prepared enough for himself, a local vegetable stew dish that both he and his brother enjoyed immensely. The smells in the kitchen must have been like some kind of torture for his brother; Duncan surveyed him with his usual cold indifference. However, to Duncan the sacrifice of the meal was the perfect point of exploitation, "What's it worth?" The war of attrition between the twin brothers left little room for compassion.

"Fuck that," Duncan's brother lurched from the door towards him and the bowl of stew, but the darling of Desma city's co-ordination was lacking. With a malicious grin, Duncan stepped back, extending the gap between him and his brother.

"Seriously Caesar, how *much* is the stew worth?"

"Fuck it Dunc, I'm *starving* to death here…" There was real desperation in Caesar's eyes, the smell of the food a torture that Duncan could never have planned for.

"I tell you what Caesar, I'll do you a deal, not only will I give you this bowl of stew, I'll give you some Diaze; if you sign *your* rights as first born over to me."

"Fuck it Dunc, what good are titles to me now…where do I sign…"

"Follow me." Caesar had always been short sighted, aware only of his prowess and reputation, he'd never really taken time to consider the realities of the world that heralded him and ignored his younger brother. So, Caesar followed Duncan to the study and for a bowl of stew and a quick fix, Caesar signed away any claims to the family. Nothing more was said between the brothers, though having finished his meal and popped his pills Caesar left the business transaction the most relaxed Duncan had ever seen him. Only years later, when Duncan's had tricked his Father into signing over the inheritance, did Duncan begin to gain inkling as to why it would be a relief to lose the rights of inheritance.

Death *could* be a relief; it was the second clear though Duncan had managed in hours and it shook him to a standstill. His life was a shambles. His riches had sailed away, his wives were at war with each other for something he couldn't give them, and all his victories had turned against him. He'd lived on his wits, his charm, his cunning; he'd paid through the nose to establish himself and it had brought him to a singular point of isolation, he'd only experienced this deep abiding sense of anxiety once before in his life, after his exile from his Father's house. Perhaps it was time to face the executioner and see what the next dimension had for him; did it matter that his benefactor *had* promised to protect him? Regardless of the past Duncan wasn't sure of the value of that promise. Yet, his benefactor was the same person/organisation/being that reportedly bailed out every generation of his family, but was it right to save him from Caesars wrath? He'd faced suicidal thoughts before, but there was something particularly seductive about the impulse; his brother would have his revenge, he would leave his family alone and they could live their lives in *peace*. He knew the word, but it never came with him, conflict, pain, retribution…those were words he understood, experienced and lived in. Death would silence those words and bring *peace* and it would be quick. After all the hit man, incompetent as he had been, wouldn't miss if Duncan just gave up. Yet it didn't sit right, in the shadows of the night of peace, past his responsibilities and deep inside, he knew that suicide or giving his life away without a battle was *wrong*. It was best summed up as instinctual; maybe for once he didn't need the clarity of thought that had defeated his Father, Brother and Father-in-Law, maybe he needed to become de-base and live. Perhaps it was time to turn the tables; the assassin had already shown a staggering amount of incompetence and had failed to hit his target with three attempts. The conclusion was: this was the assassin's first time and that even when the target was weak and vulnerable, they had frozen. Duncan was not without his own skills in personal combat, there was hope. He could turn the tide on his brother's assassin, and maybe he could turn the tide on Caesar.

The fourth bullet he *felt*, the movement of the air, the heat of the projectile, it was a whisper that shouted to all his senses and again

Duncan was moving. He'd been complacent and silhouetted himself against the massive opening of the factory door, but the would-be assassin had once again missed another perfect opportunity and to Duncan it was confirmation that the hit man's skills and experience were limited. Time to change the parameters of the pursuit, Duncan ducked and rolled out of the door and sprinted away. He needed a place to set up an ambush; to his left were another collection of large storage buildings like the one he was sprinting from, circling back really wasn't an option, but with this new attitude he recalled an office building three blocks to the west and back towards the river. Like everything else it was undoubtedly disused, but its space would in theory offer a greater opportunity to turn the tables. At least it was a plan of action, a plan to take back his life and wrestle it away from his brother as he had from the day of conception.

<u>Malkus; Hub Actual</u>

Don't trust narrators, story tellers, anyone who is casting a narrative where they want you to invest in what they are saying.

Finding Varses was not always easy, his ability to shape shift meant that often he slipped out of Malkus' view. It was frustrating and to manage this Malkus would dance away to a completely irrelevant data-stream. The stream itself was only a few moments long, a strange intersection in a discussion that led nowhere in particular. For Malkus, it was a pause in the pursuit; normally he would allow the two narrators to go through the motions, but in the current climate such an extent of time away from the plundering for information would be noticed. Though the Elder designated data streams were disappointingly sparse, Malkus had not withdrawn from the space to discover how things were. Ki would happily inform him of any positive changes, the current silence suggested that the other DRA's were finding information on the *world storm* difficult, or what they discovered only confirmed what they knew. *I don't particularly care if they have accreditation or not, actually the accredited are the worst;* having passed on the failure to find anything on the Elders data stream, Malkus had been given two new streams to pursue; one was potentially a mass of interconnecting streams, centred around a King called Kelias and the other was a tracking the life of a Professor Eddings and his pursuit of a Nestor Earland. The *world storm* didn't beckon, but Malkus would obey and hope that Varses was in a more obvious mood.

<u>Varses. Planet A63921F, 2.31 Data Stream. Data translation required</u>.

Duncan was now in position, the long sweep around the shipyard had been successful, though excruciatingly tense; being the bait to a trap you intended to spring, was no easy task. Concluding that his *pursuer* was both incompetent and unprepared, Duncan intentionally revealed himself in the darkness, making sounds that would clearly alert the *pursuer* to his movements. It had nearly been costly, halfway back across the ship yard the *pursuer* had once again attempted to shoot him, but had missed yet again. Nevertheless, Duncan waited in the shipyards offices and tried to compose himself. Exhaustion flooded his mind and he slumped into the smaller officer on the second floor. The preceding trauma of escaping his Father-in-Law, sending his family away and setting the trap for his *pursuer* almost wiped him out the moment he paused inside the office. The ground floor had been a write off, an open plan office left no blind spots to launch his ambush. However, investigating the second floor led him to discover a maze of interconnected rooms, any of which would give him an advantage when the time came. Yet he didn't have time to rest, his opponent was only shortly behind him and would soon be in the trap. Stirring himself once more, he slid towards the doorway and waited for the approach of the hunter. For all the assassin's incompetence, he'd not fallen that far behind and had taken the bait, his footsteps heard on the stone stairs up to the second floor. The analysis was simple: disarm, disable and interrogate. Surprise *was* his greatest weapon. Though he had a good knowledge of physical combat, his opponents were unknown and if the gun was not removed from the scenario then no amount of skill would matter. Duncan tried his best to still himself, but the adrenaline was back in his system as he considered possible scenarios and his potential death. He had chosen to *live*, but thoughts of death wandered in on each scenario. Everything had to be *fast*: attack, defence, death, victory. Duncan wasn't sure he could face the ignominy, shame and sheer brutality of a tortuous death; he ignored thoughts about the actual pain.

Suddenly his mind was clear. A heavy foot scraped the other side of the wall from where he crouched. Duncan's heartbeat rose and he tried his best to keep his breathing quiet. He counted off the steps; unbearably loud in the darkness. Duncan knew it was time, even in the deeper darkness of the office he perceived the assassins' entrance. *Launching* himself up, contact was around the kidney area and drove him towards the wall. Both men crashed into the wall as it buckled under the pressure; bulging outwards and denting with impact. In a millisecond

Duncan realised that he had made a glaring error: all his running, plans for ambush, focusing on the apparent weaknesses of his opponent, meant he had initially forgotten to arm himself. The *real* potential of his surprise was lost. Any opportunity to wound, cut, stab and harm, were now reduced to blows from his body. Nevertheless, Duncan drove a fist into the man's kidney and a knee into the thigh. Disorientation was his best change of disarming and overpowering his opponent. *Elbow* to head, everything connecting and finally he went for his opponents' true advantage- grasping for the gun. Cold metal greeted his fingers and with all his might Duncan ripped the weapon from the failing-assassins grasp. Duncan's world went sideways, pain sensors erupted through from his abdomen. His equilibrium informed him that he was falling back, and he took the would-be assassin with him- Duncan was now being assailed. Crashing to the concrete floor, vision flashed white and the gun flew from his hands, disappearing into the dark. Air flood from his lungs, but the adrenaline of his body reacted before his mind could engage with the loss of his advantage. His free hands rained two blows in the sides of his opponent's head, who responded by releasing Duncan and rolling away. What gain Duncan had was slipping away; perhaps if he could recover the gun then he could bring this to an end quickly. However, he too had been disorientated by being tackled to the floor, the darkness of the office wouldn't reveal the prize with ease. It was time to change tactic.

"*Wait*, look, I'll pay you *double* whatever my brother is paying." Duncan rose to one knee and looked to change the rhythm of the battle; maybe he could turn the aggressor into an ally and once again outsmart his brother. "Come and work with my bodyguard..." Duncan returned to his feet

"*Mister* Eaves, for all your analytical skill, you are not a great listener; I *do not* know your brother." The assassin was insistent, bringing his breathing into order.
"Well you might not *know* him, but he's the one who's put the contract out on me…" Duncan slowly edged away from his opponent hoping that he may stumble on the gun as he moved deeper into the office. It wasn't a massive room, but the empty space was more than enough to disguise the weapons whereabouts.
"Well it wasn't so much a contract as a verbal agreement." The more Duncan surveyed his opponent; the more things began to *concern* him. Firstly, the opponent was eerily calm, his voice, his breathing, and the stance were systematically composed. They had just clashed *violently*, Duncan had managed several significant blows, yet the would-be assassin seemed to carry no injuries. Something was *wrong*, actually a lot of things were wrong! Nevertheless, he couldn't change much until he escaped, hired or defeated the man in front of him.
"Look, I have a *family*, let me return to them and you can name your fee?" Another step back, but this time the stranger came forward, matching his step.
"Is *this* how it's always been *Mister* Eaves, offer the deal, offer again and again, wear your opponent down with words until they agree to *your* wishes? Do you do *this* to everyone?" The question stung and suddenly the analysis of the man's competency was very much in question. Duncan may have ambushed the man, but now it was turning in on him, he needed something- an edge. There appeared little physical difference between the two men and though this man had appeared incompetent with a gun, his recovery rate was just a little bit terrifying. Duncan needed a place to bond, an opening to show that they could get along, they weren't *enemies* and crucially that it would be

worth swapping sides. Yet Duncan couldn't see the features of the man's face in the dark and so placing his family heritage was out, as was any scent the man wore to mark himself out, as all Duncan could smell was himself.

"Okay, okay, look we got off on the wrong foot…you know my name, what's yours?"

"Getting a little desperate aren't we *Mister* Eaves. Oh, and by the way, my weapon only responses to my genetic imprint, so you can search for it as much as you like, it will be useless to you." Duncan stopped moving backwards.

"What was *really* disappointing was that you didn't arm yourself, you had plenty of opportunity and it would have made things more *interesting*…" Duncan's analysis of his opponent was now fundamentally flawed. An amateur may have shown a brashness to cover being blindsided and disarmed, but the response of the man was unnerving. The stranger was unmoved by entering an ambush, instead there was a calm preparation for anything that Duncan was considering.

"Though credit where credit's due, the ambush was a good idea and well executed for a *coward* like you. Must be a strange thing to actually get *your* hands dirty, well directly anyway." There was a glee and spite in the tone of the man's voice, which was slowly deflating the concept that Duncan had turned protagonist.

"Who the *fuck* are you?"

"That's more like it *Mister* Eaves," The man goaded and Duncan snapped, launching himself at the him, yet the mystery man made no attempt to avoid the collision. Duncan's drive took them out through the office doorway and thumping into the hallway wall beyond. Pursued, cornered, embarrassed and becoming desperate, Duncan's instinct was in charge. His hands sort out the man's throat. In response, the man forced him away, Duncan crashing into the wall he'd once hidden behind. This time Duncan anticipated and having bounced off the wall he leapt forward, his knee taking the lead. Contact was made, but the man deflected the lunge away from himself. Duncan had to place his hands out to cushion the resulting connection with yet another wall.

"Is this part of the contract, to humiliate *me*?" Duncan growled as he regained his feet.

"Why don't *you* run away again and see. You're good at running away?"

Fury emerged, Duncan's body attacking with fist and kicks. All of which seemed unbelievably slow, as the man blocked each one. Nevertheless, the ferocity of the assault drove them down the corridor. Glimpsing equilibrium of thought, Duncan was surprised by the stamina he was showing. Yet so few of his blows actually connected that he was recognising the futility. At some point however the man would tire, hopefully before he did- the assault continued. After roughly thirteen more attempts to strike with fist, elbow, shoulder, knee and foot; Duncan lost his balance and crashed a fist into an empty office wall. Whatever material the office walls had been made of was cheap and the particular wall Duncan struck had suffered badly- his fist went clean through. It surprised both men and they paused; Duncan swore he heard the other man stifle a snigger, yet he didn't attack. He didn't need to, pain and exhaustion ruptured through Duncan, his hand throbbed and was potentially broken, every muscle protested, and his vision blurred.

"Well that is disappointing *Mister* Eaves, you were doing *so* well."

Duncan wanted to respond but he was feeling faint. "Breathe *Mister* Eaves, you'd be best advised to try and slow your heart rate…"

"Fuck off!"

"Really *Mister* Eaves," Duncan ripped his hand out of the hole, blood running free from the smashed and scrapped skin. He lunged. His body failed him, and the lunge turned into a stumble, leaving him to fall into the man- who caught him. "Hear me if you can *Mister* Eaves, the verbal contract that I agreed to was simple, Keep you here in this shipyard until dawn…" Duncan heart was pounding in his ears, "I don't know the name of the person who employed me, but he wasn't human, Neelonian and clearly *not* your brother or father-in-law." The man allowed Duncan to slump onto his knees and stepped away, it was little relief to know that this man was not going to kill him. Instead he was assured that he would have to face his brother and the *wrath* he brought with him. With Duncan's vision darkening and his body failing him, he couldn't really comprehend the information he was being given. Nevertheless, as the man looked to walk away Duncan lunged once more and wrapped himself around the man's legs.

"Mister Eaves, *really*?"

"You have to give me *something*! Do you *know* what's coming for me? I won't let you go unless you join me!" Duncan was slowly slipping towards hysteria. Even in the shadows of the empty office corridor he could perceive the coming sunrise and everything it represented. The reality was he'd wasted a whole night and the reports had Caesar arriving at the crack of dawn to confront Duncan, the traitorous, thieving younger brother. He needed something,

"I have to leave…" The Man tried to take a step forward, but Duncan tighten his grip, "Okay Mister Eaves, I cannot join you, tell me what your name is?" There was almost a hint of sympathy in the man, he'd completed his assignment; Duncan may have been warped around his legs, but with one blow the Man could have freed himself or eliminated him.

"You *know* my name." There were tears in Duncan's eyes
"No Mister Duncan Eaves, none of those is *your* name…" For the first time Duncan looked up to see the Man's face, it was a collection of sharp lines, jaw, cheek bones, nose and brow. It was still too dark for colour.
"My name…my *name,* is Diego…"
"That is not your name. No. According to the one who hired me, your name is Hector." A searing pain ruptured through Duncan's head, his grasp going from the man's legs to his head and a *howl* of pain exiting from his lungs. Images and memories flooded his mind, places, people and events that he had no recollection of, suddenly returning. The pain increased another level and the man once called Duncan, passed out.

Varses smiled grimly as he watched the target twitch and shake in the dark corridor, it had been a strange and at times complicated assignment, but even he couldn't turn down this man's benefactor and the payment was worth the restrictions. Varses watched over Hector for another hour, until the convulsion subsided, and his breathing became more controlled. It had been an incredibly long time since he had watched over anyone as they slept, at least without the intention of killing them. It was refreshing, though not much more than that. Content and with the spectacular rising of the sun only an hour away, Varses left Hector to wake and face the consequences of all his pasts.

"Hector" Planet A63921F, 2.31 Data Stream

What had they done? His own flesh and blood, did they not understand the consequences, could they not see past their revenge? Had they learnt nothing from their uncle? The streets ran with blood, the sun beginning to dry pools into a stench, which drew those who feasted on carrion.

Diego was trying not to feast on despair, a whole community massacred and at the hands of his two boys. They weren't *boys* anymore. For once in his life the man, formerly known as Duncan, thought he had 'peace'. He'd *dared* to believe that he would shake the family inheritance of conflict and raise his family without having to look over his shoulder or outfox his neighbour. After all he'd managed to not *just* survive the meeting with his brother but was reconciled to him and his family. It had been like some kind of dream, he'd woke alone in the dockyard; dew covering his head, but a blanket resting over the rest of his body. There was no memory of going to sleep, just clinging to the shadowy figure who had whispered his name. 'Hector', he wasn't even sure what it meant or why the strange figure had answered his desperate plea in such a way, but the conflagration had cleared up one thing, he *had* to face his brother. The day of reckoning was a boat ride away and he analysed his crime once again to see, if maybe, just maybe he could find a way to justify his actions. After all, he'd stolen everything from his brother, but as far as Duncan knew there had been no other way. If he had not made his move, then, in his younger mind at least, he would have faced a life as his brothers' lackey or worse, an early grave. A few years after he had blackmailed his brother and their division was effectively written in ink, Duncan's beloved mother came bursting into his room.

"Diego, your father has finally lost it…he's going to give *everything* to your brother…" Diego was his birth name, given to him by his midwife; he'd taken the name Duncan to protect his identity.

"What?!"

"Yes, he's giving him the access codes. That *ingrate* will get *everything*..." Two decades later Diego could still remember every instant of his mother, her smell, the fire in her eyes and the pent-up rage in her body. Years of conflict with her husband and the rivalry of her children had stripped years from her. Wrinkles had assaulted her almond eyes, stress had tightened all the muscles around her mouth so that she barely ever smiled and her once lustrous golden hair was thin, cold and grey. Yet those almond eyes burned with intensity burgeoning on fury.
"He's sent him on a *fool's* errand into the reserve to bring him game…*always* his belly…" Her momentum from entering the apartment carried her into the living area. Diego was still recovering from the initial statement. "Diego, *what* are you doing standing there like I've taken candy off you…get over *here*!" When she was in one of these moods her western tribal heritage assaulted her vowels and gave a brutality that made even the most affectionate verse cut to the bone.

He'd loved to recall how he'd stood his ground and calmly responded to his mother, but he's pretty sure that he'd sprinted to where his mother stood with a suit bag.
"Your half-witted sibling has *generously* loaned you this…" His mother withdrew Caesars family ceremonial suit, a simply magnificent item of clothing made from some of the most expensive silks and fabrics that money could buy. With a predominately purple base colour, detailed and wrapped in crimson, and hemmed with green. Gold thread marked out the family crest and a design of a hunter with a bow, which Caesar had specifically requested. Though Caesar's style was quite restrictive and underplayed, when he did show up for family events then he made sure he was noticed.

"I thought he'd taken this with him?" Caesar had recently married, not just to the furious dismay of mother, but to the grievous disappointment of Father. To such a point that their Father had even mumbled about excluding Caesar from the inheritance of the first-born, which was why Diego was so surprised when his mother had entered the apartment claiming otherwise. Clearly absence had restored Caesar in the eyes of his Father.

"Don't...*why* are you still dressed..."

"Mother...you can't imagine..."

"Yes, I can, you're *going* to be your brother..."

"But Father will know! I'm not built like him, my skins different and you know the way he smells...and *what* am I going to offer?" Mother had looked at him coldly; Diego knew what was coming and silently prepared himself for the onslaught

"My *dearest* child, I *know* all these things, I *knew* all these things from the moment *your* idiotic Father, *my* husband, considered it a *valid idea* to restore your sibling *not* just to a place in this family, but *above you...that* boy has been *nothing* but trouble since he came out of me and I regret that day, *I regret* not having the strength to kill him! And so *yes my dear* Diego I had all your brilliant insights as soon as I heard of your Father's stupidity...and if you continue to arrive at such *deep* revelations then you will have nothing! So..." She finally paused to breathe, but Diego *dared* not interrupt "You *will* put on the suit, you *will* take the fragrance from the inside pocket and you *will* drench yourself in the *foul* stench, as for your skin...put on the gloves in the outer pocket. As for the voice...put *this* around your neck..." Mother had retrieved a thin necklace with a pendant size medallion hanging off it.

"It will make your voice deeper, as for the gloves they will go up to your elbows and I'm off to make sure the chef gets the meal right…be outside our apartments in fifteen minutes…"
Diego didn't like to recall what happened next, at the time, he'd *hated* his Father; for all the things he'd been deprived and for continually choosing Caesar over *him*. So, it had been easy, to take the food, to enter the apartments, to lie again and again and *again*. In hindsight, as good as the plan was, just *maybe* Father had decided that it was easier to be deceived than reveal the conspiracy. So, he'd graciously handed over the inheritance codes, proclaiming Diego to be Caesar. However, when Caesar had returned and discovered the deception, Caesar's fury turned to murderous intent and Diego disappeared into exile, becoming Duncan.

It had been *this* fury, marinating over two decades that Diego, as Duncan, had expected to be consumed by. There was some vain hope that on receiving the gifts and seeing his family that maybe, just maybe Caesar would reconsider execution. Yet as soon as Diego stepped off the boat on the other side of the river, utterly dishevelled- with his top ripped, trousers torn and hand bandaged by the stranger- he began to tremble. Not significantly, but the muscles around his knees seemed shaky. And then *suddenly* his brother was there. The dock was lined with men and behind them were his family, *alive*! Yet his eyes were drawn explicitly to his brother. Caesar had always been an imposing figure, as first born he had established a pattern of growing first and being celebrated for it. However, when he was young the imposing physicality came from the coil like tension of his lean muscular body, now his frame was filled out. It accentuated the stalking manner to his stride, the efficiency of movement, the containment of his *ferocity*.

Though Diego had stripped him of all claims to the family inheritance, Caesar moved with the confidence of a king. In the sight of this, Diego couldn't conceive of anything else to do, but to walk towards his brother and accept from his hand the punishment that was due. His knees nearly buckled on the first step, but Diego managed to push through, keeping his eyes lock on his brother. So much and so little could be read into a man's body language; to Diego his brother was a blur of counter signals, but then he knew that his perceptions were completely untrustworthy. The gap between them shrunk, Diego could see that his brother's orange hair had not faded in colour, though it was tied back into a ponytail. Diego would have loved to have claimed that he was looking in a mirror, they were twins after all, but if anything, they looked like strangers from different worlds. Of course, being the outdoorsman, Caesars darker skin had faced a toll, yet he radiated vitality. Somewhere, Diego had pictured Caesar as being similar to their mother, eaten away by bitterness, but Caesar, dressed in designer t-shirt and slacks, seemed not to have a care in the *world*, other than to *get* to his younger brother. Yet this was the confusing part, he had expected Caesar to pounce, to attack and savage him…was he being cruel? Had Caesar's wrath turned him into a torturer? Diego could take it no more, the trembling in his body was crippling his composure and on seeing his brother's hazel eyes for the first time in 20 years he fell to his knees. It was more a *stumble* to his knees. Diego couldn't understand the *look* in his brother's eyes, it made *no* sense; he tried to right himself, but again he stumbled to his knees. Tears appeared and started rolling down his face, he'd fought so *long* and so *hard*. He'd overcome his Father's madness, his Father in Laws duplicity, but his brother had him now. Five more times, he tried to move forward, but eventually he slumped to his knees for the last time. His brothers' shadow falling across him.

"Gosh you're still like Mother, stubborn, wilful…ignorant." Caesars voice had changed; it was deeper and more authoritative, though Diego thought he heard it full of tenderness.
"Get up." Diego wanted to obey his brothers' voice, the 'master of his life or his death, but his strength was gone. He tried, but no strength for action would arise. Then suddenly arms were under his and in one movement he found himself on his feet and face to face with his brother. He couldn't remember a time when they'd been this close, they'd reserved physical contact for violent attacks on each other; there had never been warmth, embrace, they had been enemies since conception. Now he was looking straight into his eyes and they were full of tears and past his own exhausted body Diego could feel a sob begin to rise through Caesars body. Tears poured forth, years of pain, hurt and betrayal marked every tear dropping from each of their eyes. They kissed and then Caesar clamped his hands around Diego's face. It was different to his own, Caesar had broader cheeks, angular jaw, bigger nose, but the same eyes.
"I would love to say you look *well* little brother, but death has had a stake in you…" Caesar smiled, studying the measurements of Diego's face. "What is the meaning of the nonsense behind me, I cannot accept these gifts; I have nowhere to put them and you know how hard it is to buy land." Diego's eyes had stopped blurring and he could see the ridged family features, though life's battles had marked Caesars forehead with a scar and he had taken to wearing a beard. "I'd need to build a mansion and given I have *four*, I'm not sure that the city council would grant *me* permission for another."

“Please, accept them for what I...” Diego had found composure for a speech, Caesar cut it off.
“Little Brother, it was somebody else’s life that we lived, Mother is *gone* and Father is senile with little time left…”
“He’s still alive?” Diego had only had the opportunity to get hold of the family codes because his father had concluded that he was going to die soon and he need to establish his inheritance.
“Kind of…” In the swiftest of movement, Caesar was now alongside Diego, propping him up and then moving him from the dock. It was all *surreal*; this was not how the story was meant to go.
“Tell me though little brother, am I to believe that you are the father to *all* those children?” Tears had been replaced by a grin as Caesar escorted him back to his family and to meet the men of Caesars family. Caesar and his entourage had taken over a sea front café; his family were being served coffee by nervous looking waiters. All Diego’s sons and his one daughter were tied to their mothers, the older ones brooding and the younger ones looking for comfort. On seeing Diego every face came to life and exclamations of relief were verbalised,
“Ah well, you have something to make me envious there Diego…” Even before Diego’s betrayal and exile, it was widely known that Caesar had not been getting on with his wives; Diego inferred that this hadn’t changed. Diego’s family surrounded him and embraced passionately, with deep relief, even if it was in the context of being surrounded by Caesar and his entourage. Perhaps now, even if events had not played out as expected, they could finally understand what Diego had been worried about.
“See I told you Kartina, my little brother is a survivor…” Clearly Kartina had been vocal on Diego’s wellbeing and she immediately lifted Diego’s smashed hand for inspection.

"Not his work Tina, I'll explain later."
"Give your Father some room children." The voice of his first wife Uli brought an instant reaction, obedience. She sat in her usual defiance, with their eldest son at her side; in fact, his four oldest boys had strategically positioned themselves close to each of his wives, even if they were not their actual mothers. Diego smiled to Uli, even if she couldn't see, her sensitivities would be aware of the gratitude. Caesar kindly escorted him to a chair in middle of the café's enclosure and released him so he could sit down. He could feel everyone's eyes on him, wife's, children, security and strangers.
"Waiter, coffee, strong black, no sugar and a pastry." Caesar took the seat opposite, as a waiter took the order and disappeared.
"Come on..."
"What?"
"Diego...only I was really capable of making you look stupid..."
It was surreal, he was sat with his brother, surrounded by his family and wasn't dead. In fact, his own personal wounds were self-inflicted, and it seemed for all intend and purpose that his brother had, shockingly, moved on.
"The wounds?" Diego played dumb.
"By the *eclipsing moons*...I have actually seen blood come from a stone..." Caesar shook his head and passed a look to one of his entourage. "Alright, alright, we've all been out on a heavy night and not really wanted to talk about it, did you win...no, no I don't think so, but as I said before, I can't accept the gifts." Again, Caesar's generosity abounded. His entourage radiated warmth, even the obvious stress his family had been under was beginning to ebb away. It was hard to put down his expectations, harder still to renounce the guilt that whispered

a form of insanity which suggested that he should provoke his brother. After all, it was only right.

"Coffee sir and a freshly made pastry." Only later would Diego realise how grateful he was that the coffee had arrived, it broke his train of thought.

"Okay, okay, though you are taking at least the Chabal's, you will find room for them..." For Diego, that first sip of coffee was perhaps one of the finest he'd ever drink.

"Mule," Caesar roared with laughter. "Alright...I give in, on one condition...how did you end up in such a state?" Caesar may have moved past the travesties of their youth, but the wrestling still went on. Diego decided to give a little ground,

"You remember Father used to talk about his and grandpa's benefactor...well he sent someone to make me see things differently..."

"Man...I always thought he was a bedtime story...some kind of bogey man thing, though not..."

"Yeah, but all I can say is that he's got me out of some pretty tight situations..."

"And do you see differently?"

"It's like I'm in a different world..."

"Speaking of which when you're ready, I think it's time we headed home..." A vision flashed in Diego's mind, an instant super imposed upon the reality in front of him and it was gone, he couldn't recall a single image, but words flowed from his mouth.

"Caesar that as with everything is an *immensely* kind offer, but some of my kids aren't up to much more travelling and, well I need to recover from my perception adjustment...take the Chabal's and we'll catch you up later..." As with every aspect of the morning it was surreal; it could have easily been the sleep deprivation, the psychological trauma of his past arriving at his door without brutal consequences or the bizarre encounter with his benefactor's man, but Diego could not make sense of it. However, Caesar accepted the request, but when the time came Diego used local connections to move his family to a villa a few kilometres from the port. Life was finally good, for the first time in the entirety of his life Diego felt like he could breathe. His mother was dead, the consequences of his youth were gone, his family were around him and he was healthy, life was *good*!

Then it happened, eighteen months had passed since they had arrived in the Villa, at first, they had kept themselves to themselves, recovering from the escape and adjusting to a new family dynamic. Diego and the family had cautiously engaged with the surrounding community. The villa was surrounded by a gated community, who transited to the nearest city of Pevnost and after about six months Diego struck up a relationship with a man called Jack. A local and successful businessman, Jack had an outstanding reputation within the gated community and had some influential connections to Pevnost. Of course, such men like Jack were not given to introducing strangers to their friends without some kind of established relational credit, so tentative steps were taken, dinner parties were exchanged. However, Diego was so fixed on establishing his family and himself that he missed a trick. A catastrophic one. Diego had one daughter, Isabella, who he loved in a way; perhaps if she had been Eugenia's child...things would have been different.

He'd come back from a run to find Jacks' sleek transport in the driveway of his Villa, the driver nodded respectfully,

“Hi Tomas, how’s the family? Miss Amelia come to see Kartina?” Diego made a note of the names and faces of what he termed the instrumental people, those who you could miss, but were crucial to their employer’s lives. Tomas hesitated.

“No, it’s Mister Sikemi sir, on *business*.” Diego’s heart fluttered, he’d long learnt that paranoia was not the crippling enemy, but a beacon of survival. “He’s gone inside.” Diego paused, surveyed to see if Tomas was going to be any more ‘forthcoming’, but it was clear he was not and so Diego headed inside. His Villa was three stories high, encircled by balconies and a large veranda, encased by dry white walls and glass, much like the rest of the gated community. Ascending a flight of stairs, his ever-present limp making it look more awkward than it actually was, onto the veranda; at the automated front doors, his paranoia went up a whole step. He was greeted by Eli, holding a grimace and a towel.

“Mister Sikemi is in your office, with his eldest son, your wife Kartina is upstairs with *Isabella*. In brief, she went out with some of the local girls to a villa party thrown by Sikemi’s son Biris and he *raped* her. A doctor is on the way, Uli is visiting Pevnost as your request with Ruel, her brothers are out trying to wrap up some details.” Diego took the towel and put it to his face; *run scream fuck the little punk up violate HIS daughter murder her innocence fucking stuck up little PRICK did he understand that* ***violating*** *her was violating Diego’s whole family VIOLATING those this* ***punk*** *had never met never considered the histories of every investment and decision the blood and the tears and the joy of surviving prospering all that Isabella represented to all who cared about her Could the* ***RABID LITTLE DOG*** *keep his dick somewhere else he’d* ***CASTRATE THE BASTARD*** *and make him a stew like he’d made his brother giving Isabella the change to witness shame made flesh.* Diego felt *utterly* powerless for a moment, his eyes

covered by the towel, but his body shaking with rage. Everything was so contradictory, though he was certain of one thing, if Isabella's brothers had been home, Sikemi and his boy would be dead already.
"What do they want?" It was the wrong question, but the others for the time being had been answered.
"Mister Sikemi mumbled something about a bonding contract. I though it more prudent to secure him in your office." Part of Diego didn't understand, Eli *should* have just escorted them into the back and shot them. Nevertheless, Diego accepted that Eli knew something that held him from doing something so obvious and handed back the towel. He felt a compulsion to shower for a very, very long time, but headed towards his office.

Gaining a coherent thought was immensely difficult, so he slowed down, tried to gain his breath. *Why did this* ***little nobody*** *have to ruin everything and everything was ruined his daughter mother her sons would arrive with thunder and blood they were Diego boys and were known to be swift to violence oh what gave this scum the right to* ***savage*** *the families restoration they'd been going forward as a family for the first time ever* ***peace*** *in his time no peace now only* ***demands*** *of revenge but they were outnumbered.* Sikemi and his *animal* were the heartbeat of the community, killing them would lead to reprisals and even possible extermination. He knew what he had to do…*cut a deal.* The door to his office was closed and one of Eli's men stood guard, with a bottle of water, which he extended to Diego as he approached. Diego knew his name, but it wasn't forthcoming,
"Thanks". Diego devoured the fluid; nevertheless, his fury *burned*, but his family were as vulnerable as they'd ever been. One wrong move and the whole community would descend on them. The water cooled

his parched lips and throat, whispering sweet relief. He would be like water, fluid, pragmatic and rescue his family from themselves. Finishing the bottle, he looked to the door; normally he would be coherent enough to run through possible scenarios. He *wanted* to run through scenario's, it gave him an edge, but time was against him. His sons would be back soon, and they would be unstoppable. He looked to Eli's man again and for a moment he swore that his 'nemesis' from the port was there as the guard, but with a blink he was gone. Diego nodded and the door was opened.

Rooms communicated data and before Diego was across the threshold, he could sense the fear: *intoxicating, instinctual, biological* and almost *spiritual*. Diego may not have been able to exact a physical and just revenge upon Sikemi and his *spawn*, but he would exact retribution. Sikemi and the *murderous scum* rose as he entered, *little shit* could remember his etiquette **now**, standing, but grovelling at the same time. Diego did his best to stride to his desk even with the limp, appearing not to acknowledge them in the limited space. Originally, before Diego and his family had taken over the villa, the room had been a storage space for winter fuel supplies; but modern technology meant it was dead space. Redecorated in a balance between classic opulence and restrictive modernity, there was one window facing north, a dark wood bureau by the door, a corner sofa of animal skin, a replica master piece that took over the rest of that wall, a plant in the other corner and finally his desk with another painting above it. The Sikemi's had chosen to sit on the sofa and on Diego's movement into the room Jack Sikemi had moved forward.
"Diego, look I realise..." Diego raised his hand and gestured for silence, pointing to the chairs in front of his desk, while continuing to walk and

making sure that no eye contact was made. Placation was not an option, actually a simple option would be to call the guard outside, order him to execute Jack Sikemi and the *little shit,* disappear the driver and his car, then as a family, run. Of course, it was a stupid option…lock them in the secure room hidden behind the desk and give himself more time. But there was a clock being overridden by the wrath of his own offspring. Diego hobbled himself around the edge of the desk, for once not clipping the corner as his damaged hip misplaced his balance, and there he opened a drawer and retrieved another bottle of water. A cultural script whispered that water should be offered, but rising at his presence did not restore the right for hospitality- they were a long way from sharing water again. Diego took a long drink of the water and then moved over to the plant and poured the rest of the water into the plant. It was petty, a nuanced communication and stated his presentation quite clearly. Diego heard Sikemi take a seat, but he wasn't done, instead of turning to face them he went to survey the painting on the back wall. The silence began to make Diego's skin crawl, yes it gave him time to draw up a list of demands as restitution, but holding back the rage was not getting easier. Water knew vengeance as well as serenity.

"Sikemi you speak," The familiarity of 'Jack' and 'Diego' were also not available, "if I hear a word, a sound, a thought from *him* then the consequences will be swift…" It was a relief to speak, to find that the words were controlled, in place and communicating a united front. "If I hear the *hint* of an excuse or my flesh and blood being slandered…" The painting was meant to be an idyllic river ford, but it was full of blood, angels and demons. Silence rolled and finally Jack Sikemi braved the silence,

"I *hear you* Diego, there is *no* excuse," Diego was surprised and then pleased to hear the savage disappointment and resignation in Sikemi's voice. He recognised it well enough, it reminded him his own fathers in the day of treachery. "…though if you'll hear *me*, there is *only* taking responsibility." A flicker of understanding waded into the raging sea of Diego's being, but it was washed away. "We all know the consequences, the brutal and sad consequences for my *child's indescribably callous unthinking moronic actions…*" Diego was still looking at the canvas, but he could tell the last words were said to the *shit* behind him, wise strategy, the *shit* was no equal in this conversation. Actually, Diego thought it would have been wiser still to hide the *shit* away with the rest of the trash. There was a *but* coming… "*But…"* On this Diego span, fluid even on his dodgy hip, the *shit*, irritatingly handsome strapping-charming-considerate RAPIST shit, flinched. It caught Sikemi as well,

"But?" Diego swiftly locked eyes with the man sitting the other side of the desk and the storm waters paused. Sikemi was a mess, his suit was torn, face strewn and puffy, whereas normally he exuded power and confidence, he appeared, not quite broken, but savagely beaten and expecting worse.

"He is my *only* son and heir…" A wave of emotion rolled from within Sikemi and it took masses of self-control to not be overwhelmed, but the words were written all over his face: *I've failed as a father and man, what have done, why wasn't I there?, what can I do to make this right, they're going to take my hope and joy away?* Diego wasn't sure he'd have felt that way about his own eldest, but Yazid… "and if you report him, it will ruin him, me and *destroy* our family…" Diego saw the flash of fury, as again Sikemi looked to the back of the room where his son

cowered, and it satisfied *something*, not a great amount, but he now decided that he wouldn't kill Jack.
"So, I've come to offer terms," Jack rose humbly to the desk and slipped a list of names on a piece of parchment, towards Diego. Skimming the list Diego was confused,
"What's this?"
"The name of every companionless female of marrying age in the community, they're *yours* if you want them," Diego froze as with amazing speed he did the calculations. In a generation his family would inherit three of the most power family estates in the community and be intimately connected to four others. "I know your older boys are of age and that you've been looking for a way in…" *A way in, this deal effectively hands the entire community over to my family.*
"What's the catch?" Diego was a negotiator and he knew Jack was throwing everything he had into this pitch, for good reason, but it was too much, even for his daughter.
"Marry Isabella to my boy…" There was a two and a half metre desk between Sikemi and Diego, but it was a punch to Diego's gut, and he crashed into his seat. His thoughts flat lined, his emotions cancelled each other, there was silence in his being; a deafening silence as if he was a computer crashing. Sikemi continued to speak, saying something about Love, obsession and so on, but Diego found a single voice in his head. Calm, clear, serene voice that he'd heard once before when waking up in the abandoned dock,
'DO IT'
He still couldn't recall the rest of the conversation; he'd called Eli and a legal associate in, while Sikemi's boy had been escorted back to the villa. It would be sometime before he could consider him a *son in law*, but his decision left him facing his very own court and a justice only

family could mediate. And for a moment, for a day, for a second, he'd actually believed that he'd won. Kartina and Isabella's mother Uli had consoled Isabella, even talking her into accepting the proposal. Isabella's brothers were another matter, but he and Eli had managed to, by effectively imprisoning them for the first twenty-four hours, bring the brothers to some kind of peace with the agreement. Diego had thought that it was to do with the possibility of stability in their lives, of finally settling down and doing it well, which persuaded them against revenge. At no point did Diego ever remember being so naïve.

It was a wet morning; Diego was idling about something when Eli appeared in front of him and it was bad. Smiling eyes, unusually sad, no not sad, resigned. The anger around his mouth was terrifying,
"Who and what?"
"Simeon and Levi, they hosted a celebration at the Hamor's, they convinced all the men of the community to join them…"
"Oh fuck."
"They drugged them and killed them in their sleep…" Diego felt a wave of nausea "…they've recovered their sister and have informed your sons…" For a moment Diego felt faint and then it was gone, a chill closed in on his spine
"Were they calculated enough to cut communications?" Eli nodded.
"Good seems inappropriate…" Diego sighed. "Split your men in half, ambush what's left of the community's security, no survivors. Simultaneously secure the women and children, move them with my family outside of the gates…the story is that we are under attack, we've been betrayed and the Kohli gang have kidnapped their husbands and sons. Tell my sons they're to loot and burn everything, every house,

nothing must be left standing…here as well; get some bodies left in this house."

"What's the reason that all ours are alive…"

"Well I'd have you present those fucking idiots as corpses, but that won't do…they're blood and maybe they're right…beat them and bring them back bloodied, re-route the ambushing security team away from us, report that they went down fighting…" Diego took a small breath, but knew there wasn't time for more.

"Secure any pets and data carrying devices, consider this a hostile takeover…I will lead the community two clicks west, meet us there…if you can blow something up that would be good…" Diego paused to allow for Eli's calculations. "Get it done, I'll see you two clicks west."

MALKUS: HUB ACTUAL

"West of the great mountain range, past the trees and river is a cave, in the cave is a picture, it's a simple sketch, by a not so simple artist and it holds the meaning of everything that ever happened in reality. "

Malkus had *lost* him- he'd utterly vanished. For two years he'd been glued to the assassin across numerous interconnecting data lines. Varses had changed form and face, again and again; living lives that Malkus didn't just dream of- but watched unfold. It was an adventure, a fantasy trail painted across realities and food to Malkus' waking and sleeping. *Where was he?*

A monster of fairy tale proportions roared out the front of the hotel, skin of flame, stone, dust, glass, wood and death. Erupting, engulfing, devouring; all that dared to attack its master's lair. The sky went black, shockwave shaken buildings and troops; thunder rang all around the

Old City as the sky fell- in lumps of glass and stone. Outwards the bellowing smoke of a leviathan's devastation poured. Knocking those on their feet to the ground, its untamed anger continuing into the street. Then the true minion of death and darkness was a shadow in the smoke; a single follower of deaths commands, fearless, relentless and lethal, appearing from within the wreckage…unscathed. Echoes of devastation were joined by insistent claps of thunder, rapid and cruel, a single fire spitting in the darkness, extinguishing life amongst the smoke. Blurred movement and unstoppable insanity.
Confusion was rife, pain and death wailing in the ears of the unprepared. Wounded screaming, glass and stone, piercing and cutting. Explosive vibrations shattering internal organs, blood offerings to the monster's fury as buildings groaned in praise as damage ate at them. WHAM! Another monster exploded amid the madness, this time it was smaller, but merciless upon the fallen. Senses began to compensate for the devastation, the fear, the panic, the smells of dust and flesh and burning and blood. Code was shouted, but gunfire broke chains and the dust shrouded all hope of pinning their enemy down as he slipped from the chaos and into another tenement building. A loud crack and another building slid into the street, the belly falling around the knees, dust and debris refilling the falling sky.

Malkus had traced his man all the way back to the first time he'd seen him (raiding a data stream for medical data). Yet he couldn't find Varses there now. In fact, a *different* person was the shadowy assassin causing the devastation. It wasn't that Varses had changed his appearance, moved between realms or simply died- no one ever simply died. Varses had ceased to be. Malkus was confused, even a little frightened- wasn't minimising or downplaying at all. And the confusion increased exponentially, as the *more* Malkus looked for his muse, the less he found of him. Inexplicably it was if Varses had simultaneously erased himself from the data streams- which was impossible. For Malkus, Varses had been his guiding star, his sweet relief, his 'dirty' little secret or just a repetitive distraction. In his search a moment of clarity arose, if he didn't get his shit together, the bleed of chaos in his systems would be noticed and then he'd have to explain...a lot, the conclusion of which would be unthinkable. So, he was left with Regus' other stream as relief from a meltdown and keep his handler from asking awkward questions.

Data Stream 4.38, Irrelvant Data stream:

The Human condition and those who suffer from it are impaired when it comes to recognising the sensitivity of...well...just about everything. Blinded, by what some consider a disease, they rarely recognise the realities of cause and effect, which is mildly humorous given the number of texts which they have formed pointing to such a dynamic. Millennia worth of the creative interpretation of their surrounds and still the most obvious of information has not led them to change their behaviour. Of course, there are those who consider such unrivalled ignorance something to be punished, eradicated, extinguished etc. The primary example of this were the YZ: it is here that one must acknowledge that not every being that samples this collection will acknowledge the sheer depth of history, culture and power of that which has just been named, but when talking on the human condition one must make allowances. Digressing back to the subject, the YZ elicited the support of numerous factions and prepared for a drawn-out campaign of retribution, for the numerous crimes that the H condition had committed or were inevitably going to commit. Nanoseconds away from departure on this sacred mission, wise allies of the YZ highlighted that the plan, though fool proof, would in fact leave the YZ in a potentially devastating cycle of being infected by the H condition. Being as they are, the YZ and the supporting factions, heeded the advice of their allies and shelved the plan indefinitely. Unfortunately, not all have considered the tale of the YZ, perhaps because they had already run afoul of the H condition and thus were drawn back to the source. One could be emboldened to guess how far and wide the 'H' condition had migrated from the source, but any conclusion would be hyperbole and as some know this can be seen as the onset of the HC and though entertaining to certain aspects of the wider community, one does not have it.

So why inform anyone of these things, for most custodians none of the above information is new and it is possible that a select group may have considered it unhelpful, nay inefficient, but texts like this have the possibility of a wide uptake and so taking this into account the advisory team and myself though it prudent to add the information. In any case, the more illustrious custodians will have skimmed past this section altogether as the information that would be considered important has yet to appear. That being the case, one will continue to illuminate the HC to a wider audience. As expressed earlier, those inflicted with the human condition are desensitised to a remarkable level. Though they often grasp some of the basic elements of the reality in which they abide, far too often they draw the most peculiar conclusions. One of the more, laugh inducing suppositions is their position of importance in the galactic and wider communities; time and again they are found proclaiming a leading role in the operation, of which ever collective they are tacitly attached to. Though more often than not they are the noisy distraction elevated above their station to the benefit of those actually making the decisions of merit. Perhaps the preeminent example of this was the Carisva conglomerate on the far wing of four-three-eight Nebula. One would recommend to any aspiring custodians an investigation of the rise, fall, regeneration and eventual obliteration of the conglomerate and large sections of the star system. For those of you with sufficient technology you will find a number of access points that will support your endeavours; apologies to those who arrive at this text on lesser formats, hopefully you will find your way through other means. It is a fascinating account and if you come upon the right texts you will be able to drill down for some excellent insights into the nature of conglomerates.

The most applicable insight to the current text is that regardless of the predicament, those of the H condition have a tendency to seek privilege and authority; supported by the narratives they call science, politics and religion. Oh and of course, a large amount violence, cruelty and expansionism. Within the Carisva Conglomerate these tendencies were shaped and formed into circumstances that supported the conglomerates expansion and of course assisted in the fall, though surprisingly not in its obliteration. However, this is an unusual response to the HC tendencies the following categories are the more recognised response. ***Benevolence****: the HC's ability to produce positive aspects into their reality is considered a benefit to the wider community, the negative aspects are treated as some kind of retardation or disability and thus those taking up the role of benefactor seek to discipline, realigned and support the afflicted into a healthier way of life.*

Resource*: One thing that can never be underestimated, in regard to the HC, is the adaptability of those stricken with the state and as such others see them as a source of exploitation and as third-party exploiters. Peoples, races, conglomerates and others, trade in and* *trade with the Human Condition; abuse is widespread, reporting inconsistent and protection so varied that it still remains a point of contention for all custodians as to which description would suit the circumstance best. One would consider 'confused' to be a holistic interpretation, but the word is not something seen as viable by the wider custodian community.* ***Experimentation****: given that the HC's can be seen as a problem or something needing rescue, they often find themselves involved in plans, proposals and tests. Obviously, some of these are for the benefit of the Human condition, almost falling under benevolence, but with a large element of risk one thinks they fall more neatly under this category. However, most experiments are generally for finding some kind of 'solution' to the Human condition; none of which have been initially successful and some of which have been so horrific that they have drawn forces into violent conflicts.*

Finally, Isolation: there are occasions when the HC outbreak is considered so detrimental to effectively everyone else, including other HC suffers, in the known clusters of the universe that the pocket of infection is removed from circulation. The system is taken off-line, and the grids are re-arranged. Being the case (regardless of the form of transport invented within the isolated community, sub or higher realities, energy movements and even basic life-form carrying transport devices) escape is impossible. In fact, the manipulation of the surrounding systems is so complete it appears to those inside the quarantine zone that the rest of the universe is moving away from them, it is a cunning allusion to demoralize any attempt to re-join with the wider community. However, it does not stop there, subtle communication to the natural fabric of the system means that the underlying interaction with the HC is hostile. Of course, given the vast resources placed into such endeavours, those in position to create such areas of space, time and dimensions, leave observation of intricate and industrious means. Those of a more 'moral' disposition may see this as cruel, after all this form of quarantine effectively destroys all those infected with HC and all forms of life within the quarantine. However, having seen the devastation caused by the Human condition first hand, I as a custodian find it difficult to sympathise with this generous position; the HC is savage, unrelenting and murderous. Energies that one would assume directed towards positive outcomes; instead are hijacked by the HC, which finds new and creative ways of being destructive, to themselves and the worlds around them. Nevertheless, I have once again digressed from the topic of this text and have slipped into a custodian faux pas, of expressing my opinion on the text and thus potentially skewing a reading of what is to be presented. Needless to say, perhaps it is time that I shortened this introduction and saved myself anymore embarrassment, hopefully the text will speak for itself and any of my peers reading this will be merciful in their conclusions.

Irrelvant Data stream, adjusting parameters of search, please wait

"Oh, come on Dad that never happened? You know that the nectar was *strong* this year right?" It was late.

"Look Yazee your grandfather was *never* one to exaggerate?"

"Yeah, yeah, just like you...I've seen your record keeping..."

"Hmm, how does a dreamer like you become such a cynic? I blame your late mother, rest her soul..."

"Mum has nothing to do with this...and anyway, you *always* say that you have to seek the numbers behind the words..."

"Do I? doesn't sound like me..."

"Ha, next you'll be denying you're favourite saying..."

"Don't...."

"In the end it's the benefactor's *mercy*." Something about Yazid's mimicry cut Diego to the core, it was the way he tilted his head that reminded him of *her*. Dead too soon, buried in every way but *his heart*...and the movements of her children.

"Dad, you alright?"

Yazid was aware like...well actually, unlike any other member of his family; but whereas Diego recognised it as a blessing, Yazid's brothers didn't appreciate it, at all.

"Yeah, where was I, oh yeah so, your great grandfather gave chase...outnumbered, outgunned, but *not* outwitted. You see winning *isn't* everything; *establishing* your victory is crucial and the Niarian gang were *drunk* on victory. They chose badly, and your great grandfather and his allies over took them and smashed them to..."

"They're faking the books again..."

"Pieces."

"Not much, a little bit here and there, no one's noticed...I've sent you a comms." Along with his awareness came a sense of justice, which Diego still didn't understand and his brothers, well they despised. "You don't look *that* surprised..." Diego was certain that nothing in his body language would have given him away. A gift it may have been, but sometimes it was spooky.

"Yes, thank you for confirming the information...I have a job for you, the boys are surveying a depot out on the coast"

"The Maloran fields job?"

"Yeah, take them the updated specs..."

"Dad, *I*..."

"Have *nothing* to apologise for, but you *still* haven't learnt the lesson of the story, have you?" Yazid, his features still sharp with the hallmark of middle youth, but his eyes fixed his father with a *weary* gaze. They'd been here before, particularly when Yazid was younger and he'd talk about his dreams. To *everyone*. Even his mother had been taken aback by the audacity of her eldest boy and his wild stories, it had taken Diego *several* conversations to adjust Yazid's etiquette. On days like today, Diego came to the conclusion that he had only 'succeeded' in teaching his favourite son to not talk about his dreams.

"I'll be on the next flight out."

"Good, *don't* mention the books, I will *deal* with it." Diego tried to sound firm, but he wasn't sure what he would do. His sons were a law unto themselves and he had few sanctions left. At least some of them were beginning to settle down and have kids of their own, but his confidence about the future of his family ebbed and flowed. He wished Yazid was his first born, for all his outspokenness, at least he was honest.

"Alright, I'll see you soon." They rose from the tea table, embraced. Diego noticed yet again that for all his middle youth, Yazid's frame was beginning to fill out and every so often Diego saw something of his brother Caesar. As was family tradition, Yazid stepped away and bowed his head slightly, Diego kissed it.

"*Be well.*"

"You too."

Yazid swivelled gracefully and glided out, Diego couldn't remember a time when Yazid didn't have a grasp of co-ordinating his body. Eugena recorded the first steps and it was less clumsy young beast and more dancer. If only he'd be so thoughtful with his gifts, but there were more pressing matters.

"Eli...come through." Older, greyer around the edges, Eli was still part phantom and appeared from a separate room.

"You heard?"

"I read the comms."

"And..."
"It’s as you suspect, the Horites have their teeth into Halgan." Diego had returned to his bureau and opening the draw, withdrew a bottle of nectar and a jar of water.
"How much of a problem is this?"
"In the here and now..." Diego had given up offering his chief of security a seat, "Nothing that cannot be covered, but if it escalates...you could *lose* Nagfar." Halgan was one of the better sons, not given to the excesses of his older half-brothers and perhaps that was why he'd fallen foul of the quiet little trap. A bird in the hand that was pretending to be a ‘robin’, but was in fact a ‘*howling* hawk’ eating away at him.
"No warning. Take it away. *Make* him understand that he *must* consider his connections in sight of the bigger picture. You have *his* mother’s permission; she is of a similar opinion now." *Again*, Yazid had warned him, tried speaking to Halgan, but she *was* pretty, the other sons were marrying, and she whispered all the right phrases. She also had a fabulous bosom.
"And the Horites?" Distant shell company of his brothers multi-national, but just distant enough.
"No trace." For Diego, something's didn't chance. Yes, he dreamed of being ‘Hector’, but still Diego *had* to make the hard calls to keep his family’s legacy in tack. The nectar and water did in fact make the order slightly sweeter, if the Horites were so willing to sacrifice one of their own for a hold in his legacy then he would shed no tears. Eli moved to the bureau and tapped the top twice, the ornate desk coming alive and a holo-image being projected above it.
"As requested. You didn't *have to* see him..."
"Yes, I did.” The image was of the last surviving member of the Sikemi massacre. Only three had escaped his family’s vengeance, one had

died of a terminal illness; another had found themselves 'accidently falling off a cliff and now there was this young man. The fresh-faced youth may have been a child at the time, but he had begun to make sounds about the events of his youth, accurate sounds. Diego wasted no time and extinguished the threat.

"Thank you, Eli." The second sip of nectar did not taste of anything. For a fleeting moment Diego thought about asking the questions, but Eli was not likely to answer.

"Finally, sir, you will have a single comms. with the address of the person that you've been seeking."

"Thank you, Eli, you're dismissed." Diego moved to his desk, swept the display and the communication came alive above his bureau, he began to read the details and ponder. When he noticed that Eli hadn't left, Diego moved his head slightly to ask the question.

"I think this is a *bad idea* sir. The Laestrygones are not to be trusted..." Eli rarely spoke in contradiction, not flinching at the orders Diego had given to massacre a whole community, yet his position was a clear statement.

Diego dropped the screen, took another sip and slowly lowered himself into the bureau chair.

"Go on." Eli hesitated, recognising the nature of his interruption.

"You know *their* reputation, the rumours and the documented evidence." The Laestrygones Company had more than a reputation, the name was mythical. Connected into the origins of the current political, economic and criminal systems, the mention of their name could produce a cocktail of responses. "We have other options, the Numerian Corporation or the Alst are..."

"When I point out the limitations of each organisation, you will *then* argue about my father's and grandfather's warnings, but these aren't the *real* reasons are they?" Eli flinched,

"Your family may have served mine since my great-grandfathers time, but some*things* remain?"

Eli's shoulders fell, the weight of family history crashing down on him; he wasn't even born in the days of betrayal and tragedy, but his family's hatred and desire for revenge was as *real* ever. "You know family is a strange, beautiful, terrible thing? Take mine for instance, when we're united there is *almost* nothing that we can't achieve...you've seen that yourself..." Diego withdrew another glass from within the bureau and poured a generous quantity of nectar and held it out for his head of security. This had happened only once before, after they'd arrived safely from the Sikemi incident.

"That unity comes from *me* giving them purpose, I lost sight of that in the villa...I'm beginning to lose sight of it here, Yazid is being punished because of that..." Yazid's talents, his indiscreetness and his dogged sense of justice had not just given him a 'bad' reputation amongst his brothers, they *hated* him. They felt that Diego favoured him, maybe he did, maybe the suit *was* a 'mistake'. Yazid's honesty was refreshing, but maybe he saw *her* smile on his face.

"I'm slipping, not 'cause I'm old, not *because* I miss her, but because Yazid is *not* the only one in this family that can *dream*?" Ever since the incident at the port and the man had whispered 'his' name, a dream life had begun to grow. He'd told no one, not even Eugena. Once she had challenged him, after a particularly vivid nightmare, but he'd never confirmed it. Dreams were for two types of people, the gifted and the mad. Diego feared that any revelation would be used by his enemies to bring him and in turn his family down. Unfortunately, the dreams were slipping into reality and he would not allow this to impinge upon his family's future.

"*You*?" Diego slid a compartment from within the bureau and pressed a code in, all the doors locked, and the room became electronically secured. "How long?" Eli was actually surprised.

"You remember the day before we met with my brother, I told you that I'd run into someone and run them off...well okay you never *quite* bought that, but he triggered something that I'm beginning to lose control of..." Eli and Diego both took a large swig of the nectar simultaneously.

"So how does *this* involve the Laestrygones?"

"They have an item in their possession that I keep seeing in my dreams...it's a staff, before you ask a very *specific* staff, made of bone and threaded with Gold. I'm not even sure that the Laestrygones know that they have it, but without it I'm afraid..." Another drink, "that I'm going to lose any sense..." Diego didn't finish the sentence, instead both men sipped into their own thoughts, Eli adjusting to a new 'reality' and one he knew to be concerned about.

"So, is this why you've employed Alric"

"I *guessed* you'd catch on, but you understand why this couldn't be done in house...and you mentioned him years ago." Diego was a reader of people and he could tell that it had stung Eli to have been left out of the loop, but the explanation was soothing any narratives that had been created. In addition, Eli was now able to do that which he loved, help his master.

"So, what's the plan?"

"Simple really, we buy a field...a couple of fields and hope that they don't notice our real intent."

Diego's Dream. Planet A63921F, 2.31 Data Stream

He was back, *again.* In a place he did not want to be. A dark place where his dreams assembled to molest him. It was the meadow *again*, damp up to his knees, shadowed by trees, tripping, stumbling, falling…again! Being chased…*always* running from something that in other worlds he had long since conquered. Here it was *all* powerful, undeniable and stalking him. No smell, no sound, touch of vision and sight of fear, heart thumping, breath grasping, pushing chin from the moist grass. Fear fed anger, on haunches he turned to face the antagonist…to defeat or be consumed, to fight and die, to lose it all and give up his mind. Time of thought, breath in breathless air, eyes responding to dream moment, but the point of fear wasn't there. Instead, below a purple sky with its yellow clouds, was a flower. In all its majesty, a single, beautiful Lilly stood proud. Memories of an unmistakable fragrance wrapping itself around him, its petals ready to melt under his gaze. Soft, gentle, caress of freedom…a way out of this! Instinctually, he went to pick the flower, for it was serenity in this meadow of bad tidings. Yet on shuffling forward, hand outstretched, serenity moved away. Then it began to *laugh*, whispers of a chuckle at first, first sound for a life time…rising in volume, louder, louder, *incessant.* A rooted 'plant', chuckling sweet joy in its stalk and then the dream began to spin. The laughter became more insidious, vicious, roaring in his ears and echoing in his body. *Desperately*, he jumped at the flower, grab it, cut it, destroy it…stop it!!! It slipped his grasp and losing balance, he splashed to the grass, again. The sound stopped. Lifting his eyes, he saw the flower, vanished, a thin memory in a whispering breeze, shifting the long grass in the meadow. He looked up, back to forward, nervous. There was a tension in the air, sodden, raising himself on elbows. Chest tightening, heart faster, skin everything. A haunting of every time before, time after time...losing the sense of grip.

It was *wild* and *ugly*; Diego had sharpened its teeth on the bones of innocence. Any minute, from the wood behind, dark foreboding past, running him down, sinking its teeth in. Yet his eyes moved deeper into the dark, from where he...did he...had he, run from there? No shadows of his conscious appeared to follow, had he finally beaten it? Was this the way it all ended...was he *free*? Sitting upright, looking into the sky and tears began to flow, unexpected, uncontrolled, damp and salty as they slipped to his lips and off his chin on to the dew-ridden grass.

Ground *erupted*, spray of sod and soil arching into the air, consciousness given form. Sinuous, compact power of muscle stretched over bone; silver long, but all amongst the dirt were white fangs! A dream-thing called *Wolf* leaping out of the ground in front of him; he closed his eyes as the hot breath of insanity blasted onto his face.

He awoke...no, no, *nooooo*! Something kept him in. *Cruel* master and evil hand, bearing him more, with no answers and no direction. Looking around he had the strange sense of familiarity, but he had never seen this place before. To his left and right were searing cliffs that broke for the sky, below which were thick forests of misted menace and yet on seeing the castle something clicked, he knew where the answers to this long madness lay. The castle scorched itself in his mind, stuck between times, ancient and new, with towers made of stone and glass, walls of solid steel and water. Escalating into the sky, it belonged to the high crags around it, but rested on the plain. The answers he *knew* were within drew him to his feet and he headed to the answer. As he walked on, the castle grew into the blood red sky, misted clouds beginning to form around the spires that flagged from the towers. Too quickly, the gatehouse was on him. The huge mass of stone, metal and glass, at angles un-natural, stared down on him, as he studied the amazing patterns his madness created. The place almost looked *alive*, its arrow slits gazing upon his every breath, the arches of the gate hungry to take him in. He reached it in a heart-beat, it yawned over him, re-cast fear to him and a whisper of a price reached his mind. In all worlds a bead of sweat slipped from his brow.

A howl *cracked* the silent air. The man spun, searching, looking, how near, how far? Back from where he believed he had just been the fangs of the demon *wolf*- calling itself his conscious- sounded him out. Even over the great distance, he could see by memory the untainted orange eyes and the sharpened silver teeth, in its slobbering mouth…it moved towards him. Another step, another step, it seemed to *luxuriate* in his fear, swaying its big head, sniffing the air. For each step it took, he took a step back. A thought built in the fear, *why was it not running at him?* Again it had him trapped…had him where it could…*oh no!* The thought *pierced* through his fear. Instinctually, all inside him cried for him to leap backwards…before questions arose, he did. Movement rushed past his feet and sound crashed through him. The huge, solid steel portcullis slammed down and, in a breath, he was falling again.

This time however, he did not fall far. His back stopped, his buttocks splashed, his feet slapped onto something solid and his arms collided causing a numbing sensation to run up them. Past these senses he immediately knew that he was in the centre of the castle. His senses distorted, no smell, no sound, but his eyes focused. The room was stunning; the floor was made completely from ruby, deep in colour, the pillars and arches soft gold and the walls of pure luminescent emerald. Light came in from widows in the ceiling, looking out onto a blue sky. It was a room fit for a king, fit for *him.* Yet his 'majesty' was uncomfortable, something was soaking through the peasant clothes. The *King* looked for the place of his discomfort and leapt from the throne he had been sitting on. For here in amongst this precious beauty was a throne which spewed blood like a fountain. Worst still the throne was made from human skulls and bones. Diego could take no more; *disgusted* at his own mind for showing something so bitter-sweet, he stepped back from the monstrosity only to become aware of something large breathing against his neck. What could he do but turn? Never stable always turning to something, he found himself faced by a horse. Black as night, its coat glowed in the jewelled room, no reflections in the hollows where its eyes should have been. Diego looked up to the rider, he knew him, his name was *Hector*- it was himself, but not as he knew. Tall in the saddle, broad in shoulders, his face was framed by a silver helmet. His dark hazel eyes, nose, a dark grin…a reflection of him, but not him. It was the rider, who broke the stunned silence,

"Heb, he Kray losz on." It was gibberish, the mouth moved so slowly, but with a scimitar the rider pointed to a door in the wall of the throne room and faded away. There would be no escape from this dream if Diego did not follow, so like the lamb, he went silently to the slaughter. It was then he finally awoke.

Somewhere, 2.31 Data Stream

It was the smell that woke him up; it was unfamiliar, undefined and offensive. Perhaps it was the unknown nature of the smell that had re-engaged his consciousness, but this was all very instant and swiftly overwhelmed by the sensations of pain. 'Overwhelmed' was inaccurate, the smell was initial point of a cascade of information: stiffness, pain and a burning sensation on his elbows and knees. His brain began to process, while informing him that he was on a cold hard surface and the space was dark, he was also face down. The scrapes came from being man-handled at least once and the stiffness was a combination of his hands being bound and unconsciousness. Any further analysis of his position was stalled by the memories, recalling Ekli's fist landing square into his solar plexus, convulsing Yazid in real time, tears began to role.

He had been faintly aware something was wrong the moment he'd walked into the depot, naively he'd put it down to his brothers once again being angry at his presence. They were always angry at his presence, but some just couldn't face reality.

"Oh, the prince has arrived, hello princeee." Issa greeted him in his 'normal' fashion, the mouthpiece of the brothers' bitter discontent toward Yazid. Half-brother, shorter, stocky, the family nose and eyes. Some days Yazid considered his younger exploits to have been foolish, the proclamations had formed a barrier between him and his half-siblings. If he'd given a genuine apology, then perhaps things would have been different. However, he *knew* the dreams were real and though the words of apology had left his mouth, the content was not supporting the phrases. Of course, on top of that his brothers were murderous, lying, adulterous, dishonourable scoundrels and it was Yazid's pleasure to point this out to them and their Father time and again.

"Where's Ruel?" No one responded. Of all the brothers, Ruel was probably the most stringent when it came to business and was a respected voice within the family, but there was an unconfirmed rumour that he'd had an illicit relationship with his step-mother. However, whatever his transgressions, Ruel was still not as universally despised as Yazid. The cavernous depot was rammed full of agricultural stock crates, part of a deal arranged by Ruel- now in its final stages. Yazid continued to move into the depot and saw Ruel standing in a makeshift alleyway between the small towers of crates. Ruel, seeing he had been noticed, turned his back on Yazid. *Hypocrite*, Yazid thought in his mind. It would be no thing for Yazid to turn around and leave, but he'd already had to hire two different vehicles to get to the depot and his Father had asked.

"Ruel, why are you here? I thought this deal was happening in Drew?" The question went unacknowledged, pretending not to be consumed by some paperwork. Sometimes it took everything within Yazid not to breakdown weeping in frustration, but one day they *would* understand. Today was not that day; in fact, his brothers had a different plan altogether. As Yazid got into the shadow of the crates Ekli appeared, charged at him and landed the punch which still rocked Yazid. Yazid had fallen to the ground, confused, all his motor functions kicking in and freezing, curling up and desperately trying to suck in air. He became aware in his shock of a something small, blunt and narrow being put against his head,

"Stop!"

"What, we agreed...!" Another sound was heard, a clicking sound.

"Shit Ruel, what the fuck?"

"Changed my mind." Yazid had always prided himself on being able to read a situation, to understand the atmosphere, appearing at times to be able to 'read' people's minds. Now all he was aware of was *his* naivety and fear, which slipped over a precipice into terror, his brothers' hatred had become murderous.

"*Pussy*."

"Say *that* again." Above him, Ruel had placed a projectile weapon next to Ekli's head and retrieved another weapon to aim at his own brothers.

"This *is* bullshit Ruel..."

"Enough, I'm not having his blood on my hands..."

"You agre..."

"Shut the *fuckup* Ekli, Gad make the call."

"The call, Gad, *what* call?" Daan enquired aggressively.

"We're selling him, Galatian traders are in the port." Ruel as ever had a side project.

"On it, they'll want him in one piece...put him to sleep." Yazid never saw who reached down and sprayed the gas into his face. Nevertheless, the tears of recollection continued to stream down his face and Yazid could not stop the sobbing. At least now he knew how he'd got in the situation, but it brought no joy, details did not bring any relief to the pain. Yazid was in a freighter, heading away from his home, away from everything he loved, in the darkness, in the pain, but was still alive.

<u>KI REGUS: Data Recovery Agency- Actual</u>

Regus woke. Badly. She had swept herself into sleep with a neuro-suppressor. Any claims to side effects being 'mild', were to her knowledge, *complete* bullshit and then some additional rainstorms on top. Yes, the body slept, the mind drifted into low appropriate activity, but never had she felt 'rested'. Or maybe she had felt rested for all of two minutes, as her systems re-activated and her mind came on-line, reminding her of the *terror* that was her life. Her rested-ness was consumed by the *world-storm*, not the reality of it, but the predicted arrival and the desperate attempts to find anything to stop it. Everything was being done, but no one was coming up with any results other than...shit, *we're* fucked, completely, forever and there is nothing we can do about it. In the fourteen cycles since the initial disaster, they had hit dead end after dead end; glimmers of hope mutated in to horrible, horrible realities. The pressure was overwhelming her colleagues, she'd found Banks weeping in the recreational area, Bilzerian had locked himself in his quarters; they'd had to escort Nela from her post because she was literally screaming at her DRA. Everyone was short with each other, hollow look in their eyes; anxiety was master and commander of the organisation. Yet they couldn't stop: civilisation, unknowingly, unwittingly and without say, were relying on the DRA's and their handlers to rescue everything. This thought resonated with dreams from days gone by...were they dreams? Or a stream she'd viewed in the eyes of a DRA? A tale of super-powered, super-equipped 'champions' that would defeat the on-coming...apoca something. Perhaps that was it, maybe they would find an ancient text, weapon, code or even a deity willing to bestow a solution upon them, better still willing to turn them all into super-something's that would crush the on-coming storm in climatic battle. HA, Ki's anxious mind jested, after all she was an executive bureaucrat of a mind-fuck organisation that had her 'handling' a crippled eccentric, who some thought had long ago slipped into senility. Maybe that was a 'little' harsh, crippled genius eccentric who was an *utter* bastard, was maybe more accurate. She regretted the quip she'd made about the General executive's mistress. Yes, it had been three terms before, but the General executive had bided his time and found the absolutely, fundamentally, beautiful punishment- being assigned to Malkus. Broken, 'brilliant' Malkus.

It was time to get up. Her body took to the command, maybe a minute more than the day before, but her feet were on the floor and she padded naked over to the slim sonic shower, the rays set to augment her waking. It stung a little, it didn't have to, but it was a habit that she'd formed at some point and saw no reason to give it up. She then moved to the toilet, in a hermetically sealed room, her bowels moved vaguely, and the product was whisked away to be recycled. A beep informed her that clothes were ready, a freshly cleaned uniform that consisted of a one-piece, camo-active garment of fabric that gave Ki-Regus the ability to withstand heat, radiation and impact. Ki had been told the stats, but they didn't really matter anymore, it was time for sustenance. Before the crisis she would have sat down and eaten a chef prepared breakfast that would have been brought from the kitchens of the complex, but now the restrictions on the handlers were extremely strict. She had only overslept *once*; it was not something that would reoccur. So instead of a three-stage nutritional breakfast, which was seen to be both psychologically and physically beneficial, she placed a single tab on her tongue and headed out the door to re-engage with her most infuriating muse.

Diego's Dream. Planet A63921F, 2.31 Data Stream

Disconcertingly things had changed, originally when he arrived in his nightmares; it was in an ancient dark wood. Trees loomed over him; twisted branches and gnarled bark, whispering malevolence into the night. However, this was not to be for tonight's expedition, no, now he was loomed over by *the castle*. It seemed higher, the spires carrying dark clouds as flags, though there was familiarity in the walls of water, steel, glass and stone. He turned all around, the forest and cliffs still menaced unhealthily towards him. So, what was different…nothing *visible*, still silent, cold, waiting…no it was 'he' who was different. Diego could not feel the burden that weighed him down every time before. Yes…he was ready to face that which dared to try and tell *him* how to live; now he would stride peacefully through this place. For *he* was owner of his own soul striding into the gaping mouth of the castle, almost unaware of the portcullis crashing down behind him.

For a few moments everything was dark, an unreal twilight in his dream, but then a number of torches lit themselves and Diego paused to survey the nonsensical given form. The flames burned against walls of horizontal water, sweeping waves held in place by his fantasies; the torch light flickering patterns not even held in the stars. After an irrelevant amount of time, he walked out of the gate house and into an impossibly big outer ward, which was full of people. *Eerily*, he could hear them and smell them, but nothing moved. The actions of a market day caught in freeze frame. A fixed kaleidoscope of colours, rough textures, they were people Diego *knew*, but couldn't place; disassociated by the lack of breath in their lungs and energy in their bones. He took a step forward, where else was there to go? His dreams *always* went forward. At some point in his steps forward, he realised that the sound had stopped; the quick blast of life had fallen silent. Yet it did not shake Diego, as disturbing as it was, it was better than having that accursed 'wolf' chasing him; its high shoulders and thick arctic coat, ready to engulf him. Maybe the new *him* had finally overcome his conscience manifest; though there was a strange pang that the 'wolf' was not here, there was no challenge now, no chase, just the frozen form of a misunderstood humanity.

As if 'reading' his mind, something moved… it was unnatural, fast, slippery, momentary…it was familiar, and something crept in his soul. No… *not reading*, his enemy was his mind. The movement had been far off to his right, a blur of action between two unmoving figures. Diego took another step forward to see and instinctively knew it was a mistake, he span on his heels and came face to face with the 'wolf'. His lungs forced the air from him, blood froze, and heart stopped, eyes on wide. The 'wolf' towered a foot over him, its shoulders casting deep shadows with its long snouted face and razor-sharp teeth, Diego screamed.

"AHH!" Immediately Diego turned his fear, *anger* reached through him and he threw a punch with all his might. The 'wolf' predicted…*knew* what was coming and standing high on its hind legs, clamped a huge paw over the human's fist. Diego tried again with his right arm, but he was fighting a part of his own thought process and the 'animals' other paw covered the remaining fist as well. Finally, it was over! Just when he thought that he had *won*, when life was complete, and all had fallen into place he would lose it. Killed by his own minds' sickness.

"And about time too…" Diego opened his eyes and looked completely bemused as the 'wolf' spoke in a deep, manly voice, it was no one specific, a collection of every man he had ever known. "Friend you look confused?"

That is an understatement, this is it, you're here to finish me off, me the survivor, prince of a people, hope of a nation, the future of my people… you're meant to devour me.

"Oh, no…no, no, you've got it *completely* wrong. Okay…so you may have ignored me for most of your life, but I'm *not* what you fear in this place". The voice was soothing and hypnotic, Diego inexplicably relaxed…something about listening brought peace to him.

"So…if this is true, why are you chasing me?" The 'wolf' blinked his big orange eyes and looked dismayed.

"Chasing *you*…no, my distant friend, I was just *trying* to say hello and show you the way…" Diego grimaced at how true the answer sounded.

"I take it the way, is to that which I fear?" Diego trusted the 'wolf', *after all it was his conscience*, and the part of him that claimed to be *good,* if good existed in this place?

"Ohh dear…you're in your *own* dream and you don't even know what's going on?" the 'wolf' sighed and scratched behind his ear. "Here follow me!" With that the 'wolf' released Diego's hands and turned away. *NOW!* Diego swung…but before the impulse was in the nerve endings, the 'wolf' ducked under the cheap shot. Rising back to his full height the 'wolf's' only reaction was to shake its fur coated head and give the most disappointed look. Trusting Diego not to try anything so immature again, the 'wolf' moved into the static crowd, waving *its* master on. Slipping through the silence, Diego caught glimpses of the life going on in his dream. He passed buyers and sellers, gossips and those willing to meet with petty rumours, but the thief picking pockets was what brought the biggest smile to Diego. It was such a peaceful scene, life was so good, and he couldn't wait to wake tomorrow from a full night's undisturbed sleep. They walked, for what felt like quite a while, neither talking, as if out of respect for those around them. Finally, the 'wolf' stopped and turned to the person next to him. The 'man' was- as the rest- caught in mid-action, standing straight and shouting to someone faraway. He was just over six-foot tall, a square face and angry eyes, yet Diego knew there was *something* significant about him. The 'wolf' grinned at the thought and said,
"This is what you fear…or more what lies behind him". The 'wolf' had a strange edge to his voice now, an anticipation of what lay ahead. Diego however, just looked a little lost and tried to look behind the statuesque figure. *His* conscience shook its head and then without warning, grabbed the arm of the frozen man and pulled. Diego had not known what to expect, he could have been accosted by another orchid or sprayed by blood, but the man simply swung like a door away from the wolf. Left in his place was a doorway, the shape of a human frame.

“The fear is through there!” the ‘wolf’ said commandingly. Diego however felt in control, his conscience was his ‘friend’ and these dreams were now under his command, his bold anger and annoyance had finally overcome the dreamscape. So, this hidden room would be no different, he stepped forward and turned to the ‘wolf’.
“Thanks…I’ll try listening to you more”. It sounded hollow and got the appropriate response,
“Bollocks. Now deal with this fear of yours…being a wolf really itches!” The ‘wolf’ scratched his ear again as if to prove it. Diego nodded and then walked towards the door, but a pace from it everything changed. *YOU CAN’T GO THROUGH THERE!* Everything that was in him screamed, his emotions *froze* him to the spot…he was stone with fear. He was at the mercy of his fear, unprepared and unwilling to enter that which did not exist. He tried to take a step back, but two paws fell hard on the gold armour that covered his back.
“Call it payback for the years of ignorance and shame!” The *wolf* said with a familiar chuckle and launched Diego through the human doorway, screaming.

He had fallen in the *forever-darkness* for a long time, until he just felt the cold ruby floor under him. “Not afraid!” he said like a mantra. He could not remember crashing to a stop or how his eyes had adjusted to the sunlight, but the floor was as stark and chilled as the first time he had seen it. Looking up, he found a growing dismay confirmed, the throne was there, gently bubbling away and he was back in the throne room of his discontent. *Fear*…The fear then began to grow, as if recognising something in the high arches and cold stones that he dreaded. Yet they looked like precious metal to him. A shiver ran through him, as the chill that permeated the floor transferred itself, so he slowly lifted himself to his knees and then his feet. Standing still, he waited for the embodiment of his fear to come, the eyeless horse and its master, *doomed* to stand over him. However, there was *only* the bubbling of the throne, no sound, but fear was growing to unbearable levels. Alone with an arising terror, brought to his knees by nothing more than a dream, a spark of electricity through his brain...*how can this be?* Before anything or anyone could answer, a piercing sound wailed out into the throne room, echoing off all the walls. Diego turned in all direction, his eyes and very being fell upon the door he had seen on his last trip here. It was a plain oak door, dark wood held in place by rusting braces and a large doorknob. He took a step towards it and the sound wailed again, but this time it was clearer, it was the cry of a child. Diego had many children and knew the sounds; the child was in pain. Only *when* his hand was on the doorknob did he realise what he was doing, the door however was heavy and not easily moved. It caught, half-open, on the perfect floor and would move no further.

Slipping nervously through the doorway, he found himself in a room obscured by mist. The moist air was bright and stung his eyes, blinking profusely they adjusted slightly. He was not alone, neither in the room nor in the sanctuary of the mist. About eight paces in front of him was a toddler, standing side on and naked to the trapped mist. Diego was a little shell shocked, how could he be afraid of such a cute kid, maybe he was about to turn into a giant snake and *bite his head off.* The kid, on noticing Diego, instead smiled toothlessly and then walked away. Diego then knew the waddling infant with its long blonde hair, chubby arms and legs...the toddler was him...*Hector...him.* Like a picture from his youth, he recognised himself, not because someone told him, but because he instinctively *knew.* The young Hector was already *well* into the mist, before Diego started after him, getting within two paces, before a shadow appeared in front of the obscured toddler. Suddenly the fear was back. Diego had been so preoccupied with the child-Hector that he had forgotten how he had got here, but this shadow made his heart cold. His chest would tighten no more- the shadow was *everything* he feared. In the moment of revelation something caught around him, only metres from the truth- the real world came calling in the form of vines. They knotted around him and he screamed. He fought the 'unnatural' something tearing him away and so as he prepared to wake, Hector continued onto a revelation.

Negotiations for the Staff. Planet A63921F, 2.31 Data Stream

"Well this is the famous Diego...I have to admit, I was expecting more"
You'd look fucking exhausted you arrogant prick if you'd had as little sleep as I've had,
"As the Laestrygones know, rumours can be *greatly* exaggerated." *Little sleep recently, but still a decent riposte.*
"True, true...nevertheless you have at least confirmed your punctuality,"
Diego had been warned that the Laestrygones were known to treat friends and foe alike, with a certain sceptical distain.
"Thank you. Shall we get down to business?" Getting to this point had been relatively painless in terms of proposals and counter proposals, as ninety five percent of the administration had been dealt with by the family's representatives. This meeting was merely for a traditional signing, particularly as it was the first time that the families had ever directly done business together. However, Diego nearly missed the meeting, due to an overdose of sleeping medicines four days before; as he fought to manage his dream. Not for the first time, his life belonged to Eli. The rescue had been passed off as a moment of intuition; but

much more likely was Eli being on constant guard against his own master, and the traumatic loss that Diego was trying to process. Yazid was dead.

Was it worth trying to recall how many words had been said, were they actually words? Loss, bitter pain, as if a force had grabbed his heart and walked through him. His eldest son's utterance had confirmed Diego's fear. A *fear* placed far from his thinking; at every point it had dared to place itself on the plateau of his consciousness. Nevertheless, *Ruel's* utterance had sung clear to the loss of his best and brightest - something of himself- maybe his mortal *being*? *Not the time, you are in a predator's territory.*

Lush, extravagant carpet with a subtle weave of Khaki, three of the walls were panelled in a rich chestnut coloured wood and the fourth was a transparent wall with a stunning view out on to the sprawling gardens of Byābilanēra and the metropolis of Tian beyond. *Don't get distracted, acknowledge the view, breathe, see Tian beyond, its beauty is deceptive, and it devours the naive, return to the room.* Diego gave an impressed nod, even if he had no emotional reality to connect with what his eyes saw, no care for the rich green colours, shining city towers and the horizon beyond. Nothing stirred, his gaze returned to the room, surveying the single piece of wood carved into a conference table, polished to glass. He looked and saw the shadow man that was his being in the room. ***NO** time for that now Diego, we need that staff...*Along with the *insistent* voice in his head (which was keeping him moving, establishing his poise and living his desires) came two of his sons, Yuta and Daan. Though were they *his* sons? Criminals, swindlers, merciless butchers...*NOT THE TIME.* They were two of his more ‘reliable’ sons and Yuta was now in line to become inheritor of the family. Yuta had successfully not started a massacre, overly swindled the books or had an affair with his STEP MOTHER! *Please Diego...*everything was so edgy with him and he was relieved to have something in his being restraining the tidal waves.

"Please take a seat.” The families agreed arbiter stood in the centre of the conference table, a man by the name of Simpson, who made Diego pine for Duncan's associate Hampton. Simpson was a cliché of the legal services, suit, mesomorph, tanned skin, sharp features and exceptionally competent. A matching set of tablets rested on the table in front of Simpson, awaiting the final confirmation and bio-data.

"Thank you," Yuta responded. Diego finally focused in on the two brothers representing the Laestrygones and he had to admit they really were impressive in person. Not in terms of features, they were not handsome, but they had an aura, which fiddled with perception and made them larger than they actually were. Crom Laestrygones was to the left: bald, large soft features, big mouth, which he was reputed to not open to utter much. Titus Laestrygones carried his brothers features, except for a sharp angular nose and close-cropped auburn hair. Both men wore identical robes, the Laestrygones had skewed conventional clothing throughout the generations, but there were rumours that the robe was ‘coming back’, not that this interested the family. It had been Titus who'd voiced the *warm* welcome and he continued to survey Diego and his sons with an intense, aggressive stare; even though he appeared relaxed. Crom on the other hand was sat forward, compelling his aura forward until his face seemed to float at arm’s length from Diego. It was not an inspiring or soothing face, be it at hand or at length of a boardroom table.

"Welcome esteemed parties, before me is a contract which is for the purchase of a small number of the Laestrygones family interests as listed..." Simpson was a smooth operator; he had a voice trained to the frequency that could gain any person's attention, even when nothing relevant was being said. "...The Field of Linermaree and property..." Yuta had already arranged a buyer, "...The Negev of Enid..." Originally owned by a Laestrygones subsidiary, it had been the most complicated part of the negations, as the subsidiary had at first not been willing to contemplate a sale, but the parent company were persuasive. To the outside this part of the deal looked to be the centre piece of the acquisition; as the Negev, though not obviously productive, bordered Diego's lands out to the north. However, it was a ruse, expensive, but one Diego desperately needed to work. "...the meadow of Ustain..." Yuta still maintained that this was a 'true' waste of money. In fact, none of the family were initially convinced as to the value of the purchases and in the end, Diego had simply ignored or bullied the doubting parties into silence. Perhaps they just thought it was part of his grief. "...The warehouses of Kisunu & surrounding civic buildings..." *Show nothing, clear your mind, notice the curve of the sunlight on the desk;* the colours accentuated the smooth finish of the wood, as Simpson rhythmically flowed through the final three properties. Someone gently nudged his foot and Diego came back into the room form the coloured space of the wood.
"My apologises sir, are you happy to proceed with the signing?" Simpson had his hands upon the two contractual tablets.
"Yes, sorry..." The atmosphere of the room shifted or at least Diego felt a *shift*, but he wasn't sure where, whom or what and he knew that reaching out to investigate might release the cords of the grief. "Please go ahead."

Simpson scooped up the contract tablets, moving as tradition expected and taking the contract to the senior party. The signings were called 'death-stone' signings. Ancient tradition held that two blood marked stones would be passed amongst the parties, with the 'senior' party showing their power by bleeding first and therefore longer. History told of times when the 'senior' party had over-estimated their strength and died while signing, more recently there was rumour that the contract tablet had been a source of poison for one or both parties. Thus, Simpson and his cohort of lawyers had been employed for security as much as legal procedure. So, with a degree of confidence, Crom and Titus used personal stylus to sign within a holographic frame projected by the tablets and then placed their fingers in specifically marked slots.
"I Crom of the house Laestrygones agree to the terms of this contract."
Simpson then glided away and down to Diego and Yuta. Daan was there as a mark of respect, though he had been given the responsibility of bringing the family stylus. Signatures were waved through the air; blood was drawn, and words were said. One contract done; in turn they signed the second tablet with the same process. Simpson nodded his thanks and then glided smoothly back to the Laestrygones, thus completing the circle. Or nearly,
"I have a thing to say..." Crom spoke, his voice was not sweet. It was earth and giant, resonating, even though the volume was soft. Was it all going to fall apart now, so close to getting his hands on the *staff* and finally being able to sleep, finally being able to see some other face in his dreams than *that* child? Finally, being able to grieve, "...You have showed strength today, I am one who has *lost* a son..." The men's eyes locked across the table, there were words, deep complete communications that verbal utterances would have contained and

brought to naught. A sharing of a scar and a fresh wound, blood brothers in loss. Yazid's face came to mind and a tear escaped the dense levels of control that Diego had on himself. *Did Yuta and Daan flinch?* "...I hope than neither you or I outlive any other..." The Laestrygones were butchers, merciless competitors, barely friends; neutral to no-one, but Crom offered a reality that no other could. The gaze held for two breaths "I Crom, agree to this contract."

Diego bowed his head, in tradition- in the beginning of freedom- in hope and in respect. Tears falling to the table, caressing a rainbow on the way down.

"That gentlemen is our business here concluded, I wish *both* families much abundance and satisfaction." Simpson brought the signing to an end, a contract tablet with each family, but more than that, Diego had access to the *staff*. On lifting his head, he found that Crom and Titus were no longer in their seats but had their backs turned. Yuta lent into his Father and whispered

"It's time to go." Perhaps Yuta had *always* been destined to be heir. Diego nodded and rose.

"Thanks to you Simpson and to the Laestrygones for their generosity and wisdom." Diego did not look long for a response, but Crom turned his head and gave the shallowest nod. Daan retrieved the Stylus and opened the door, Diego leading the way.

"Are you alright Crom?" Titus asked as the door shut, he'd never heard his brother speak in such away; in fact, the death of Crom's son was almost unknown outside of the family because he simply didn't appear to acknowledge it as happening. It had taken a great amount of self-control not to give way to the shock,

"I thought it would break him, but he is one to watch."

That Evening

Everything was a shade of grey, Diego knew he would mourn the loss of Yazid for the rest of his days, but the pain was so apparent that anytime he looked at it, a storm would rumble and erupt. Or try. His reality was a shaken scene in a souvenir glass globe, not so much the movement, but the disconnection from anything going on within the globe. Except Diego had two or three *different* globes, which he was aware of, and there were cracks in *all* of them. Realities merged onto one another and he was spending vast amounts of energy trying to keep track of a thread. The drain drew on all his resources and brought his shoulders and head down. His hip complained all the more vociferously. *Hip against hope.* Perhaps tonight he could finally lift that weight or at least find some respite. However, nothing was straight-forward; after finishing the signing, a family meeting had been called (demanded) and plans spoken about for the new purchases. Eli had warned Diego that this was a very bad idea and on a superficial level, his predictions came to pass. It was an angry shouting match; any sensible constructive discussion never entered the room. In fact, Diego was so aware of what was going to happen that he ignited the fire himself and opened 'discussions' with the Ustain meadows. Ekli railed into Diego, indirectly, but Daan was having none of it and leapt to his father's defence, even though Daan too thought the meadows weren't the best options. It was then that the brothers separated into the maternal factions and it descended into a farce, the brothers bringing up grievances that had and hadn't been settled, some that actually belonged to their respective mothers and had nothing to do with them personally. Nevertheless, four stayed silent, Diego, Eli, Yuta and Ben, though tears ran down Ben's beautiful face. After ten minutes the arguments raged into a cacophony, but Diego had drifted into a day dream, as vivid as any waking reality.

He came to the edge of the gorge, a gaping darkness calling him forward and without hesitation he succumbed to the invitation and leapt off the side. With arms and legs extended outwards, gravity-grabbed him and hauled him into the abyss. Yet he was without fear in the darkness, he breathed in and knew that it was not a place of oblivion, instead he took control of falling. In the darkness, forms quickly took shape and he was aware that below were his enemies, in a ring of sleepy canvas tents. Effortlessly he brought himself to a stop, feeling the weight of the air and the insistence of gravity, but he smoothly transited from the horizontal to vertical, some kind of dark spirit floating a few metres above the camp. Fourteen people billeted below, four on watch using simplistic sensory devices, while the other ten were in states of sleep. He knew that a statement was required, but it would have to be as quiet as possible, he could not afford a full-scale exposure, people relied on him. From a gold wrist band, which was the only colour on him, a thin film moved up his hand and began to extend out into the night, taking shape and colour. Reaching out, the thin film became a curved sword and then hardened silver with a perfect edge. None of his enemies would retain their heads by morning.

"Enough!" Diego snapped out of the day-dream to see Ben standing to his feet having howled and slammed his fist into the table in front of him. Everyone stopped and at first looked at Diego before realising that it was the youngest of the clan who had risen, tears streaming and a *fury* in his being that paused the arguments' song.

"This, these petty, pathetic slights are the things that *you* show so much passion for? How *fucking* dare you, you punch of pricks, he's dead! One of *us*…and *yeah* he was a fucking prick as well, but he was *blood*

and you brought most of this shit on yourselves! Grow a pair you numb-hearted fuckers, at *least* acknowledge his shade- *fuckers* and shut your mouths." Ben was shaking with a force that shrank his once furious brothers into silence, but before a continuance or a response Yuta placed a hand on Ben's shoulder. It brought him from a shake into a shudder and then he buried his head into Yuta's abdomen, sobs muffled by the dark suit jacket. There was an uncomfortable silence, but it was broken short by Ruel;
"Our brother is right. We have suffered a *terrible* loss, maybe not personally, but as a family we *will* honour our loss. We will draw no more on what has happened with the Laestrygones, let us allow time and space for us to *be*." Ruel took centre stage and Diego admitted that he spoke well and appropriately, "If it is alright father shall we adjourn any discussion till after a period of mourning?"
"Eli."
"A memorial service will be in five days; we are shutting down all our operations on that day. An itinerary will be forwarded to you when we leave this meeting, roles have been assigned. Directly after the wake Diego will be taking a holiday for ten days, during this time Ruel will be chair of any meetings, but authority will reside with Yuta. That *is* all." Eli may not have been blood, but there were days when his voice held more authority and respect than that of Diego's.
" You heard Eli, let us retire and begin preparations for the service." Again, Ruel spoke and after a few moments ten of the brothers began to leave, as they passed the still sobbing Ben each one, in turn, placed a hand on his shoulder, patted it and headed away. Most likely to brood, but at least some of the pent-up stress had been expelled and for Ben, his grieving had begun in earnest. He had also stood tall against his brothers, Yazid would have been *proud*. Yuta looked to his

father and could see the tears now at the edges of Diego's and escorted Ben away.
"It was worth it..." Diego held those tears- yet again.
"It would appear so, let's hope that the purchase was as well." With that Diego and Eli had departed the room. Eli had stopped to tell one of his assistants to send the itineraries and then they headed to a waiting transport. Diego's eyes were heavy, and the comfort of the vehicle saw him slip towards sleep.

He was travelling as part of a team, he wasn't Diego or Duncan, he was the other and people relied on him. A team of individuals trying to broker a peace treaty, young ambitious, naive...in need of his help. So, he had called upon his avatars Tamerlane and Nemesis, drawing them from the night; those he protected would awake with greater security. Each avatar stood at the same height of six foot two and both were cut from rock and rippling muscles. Neither however shared the same looks, Tamerlane had a narrow face, high eyebrows, pale skin and intelligent turquoise eyes. Nemesis had a more rounded face, with a character-less smile and warm brown eyes. The appearance of these reinforcements did not go down well; the delegates knew what they represented and that a real and present danger was at hand. Breakfast was eaten in silence and then they returned to the main trail. He took point on the wide track, flanked by grass to which the new Avatars moved, while the other avatar Sal brought up the rear. The tension had brought a daze to the group, their anxiety keeping them from noticing the beauty of the trees and fauna around them. Then after an hour the tension broke, the two new avatars picking up a conversation, Nemesis telling tales of the great adventures they had been on and Tamerlane continually correcting him. But he knew now that the decapitation of the those in the gorge was not enough to persuade the pursuers to desist and they came on. Subtly the pace began to increase, slowly at first until they were walking faster than they could jog. BANG! A shot rang out in the wide valley, rolling like a peel of thunder to the far hills, as one of the group was blown off their feet.

"Sir," Diego woke with a start, blurry, confused...had someone just *died*? Competing information rallied to his waking reality, he'd been dreaming, *so vivid,* he'd been travelling to take hold of the price, *so close,* and Yazid was...

"Are you okay?" Diego's spacial awareness told him that they were in a transport vehicle, it was now evening and that someone smelled, actually *he* smelled.

"Are we here?" He was tired, complicated sentences would lead to blurred communication, so he kept it simple. Whatever sleep he'd had, was deep and his body had suffered not being in a bed: aches began to signal in his neck and shoulders. *How did we get here?*

"Yes sir, this is the place, sorry for the delay, we were being followed and thought it best to lose them." Diego knew that to get to the meadows that they would have had to fly, had Eli carried him from one transport vessel to another?

"Any idea who?"

"Not at the moment, I have someone on it." Eli sat facing Diego in the stretched transport, he held a cup of warm stimulant and his face was unyielding as ever. Diego took the cup and for the first time with his own eyes looked upon the Ustain meadow storage. It was thoroughly un-impressive, and it gave him Deja-vu as his hip ached, he hoped that his benefactor did not have an agent awaiting inside the cavernous warehouse. The stimulant flowed smoothly, if a little bitter, but he needed his wits about him. Just because he now had access to the staff, didn't mean that suddenly everything was going to be set right. Life had offered him many lessons on this.

"It's time."

"One moment sir," Eli reached to his ear, "Clear? Good, secure the exits, we're in bound..." Eli's focus returned to Diego "We're ready to go." Eli opened the door stepped out, moving himself so that he could view the barren wasteland that was the meadows and then signalled for Diego to depart from the vehicle. "We're on the move." Eli said to the air as Diego stepped out into the biting cold, his stimulant mug overflowing with steam.

"How many are we?"

"Four, it will be enough." A tingle slipped through Diego and for a moment he saw the green forest again, twenty-five enemy combatants in bulging environmental armour bearing down on those he sought to protect. The glass of his realities were crumbling, but he stepped forward towards the meadow warehouse and the staff of gold and bone. *One of his avatars had fallen to a sniper's bullet, he would arise soon, but the others responded to the threat with precision, the civilians launched themselves the floor. Simultaneously, Tamerlane and Nemesis, in flowing moves, brought from within their travel bags, beautifully crafted, multi-barrelled pulse rifles and with them returned fire.* A strong breeze tugged at Diego and Eli as they crossed a few metres to the rusted front door, Diego just kept putting one foot before another as in his *ghost reality* weapons fire raged, blue plasma pulses tearing wood, armour and flesh. While the wind howled in the wilderness of the meadows in what Diego accepted as real time.

"Sir are you alright?" Eli knew something was up, but Diego couldn't say, they were to close and he had finally lost it...the staff of gold and

bone was all he had. Looking back over his 'actual' shoulder he could see the avatars of the *other* him not retreating but advancing on the enemy, forcing them to adjust, buying time. He *would* take that time.
"Yes, I'm fine...this place is eerie, reminds me of another time." So much of his life was circles, intertwined, intersecting and leading him through yet another threshold. Eli opened the door and Diego was for a moment swept into darkness, eyes adjusting to the darker space of the warehouse.
He was standing alone on a bluff which looked down on the valley, below his avatars fought valiantly, holding the line and removing the sniper. Nevertheless, they were being outflanked. More than that, in orbit the enemy had sealed any easy exit, it was not enough to just remove the current threat; to protect the team he needed to pull off something more complete.
"Here sir put these on," in the dark Eli placed a set of glasses in his hand, unfolding Diego placed them on and was given sight in the dark, in full colour. The warehouse was not empty, in fact it was full, rows of cargo crates, all completely irrelevant. A joke was circling about burning the place and claiming some kind of insurance.
"Where is it?"
"Two over, three down. Marked Es fourteen"
"Thank you," *Eli is a hero, a man who has rescued you from the fire, who has chosen you over his family, you over his own safety and above all brought you here...thank you, really?* Diego had never been criticised by the *other* voice before, but he turned away and marched towards the prize. The air was stale, the roof high and the storage crates unremarkable, Es Fourteen appeared. His father had told him once, well at least he attributed the statement to his father, that some of the most profound answers came in the simplest packages. The simple

package however was very expensive, even if it was a wooden crate just over two metres long, half a metre deep and wide.
"This one?" Diego asked Eli, putting a hand on the crate. Eli wearing the same glasses nodded and together they slide the crate from the shelf, dust sweeping into the air. Gently they placed the crate down on the floor and Eli retrieved bolt cutters for the padlock. With a nod from Diego he cut the lock and Diego lowered himself, opening the crate. The globes of his realities were popping now and so Diego took what little control he had left and looked into the crate. According to the inventory, the item stored was a minimum value item of some historical note, any attachment containing the historical data had been lost or simply not created. Alric had called it *fate*, because even he could only take some of the credit. Diego had paid Alric handsomely for the discovery, but he had the suspicion that at some point the *benefactor* had stepped in because the probabilities of the discovery were astronomical. Nevertheless, the 'item of some historical note' had been packed well in secure foam, but it was simple to find the purpose-cut slit which revealed the metre long, vacuum wrapped staff of bone and gold. Diego's breathe caught; he'd been looking for the staff since before the villa massacre. With Yazid declaring to his family his *gifting*, Diego had sought a way to help his favourite son. However, now he *desperately* hoped the myths surrounding the staff and its power, would rescue him from the dreams that bled into his reality. No more hesitation, Diego grabbed the staff and he arose as someone else.
The scene below was in the balance, though his avatars were punishing the pursuers and those he protected were making for a safe point, it was not enough. In orbit, an ambush waited. The planned route of travel, (through interstellar cargo vessel) had been intercepted and it would be a death sentence. The circumstances required more, so he

brought the staff to bear, the relic remembered things and would reshape the battle. Below the peace delegation had reached the safe point, it was time.

"Avatars, fall back!" The avatars without fail followed the command, launching a volley of plasma grenades and then beginning a strategic retreat. Such a sharp change of tactic gave the enemy forces pause and Hector believed that this would be enough- *it had to be. So, on the bluff, he lifted the staff to the sky, arms outstretched as if calling on a God.* The entwined gold glowed and two heartbeats later a tearing sound exploded through the valley and a tornado roared into life. Arising from the ground, with not a cloud in the sky, the swirling force of wind and moisture began consuming: trees, roots and soil. Growing into the clear blue sky, the tornado began to move towards *Hector, cutting off the advance of the enemy and undoubtedly causing massive confusion. But this was just the prelude, the howling winds continued to roar and with a flick of the staff in Hector's hand something began to take shape.*

At first a confused outline, a mess of tree and dark funnel, a form not familiar to the eye, but to the imagination, to fairy tales. A Dragon, wings the size of two storey houses, a towering body, massive legs and a line of razor spikes running from the tip of its head to the end of its tail. Hector swirled the staff again and in the roaring funnel the hard form of scales filled the outline. For a moment 'it' seemed unaware, oblivious to its surroundings and the fear it cast into those who looked upon it. Then it yawned, its block square jaw showing a mouth full of keen looking teeth, it shook clear the kinks in its body, stretched its wings and opening its eyes it turned its attention to those ground forces that pursued the peace delegation. With a glint in its blood red eyes, the green dragon grinned, nodded to Hector and then proceeded to rain fire down upon those below. Blue hot flame came roaring from its mouth, proceeding like missiles to their assigned targets. Crashing, connecting, exploding, engulfing, whole areas of wood and anyone who stood in it. Quickly the heavy armour of the enemy forces became boiling pots for those inside, contents and all exploded in a burst of flame. Fire danced from tree to tree, but the dragon was not done, flexing his back, he lowered his head and opening his mouth poured lava fire over the trees in front of him. Soon the whole area was ablaze, fire licking at the dragon's feet, as all around trees and soldiers exploded in death cries. Yet the dragon would not stop, firing again and again, the missile-balls of flame shuddered from its mouth to the ground. Hector brought it to an end. Bringing the staff to the ground in an arch, the dragon rose onto its hind legs, turned to the delegation bowed, and with a roar, flap of its great wings and tore into the sky.

ORBITING Assault team:

"Sir we have lost contact with Jora's team…there are no vital signs!"

"Sir something is coming up from the planet!" Both officers shouted in unison, the assault craft captain appalled by the news that touched his ear. It was chaos and he had little control; they'd had them…what the Sangra had gone on down there? They couldn't make any sense of the communications, the dead rising, superior pulse weapons…huge lizards! Were they chasing a peace delegation or some mystical demons? It did not matter, he had more Special Forces units…twelve in all, they would finish the job, but before he could give any orders the second officer was speaking again.

"Sir, it's coming straight at us!" The officer punched up the screen, a shallow picture of Gilino's atmosphere. For the past few weeks they had orbited the planet, a shadow against the stars, the captain getting used

to seeing banks of weather clashing for the world's attention, but now it was what rose from the clouds that shocked his soul. Coming out of the atmosphere, between them and the trading spacecraft, was a winged lizard, the size of a shuttle.

"Live link from the other cruisers sir" The tall captain didn't respond; his eyes were fixed on the unbelievable.

"Captain Halnon, are you seeing this?" The question flew between the six cruisers in high orbit, long knife shaped vessels, pointed at the planet, white hulls and red superstructures glowing the sun. Captain Halnon, a thirty-year veteran of twelve campaigns was silent…he couldn't find the words, so he just nodded. For a moment the lizard hovered in the vacuum of space, its razorback shining in the sunlight, and then it tore for the trading vessel. No one on any of the six cruisers could believe their eyes as with balls of fire, the winged lizard attacked a freighter fifty times its size. The conflict was short lived; first the shields collapsed and then the whole craft shuddered as the huge lizard thundered into the vessel. Flames erupted, as the lizard battered and bathed the spacecraft in flame.

"Gunner can we get a lock?" Finally, the captain found his senses.

"Gunner!"

"I'm not sure…I can only find the freighter…"

"Fire, widespread, high yield! Shields up! Start engines!"

"Sir!"

"Sir we have people on that craft!" The first officer finally realised what was happening.

"For the sake of all the gods Fire man!" The Captain bore down on the weapons officer, who shook under the assault, but from the black under belly three missiles tore away. Without fail they streaked across space and splintered into the freighter. Instantaneous, white, yellow, blue,

orange, licking, smouldering, eradicating. The three missiles struck bridge, engine and centrally. Silently, the dragon beat on, oblivious, but the vessel gave up and erupting in orbit, the explosion engulfed its enemy in one last act of revenge. The bridge was silent as the night lit up in front of them,

"How many men did we have on that vessel?" the captain asked, sombrely.

"Eighteen sir!" a crewman answered solemnly.

"Sir what in the name of Yasuo was that?" The first officer asked, but he never got an answer.

"By the Gods!" The Captain leapt to the view screen, but his eyes were not lying, the freighter was still roaring outwards, but within the debris, shadows took form. What was once one was now six. Six multi-coloured lizards, smaller, faster, but still as menacing. Six dragons for six cruisers. The cruisers were two kilometres long and one wide and though the dragons were a third the size of the cruisers, fearlessly the gold, red and blue beasts crashed into Yasuo's Special Forces cruisers. Captain Halnon's whole vessel shuddered as first the dragon crashed into the shield, flame racing over it, obscuring the hulls view. Giant beast on the edge of a knife, wings asunder, flame alive.

"Shields failing!"

"What! fire something!"

"Sir the weapons will not target!"

"Sir shields have failed!" The dragon dug in and the whole vessel lurched under the weight. "Hull breaches on levels three, twelve, eighteen and thirty!"

Three different officers shouted up the bad news. A strange silence filled the bridge as everyone looked to the dragon, myth given form, huge arms tearing chunks, cold eyes fixed on the bridge, its mouth firing out burning hot lava.

"Abandon ship, programme the pods to land away from civilisation…send a distress call". With that the captain got off his seat and headed for his pod, leaving his precious ship to dragon's teeth.

Diego knew now what the mystery man had meant, knew now who Hector was and the depth of the power he wielded, not in the staff, but in his own hands.

<u>Ki Regus, Data Retrieval agency, Hub Actual:</u>

Regus woke. Badly. She 'swept' herself into sleep with a neuro-suppressor. Any claims to side effects being 'mild', were to her knowledge, *complete bullshit* and then some additional rain storms on top. Yes, the body slept, the mind drifted into low level activity, but never had she felt 'rested'. Or maybe she had felt 'rested' for all of a minute, as her systems re-activated and her mind came on-line, reminding her of the *terror* that was 'life'. Her rested-ness was consumed by the *world-storm*, not the 'reality' of it, but the predicted arrival and the desperate attempts to find *anything* to stop it. Everything *was* being done, but no one was coming up with any results other than...*shit, we're fucked*, completely, forever and there is *nothing* we can do about it. In the twenty cycles since the initial disaster, they had hit *dead* end after dead end, glimmers of hope mutated in to horrible, horrible realities. The pressure was *overwhelming* everyone, eyes were vacant, half nods were the only response to each other's existence, anxiety was *master* and commander of the organisation. Yet they couldn't stop, civilisation, unknowingly, unwittingly and without say; were relying on the DRAs and their handlers to *rescue* everything. This thought resonated with dreams from days gone by...were they *dreams*?

Or a stream she'd viewed in the eyes of a DRA? A tale of super-powered, super-equipped champions that would defeat the on-coming...apoca something. Perhaps that was it, maybe they would find an ancient text, weapon, code or even a deity willing to bestow a solution upon them. Better still, willing to turn them all into super-somethings that would crush the on-coming storm in climatic battle. HA, Ki's anxious mind jested, after all she was an 'executive' bureaucrat of a *mind-fuck* organisation that had her 'handling' a crippled eccentric, who some thought had long ago slipped into senility. Maybe that was a little 'harsh', crippled genius eccentric who was an *utter-bastard*, was maybe more accurate. She regretted the quip she'd made about the general executive's mistress. Yes, it had been three terms before, but the general executive had bided his time and found the absolutely, fundamentally, beautiful punishment- being assigned to Malkus. Broken, brilliant Malkus.

It was time to get up. Her body took to the command, maybe a minute *more* than the day before, but her feet were on the floor and she padded naked over to the slim sonic shower. She suppressed as best she could the ache that existed in every sinew of her frame or what felt like it. She was horny too, more than that, she was lonely, but she took the subscribed pill by the shower stall and stepped in. The showers rays stung a little, it didn't have to, but it was a habit that she'd formed at some point and saw no reason to give it up. She then moved to the toilet, in a hermetically sealed room, her bowels moved and the product was whisked away to be recycled. A beep informed her that her clothes were ready, a freshly cleaned uniform that consisted of a one-piece, camo-active garment of fabric that gave Ki-Regus the ability to withstand heat, radiation and impact. Ki had been told the stats, but they didn't really matter anymore, it was time for sustenance. Before the crisis she would have sat down and eaten a chef prepared breakfast that would have been brought from the kitchens of the complex, but the restrictions on the handlers were extremely strict. She had only overslept once; it was *not* something that would reoccur. So instead of a three-stage nutritional breakfast, which was seen to be both psychologically and physically beneficial, she placed a single tab on her tongue and headed out the door to re-engage with her most infuriating 'muse'.

Ki turned right, nothing had changed, the cleaning machines kept the surfaces spotless; the holo-walls projected a warm pastoral scene, which even had a seasonal algorithm. Yet as lush and peaceful as it had once looked, to Ki it was a *torridly* boring, un-inspiring and irritating piece. Which was unfortunate for the first person she saw, Tel-an Maxwell; an intern, who had been drawn into the agency early- due to the multiple breakdowns of her colleagues. They'd talked a little, coupled once, but Ki generally didn't care enough to invest in a relationship that could end at any instant. *Regardless*, he smiled, a fetching, handsome smile, but they both turned into the crucible.

"Morning Ki" Tel-an said. The 'Crucible' was the new nickname, originally it had been nicknamed the 'vault', the room housed the data retrieval agents, encased in the intricate bubble that was the boundary of their physical existence. Ki thought of it more as *dungeon*. Both handlers paused, allowing the multiple levels of security to read their bio-scan,

"Tel." They couldn't actually see the DRA's bubbles, they were shielded in a vacuum space three kilometres below the crucible itself, instead the handlers were positioned in the analysis den. A porticus of cubicles where an individual handler received the raw and processed data forwarded by the agents. Each cubicle was a semi-immersive experience, with the handler having a virtual experience of the data, but not the intense sensory experience of the agents. Which would simply be too intense, even for the analysis' superior physique and psychology.

"Hope you find it..."

"You too." Ki had been a relatively 'successful' analyst for the agency, recovering an algorithm that would allow the solar collectors to work a few percentages better. Which was well received, but much of the great breakthroughs had happened a generation before her arrival in the unit. Directly across from her cubicle was the last of the *finders,* a tired, nervous looking man called Nin, slim, dark-skinned. He nodded to his colleague, as he had for the last thirty cycles and returned his focus to the feed. The *world storm* was *eating* them all alive. Ki stepped into the cubicle, it synched to her body scan, DNA and embedded chip tech.

"Welcome Ki Regus, shall we forsake the niceties," the central AI had a very particular relationship with Ki and could be relied on to adjust appropriately to Ki's moods. It wasn't to, difficult, as the Central AI had been tracking her movements since she left her room, having observed Ki's movements, biology and corresponding moods historically. The AI didn't even have to wait for a response but began to show the encrypted feed from Malkus; only Ki could access the feed, unless there was a crisis, even the AI had restricted access due to concerns that the AI would use the feeds to make itself 'God-like'.

However, decryption did not reveal anything that would have given the AI 'God-like' insight, instead it caused Ki significant alarm; Malkus' feed had become a mis-mash of streams, intersecting around a man called 'Hector' and his other realities, it was a beautiful and confusing collection of massive possibilities, but crucially there wasn't a trace of the *world storm*. Worse still, the shape 'shifter' had disappeared and with him any trace of the *world storm* data that Malkus had assured her would be available. Both of them had lost sight of the mission and its objectives, any review by her superiors would cause significant consternation and undoubted sanction.

"Central, patch me through to Malkus."

"Live"

"Malkus, what's this gibberish?" There was no response, it was unnerving, Malkus was always on the front foot, one step ahead of handlers, commanders, generals…the whole *fucking universe* in his mind. "You *assured* me that this wouldn't happen, *you've* lost sight of the data and there is simply *no* trace of the shifter..." More silence, the communication was bound to the voice, no visual for either, and even the voices were encrypted. "Malkus are you sulking?" Ki thought she heard a sigh, a resignation or deep frustration. "*Right*, fuck you, you prick; *screw* you're fucking head back on..." Weeks of blurred stress began to motion to the surface of Ki's reality and found focus on Malkus, "...we're dropping Hector and *you* can forget any further investigation into the *shifter*, I'm going to reassign you to..."

"You just can't disappear." Malkus finally spoke, the encrypted voice a collage of different emotions.

"What?"

"He's *gone*, vanished, there is no trace of him at all...it's as if he never existed." Ki continued to seek new streams to put Malkus on, but something about his words were deeply disturbing. "I've looked *everywhere*, even to streams he was in before and he's gone...someone *else* is there, but not Varses."

"Malkus, do I need to call in *the team*?" She had never had to use the threat before, Malkus for all his vanity, knew how to play the 'game', but his communications were past disturbing, they were madness. The question of *really, if so, how?* pulled at Ki, but the *storm* was coming and what Malkus was saying simply couldn't be.

"Fuck you Ki, *look* at feeds..." Even with encryption, the communication was like a slap in the face and it stunned Ki enough for her to look across to Nin. He was looking at her intently, aware in part of the struggles that were happening in Ki's cubicle, it made Ki feel naked, vulnerable and she could feel her anger rising. *Breathe.* Clarity came to her in the moment, what Malkus was talking about was impossible, even if, for some reason the 'impossible' had happened, it brought her, Malkus and the DRA's no closer to a solution for the *storm.* Ki had bought into the myth of Malkus' for too long, it was time to be his *handler* and not his 'co-conspirator'.

"Malkus, I *will* review the feeds, but we need *you* back on point. I'm placing the stream data in your system, clear your buffers...store it if you want..."

"But..."

"Malkus, the *storm* takes priority, you *know* this...you resist here and whatever's going on with the *shifter* won't matter at all, I'll be reassigned; you'll be back on gardening leave and they'll delete everything..." Normally Malkus would start trying to interrupt, but the resignation that Ki had heard early was in the silence, "...find us *something*, I'll look into the *shifter.*" It wouldn't be a priority, but perhaps having something else to do would give Ki some respite from the *storm.*

"Your word?"

"*Fuck you* Malkus, buffers clear?"

"Saved, you know what Regus, you're a bitch!" Whatever was going on at least with this Malkus sounded a bit more like himself.

Data Stream 5.58- Relevant

Light fell cleanly onto one spot in the room, in the centre of the circle and onto a cold and decaying corpse. Eyes watched from a dark corner, in a room that was usually ablaze with light. A circle of figures fixed each other with gazes that sought information from the slightest physical response to the proposition in front of them. The 'proposition' was formed into a question, an utterance silent, but convicting of those who carried the responsibility of the peoples outside of the dark room. *What do we do now?* Corpses didn't give answers, they proposed questions; such as: *how did I die, quietly, brutally, witnessed or unseen?* Often simple interpretations of data fulfilled the expectation of the question, but this corpse carried a ramification that was causing a shockwave. These passed through the darkness and into the community beyond, even as the Elders came to terms with the small 'stone' in front of them.

"You know what *this* means?" the Elders stood in a circle around the table, a male Elder spoke, his designation seventh. As it was the Elders of the community understood, perhaps not the full breadth or how far the waves would travel, but the interpretations baring down on them. Ten elders, three males, four females and three without sex, looked from the corpse to each other, everyone wore the same dark purple cloak. Each Elder knew exactly who the other was, but this was tradition, only the voice distinguished the differences in the group.

"Could just be a stray or another reject?" A voice as light as a breath of wind, designated number nine,

"Tomos says that *it* was armed," deep and foreboding, elder three.

"It's our *worst* fears then?" A stream of light babbling tones, elder five.
"Let's not overreact." Elder two, a confident mid-range tone of pleasant resonances.
"Savages, I say *we retaliate*; this is a clear incursion." Elder four, aggressive with undertones of stones being crushed.
"Attack, are you…those are consequences *we dare not* face, as powerful as we are…Tomos says that there were three savages all armed and clearly scouting intently." Elder ten, firm with robust conclusion.
"Did they attack first?" Elder four.
"Yes." Elder three.
"See, we *have* valid ground, even *they* could see that?"
"Look, we're not on best terms even with a righteous claim." Elder six, a voice on a string, plucked and muted. That stopped the silent conversation in the fire lit hall, every cowl swayed towards the chief elder.
"Call Tomos, tell him to take five, no six of the finest and to scout out the savages' movements. Minsel as Elder for communication I want you to take down a simple message and take it to the high council. In the meantime, everyone else prepare to move the people."
"But Elder!"
"If it is not as Dasan fears then we *will* return, but I will not risk our people for what is left of the harvest. Are we agreed?" Agreement was given with a solemn bow of the head, a unified acknowledgement that an interpretation had been found, "Thank you, may our choices be wise; bury the body by the river. Please complete your tasks swiftly. Minsel with me." Two of the elders wrapped the corpse and four took the burden, songs would be sung, even for the one who had trespassed. Minsel and the chief elder headed for the back of the small feasting hall.

As they entered into the light of the bright day, Minsel dropped her hood. She was stunning in her beauty, the angles of her face flowed in perfect symmetry, large almond shaped green eyes, flanking a thin ridge of nose over the full lips of her delicate smiling mouth. Her oval face was given character by an inverted jaw line and chin, framed by thick curling auburn hair which formed beautifully around her slender neck and shoulders.

"Are you *sure* Karith?"

"I will not speak of it in the open." Karith, Chief elder remained covered, as was his way, his voice low and warm.

"Sorry that was indiscreet me." Minsel's sweet melody of a voice was apologetic.

"It is a shock to us all, but we must remain peaceful for the appropriate course of action." Minsel entered into Karith's house as the door was opened by the servant therein, Karith bowed to his servant and entered.

"I'm sorry that there is no hospitality, but I have a mission for you." Karith was famous for his hospitality, but they had yet to leave the hallway. It was a large area of dark wood, but to stay here was normally considered an insult.

"You actually think it's that bad?"

"*Yes*, take your family and go to Malahman." Karith's servant brought him a piece of cloth and a feather inked, he began to write on a smooth wall.

"When you get their go *straight* to Lucian, he will know what to do." Minsel waited quietly as Karith finished writing, it was clearly graphic and full of emotion, out of respect she did not probe the words. In a sense she didn't need to, she had a fair idea what these phrases said and why they were going to the permanent dwelling of Malahman and Lucian within- they were the communication hub of their people. With the rising number of *savages,* their incursions and growing animosity towards her people, the only reasonable conclusion was *war.* A war they could not win, because at the simplest level her people didn't have the numbers. Karith finished writing, dropping his hood for the first time and looked upon Minsel, he locked his eye upon her.

"Though you best prepare yourself for a long journey, this message must get to the upper chamber, we are enacting *Silab."* It was the first time Karith had actually used verbal communication to speak to anyone, having used telepathy instead, and in verbalising those words tears fell from his silver eyes.

Data Stream 6.34, Semi-coherent connection

Malkus clashed with his own being; Ki's words of rebuke had cut, but restored the perspective he'd lost. He couldn't keep behaving the way he had; they'd take everything, there was even a chance that *if* they all survived, the Elders would put him on gardening leave permanently. He needed to turn things around or at least show willing, so he'd adopt a different stance, even if losing Varses was- *no* he couldn't go back there. It was time to focus, there were several ways to ride the data streams. Often the DRA's skimmed to surface of a stream, which allowed for a wide focus on information that fell into very specific categories and was often processed at length by the handler, it was nick-named the 'all seeing eye'. The *Birds eye view* was more intense, both in the intricacy of information retrieved for the buffers and the demand on the agent's senses. Finally, *the real world or ghosting;* effectively this was as close as a DRA could get to being part of the data stream and the impact on the agents was profound. Interacting physically, emotionally and psychologically, but never connecting with the *other* reality was consuming. It built an unrelenting tension in the agent, a dissonance between realities; it required careful management by the agent themselves and their handler. This being the case, Malkus flagged on the system his intention and he sort to *ghost* the semi-coherent stream, something about the form of the stream intrigued him. *Ghosting* was significantly easier when an agent had a consistent way point, which was usually a building, person or perhaps a family, otherwise grasping something from the stream became like picking a twig from a raging river. The initial stream, five fifty-eight, had offered a few potentials, though nothing convincing. Instead Malkus' marker was a person named James Eddings. Professor of Archaeology at the University of Kalinacta, Caucasian, ectomorph, sixty-eight kilos, one hundred and eighty-five centimetres, fifty-eight years old according to the cycle of the planet, green eyes, a prominent birth mark under his right arm. Parents Nemian and Patrice, deceased; two siblings, divorced with three estranged children and a significant estate, managed by his brother. The professor may have been separated from his family, but he was embraced as a global superstar. According to the stream, his team had re-discovered the lost city of Ēṭalānṭisa, he'd been heralded, wined and dined, some kind of entertainment phenomena. However, he'd deceived them all by admission, for within Ēṭalānṭisa was a greater prize still, a map to a time without words. After the hype had died down and a long battle to get additional funding, Eddings and his team had travelled into a disputed region of dense vegetation, setting up camp on a plateau, here Malkus decided to become ghost.

Malkus flickered just a little in his cocoon as he contacted with the 'reality' of the trifling, oppressive, unrelenting humidity which had not been given a change to fix its torrid life- sucking form onto every nanometre of reality. Instead a vast storm had swept in and driven the humidity off, for now. The team had been pre-warned of the severity of the storm, by equipment left behind by the Elmander corporation team. Who had begrudgingly, retreated from the oppressive reality of the plateau after failing to discover fresh water. Not that this turn of events had been met with celebration by Professor Eddings and his team, the Elmander corporation had under written much of the project. If not so much in hard currency, they'd supplied political and, some of it not exactly 'legitimate', influence. Professor Eddings and his team were archaeologists, brilliant, world renowned archaeologists; but they had discovered early in their careers that being 'world-famous' in some areas just didn't mean anything. Even if an occasional cultural expression presented your chosen profession in an 'adventurous' light. They also understood that contracts were not *that* binding to multi-global corporations and even though Elmander had left significantly valuable equipment and contracted military support, the 'sands of time' were moving against the excavation. To compound the pressure, Professor Eddings had also misjudged the emotional bond that had been formed between the two groups, some quite personal bonds and so, exacerbated by the demanding hours, a fight had broken out. Surprisingly, for Eddings at least, it was between one of his senior staff, Doctor Thomas Sheng and a young assistant by the name of Riband. The fracas had got so vicious that the local military liaison officer had actually discharged his weapon, which was swiftly followed by the officer publicly dressing down Eddings. The liaison officer declared him a 'slave driver' and 'obsessed' about something he would never find, because he didn't know what he was looking for and the climate had driven him 'crazy'! A particular grievance and concern was that though the team had made numerous, 'incredible' discoveries- Eddings just passed by. These things were 'sacred', to be honoured, mapped, documented, *what kind of archaeologist was he?*

.

Something in the crack and distant echo of the bullet seemed to unleash a wave of exhaustion. Eddings had collapsed. No show, no emotion, his system just shut down and he woke ten minutes later with Doctor Lindquist standing over him. *Stupid commander*, didn't he understand that no one else could know, *no-one*! Eddings could not have a vulture stumbling on the secrets of the cylinder. Nevertheless, his fainting gave him an opportunity to manage the situation; he gave the green-light for *his* team to call in help from the local government, but only to excavate the already established discoveries. The junior members of Eddings' team would head up those units and start at the far end of the plateau with the first discovery. In the meantime, he and the 'advanced' team would carry on, only returning if the teams discovered any new caves. This was an 'acceptable' course of action for the officer and fifty of the nation's archaeologists were called in. The sands kept running, though. It wasn't for another two months that finally they found what they...what he was looking for. Eddings had driven his team south, arriving at a strange phenomenon within a low risen mound. At first the team had considered it nothing more than an aspect of the plateau, but the sonar system conceived that within the mound was a structure, which it could not pierce. Focusing on the spur, the team found a vein of weak sediment and cut through to the heart in no time. With the debris cleared, the sonar imagery revealed a dome surrounding a sealed room. It was twenty metres high and fifteen in diameter, only three metres of which actually breached at the same level as the plateau. Though hollow the room was not empty, on the west compass angle were a set of two forms that looked like thrones and upon one was a mass. *This was the site*. This was the place the scroll in the cylinder spoke of, which ancients had spent untold riches and resources sealing up, they may have even buried a city in water. Words were always limiting, there was just the silent groan; *he'd found it*, a place that had not been *desecrated*. His head was spinning, but his heart and guts were cold. He ordered them to dig. Yet the news of difference stole his vitality.

Nearly sixty, 'vain', 'egotistical', estranged from his family, mildly 'obsessive', surrounded by professional obsessives who were digging into a past that wasn't his. He had no past, just a string of dig sites and pictures scanned and edited. There were those who thought the whole mission was a delayed midlife crisis, now, near the pinnacle of his greatest *desecration* these thoughts had become real. The very mortal feeling of his life magnified, spun him back to looking at the pale hue in the skin of his mother's withered body before it was cremated. He'd not mourned, instead he'd excavated the historic site that became known as 'Ēṭalānṭisa' and buried the grief there; *he would not let it arise*, behind it was a tsunami. Instead of facing the wave, he'd used the cover of his teams' celebrations of the discovery to seduce one of the Elmander security guards- a submissive proto male- and they were with him until dawn. The next night he found one of the local amateurs, a little dusk skinned girl with big brown eyes and bigger curves, got her drunk and simply violated her. Yet he found no strength, no resurrection, no accusation; just the cooing of success. He faked his enthusiasm, went through the motions, but that was a mask that would crack. The guard said nothing, but the little amateur girl continued to share his bed, even if he was simply forcing himself upon her; after all she was grasping at opportunity, she got to work at the main site...perhaps she was angling for what came after. Daily he watched the slow progress of the dig, nightly he fucked the amateur, *weeping* as he did. Eight days after the discovery; they were ready. Eddings, Nilsha and Sheng had been lowered to the base of the submerged dome with laser drills to cut the last metres, it was the 'Eddings show' now. The coldness in his guts was creeping up his spine; it wasn't even worth explaining to himself now. A train was runaway, he'd started it and sabotaged it, he had always desired the crash. With tender care and a rhythm-less heart he removed the last stone and put the hydraulic joist in place.

He wanted to run, far away. *The professor was not the only one, what was it for a ghost to shiver? Malkus was shaken by the anticipation and dreaded going across the threshold. These were his feelings, but never before had his ghosting brought such massive levels of feedback, he was aware of his own perspiration in the cocoon, moments before the system took it away for analysis and recycling. Procedure stated that he should step back, but the darkness begged the light, calling for revelation.* Professor Eddings could feel all those watching through the enviro-suits camera's 'pushing' him on. It was a moment of 'faith', not in a higher power, destiny or fate, but that he could survive the next step. He ordered himself forward.

"James, it's waited long enough." Nilsha voice cut into the ragging torrent of stillness, James Eddings could not move.

"You're acting like a virgin Jay, if you won't I will." Sheng shoved him gently, a light mocking pat, but James was so rigid in his suit that it put him off balance. He stumbled into the dome and the moment of 'desecration' was gone. Eddings took too long to regain his balance and he reached the centre of the dome by the time he steadied himself.

"Jay are you alright?"

"What's up with you?" Nilsha moved more cautiously, letting his eyes sweep over the dust covered floor. "Is the vacuum still in place?" Though Eddings was struggling, Nilsha was all business.

"Yes Professor, we're not reading any change."

"Once we've completed an initial sweep begin pumping the air."

"Yes sir"

"Beginning sweep now." Nilsha and Sheng went about business as usual, carefully and cautiously moving in a forensic manner but James just stood dumb-founded. Time was blurring and he couldn't see beyond the Plexiglas face guard, he couldn't seem to take breath properly. James had *never* felt like this before and had no way of narrating to himself a viable way forward. He just stood, allowing his body to take in the necessary oxygen, but not much else.

"Are you getting the feed base?"

"Yes, professor Nilsha, filtering and processing already began, but the place looks…"

"Empty. Clear, except for the thrones." Sheng cut in; he had returned to James but this time he was in front. He tapped his arm to request that James moved to a personal frequency on the blue tooth communications device.

James reacted without thought.

"What the *fuck* is up with you James?" He couldn't find a response.

"You actually look like, well either you're having a breakdown or *Great Spirit* forbid…a religious moment." Something ticked over in Eddings, perhaps it was the line of accusation or the tone of the voice, but he returned to the moment. He'd desecrated for the last time, he couldn't go any further, there was no further back. Yet to fail to be the archaeologist he was at this point would be a disaster he would never recover from.

“Only you have religious moments Sheng, when you're taking a dump.”
“Well that was my third option, you’ve been banging that *piece* so hard that you’d become constipated.”
“How does that work?”
“I’m an archaeologist not a doctor, don’t ask stupid questions. Now confirm that you’ve not just released your bowels by going and studying our friend on the throne. Nilsha and I will begin beta sweep, try not to step in anything.” Nilsha had returned. James tapped his head in mock salute and putting his thump up, finally engaged with the dome room of legend.

There was no light, natural or otherwise, and wouldn’t be until the second team moved in, night vision highlighted the hollow space. There were no obvious carvings in the floors or walls, even with advanced night-vision one couldn’t make out the textures of the dome with ease. James moved toward the thrones which rested on a two-step dais, like the rest of the room they appeared to be unmarked. It was immensely unusual for a site such as this to be so lacking in elaboration; the doom structure was an outstanding piece of engineering; it had been remarked that technologically it could have been built recently. The assumption was that those who had created the structure would have extravagantly arrayed the internal space, but this was not a place of celebration, even the poorest surrounding burial site was more adorned. The thrones then remained within the overall theme, simplistic and unmarked, rising to form traditional arches above the main seat. On the right throne was the mass; a vague humanoid shape covered from head to toe in a ragged, colourless cloak, the expectation was that the body within would be mummified. Eddings *drew* closer, flicking his vision over the metre in front him so that he would not step on anything of note or worth. He took two more steps and got to the bottom step of the dais and for a moment he could see under the hood of the mass, but something was *horribly wrong* and then he passed out.

Data Stream 5.58

WAKE UP MALKY, WAKE UP YOUR DREAMING...Malkus dreamt. James Eddings becoming a 'memory' on a buffer, a relevant stream to drift into the state of rapid eye movement. Malkus was not meant to dream, was he? How could he know, but it was the only frame that could find to explain how he floated on the river of data. *He flowed* with the *goddess* Minsel as she travelled with her family toward the beacon community, traversing the densest forest, moving to the rhythm of the wind. They travelled light, Minsel's culture was not one to believe in possessions; identifying with each other and the *great spirit* of the land, with whom they now pleaded for safe and swift passage. Swift feet that brought her people the news they had dreaded from the before time, the prophesied rise of the darkness and the escape to the light. There had been false rumours before, whispers when the land had swallowed up whole villages, but this time it was different. Minsel's mate had known instantly and even her beautiful children's developing awareness was keen enough to perceive that massive change was upon them. So, to Malahman, carved onto a mountain, it was a pinnacle of construction and beauty, but Minsel could not see it, a grey lament had followed and overtaken her. Minsel sort Lucian. The 'one' to take away the burden that drew life from the *goddess* Minsel and give her renewed hope- the people had a future far from the dark lands. At least the children had enjoyed the journey, seeing Malahman for the first time was an ecstasy. They skipped ahead, dancing up and down the steps, amongst the hunters and gatherers who went out to control the local animal populations. Minsel could sense the curiosity, visitors were always heralded; ceremonies were performed, generally swift, and stories were told, but not today. Such behaviour did not go un-noticed and at the gates of the city, a guardian paused their progress.

"I intrude on my family to ask where they journey from and to?" The guardian was an aged man, but his weather-beaten dusk skin was glowing with youth and his eyes pierced with colour of a winter cloud. It would have not gone well to assume anything about the guardian.

"Honoured Guardian we come from..."

"Ah, I am informed, beautiful Minsel, my family. It has been an *honour* to have met and received your presence, please, Yalom here will escort you to Lucian." Clearly Karith in his prudence had sent messenger birds ahead to smooth the transition and also to protect the sensitivity of the message Minsel carried. In the instant of the guardian's declaration Minsel had assumed that a 'younger' person would be assigned to the task, but Yalom appeared to be as aged as the city itself; valleys and creases carved into his face, skin like his comrade and eyes rich in a lush green. An exceeding warmth exuded from him and brought calm to Minsel's being. For the first time in days Minsel smiled and the world found some colour,

"Yalom, in your kindness, the crystal rooms via the memorial residence. No one speaks to her but Lucian. It has been an honour to share your presence friend." There was communication beyond the words, twitches of the shared experiences marked upon their faces, understanding and the slightest bow. Minsel felt humbled, she and her family were being heralded in a way that was almost unheard of, these persons were legends and they moved with generosity.

"It is my honour my friend, your presence has been *most* fulfilling, may it go well with you." Yalom titled his head at the children,
"Welcome younglings, I sense your names still await, that will be a joyous day for your Kinling, but can you help an ancient like me by restraining your beauty for a time as we travel. You know how to *embrace* the moment?" Minsel was as transfixed as her children, Yalom was a river running in pleasant places, his voice a rolling song, and silently everyone in the party nodded. "Ah good *as* expected of those who attend with young Karith. Shall we depart?" Again, everyone nodded.
"Guardian, it was an honour to be in your presence..." Minsel's mate bowed low, offering an open hand gesture above his heart and Minsel could have wept at his beauty, the attentiveness of his being.
"Go in life." And with that the Guardian's gaze returned to beyond the gates of the city.
"Thank you, my heart." Minsel whispered as they took up behind Yalom, a brisk pace was established by the slight figure of Yalom. As with the first Guardian however, the age, build and greying hair described nothing of the latent power that these persons had. The grace of his movements were as invigorating as a cool breeze on a hot day, Minsel was mesmerised. Colour, smell, form, beauty, movement; each step a cacophony of sensual experience as they moved further into the city. A dance of acceptance, becoming one with community, unhindered to the memorial residence,
"Minsel, I will watch over our children." Her mate, bonded heart, complete romance; attendant to the moment. *Irritating*. Just a little, because he was being everything she wanted him to be, but the little voice in *her* dialogue wanted him to help her into the crystal rooms.

"Yalom will guide you well." Not the words that she wanted to hear, but the best words. Yalom smiled and offered an arm to Minsel.
"I can see why Karith guided your pairing, please I will help you carry the burden of your words just a bit longer..." Minsel smiled at her mate whose noble hands rested lovingly on their children's heads'; it was not the time falter.
"Continue in the moment, *my* life I will return soon."
The family simultaneously kissed the inner knuckle on their hand, as was their way, and then Minsel took Yalom's hand.
"*Exceptional*, Karith has done well to keep you and train you, you do have *all* the form of an elder, but yours is a sad song at the moment isn't it?" Yalom's arm was warm and reassuring, Minsel looped hers through as Yalom spoke to her inner dialogue without words. Minsel nodded. They stepped away from the memorial chamber and deeper into Malahman.
"Do not brood on it, there *is* not blame for the messenger, especially one of *great* generosity as yourself. Make no mistake there was a time when messengers would arrive and speak words, but even the *kindest* words can be poison when formed around a particular intent. I once remember having to discipline a Kin of mine because though they spoke accurately the intent was clear...do you *understand*?" Yalmon's river turned and Minsel again nodded. She could sense her own foreboding, *Silab*, was slowly consuming her. For the first time since her pairing, dark dreams had come to 'speak' to her on the journey to Malahman. *Silab*, the inevitable reality of decisions made a thousand generation before. The slow creeping reality of the interfering, the great disconnection; some had begun to think that it was an unnecessary precaution, a hopeless supposition. Even she had placed it *far* from her, after all if the seers could not conceive of it would it ever come? The

dark dreams whispered the reality of its coming, of the shock, consternation and resistance. SILAB. The end of her people. The steps to the crystal hall grew heavy.

"There's no way out Yalom."

"Then embrace the freedom of that assurance." With that they fell into silence, Yalom did not probe or speak, Minsel noticed the intricacy of carvings, the stories of yesteryear interwoven with recent events. *All soon to embrace Silab shadows cast* and then they found themselves at the entrance to access to the crystal hall. Minsel's mate had once been given access to the hall, due to an emergency for which he was still bound to silence. Through his silence, Minsel had sometimes imagined what the hall actually looked like, as he'd given nothing away, but to her disappointment the entrance was way past underwhelming. If Yalom had not been guiding her, she would have walked past the bland wooden door that was the entrance, cut as it was into a recess of stone on the curve of the main walkway.

"We are here." Clearly there was an intent behind the subterfuge, this was the centre of communication within the region and any breach would be catastrophic. Yalom paused Minsel with a gesture and approached they very thin door with reverence. Two paces from the door, Yalom lifted his left hand and stood for a few breathes with his palm directed to the door. A few beats more and a click sounded, the door slid into the rock to be replaced by darkness.

"Ah beautiful Minsel, your presence has been a *great joy* to me and you have lightened my way. Go in life. You will have to enter sideways, after about ten paces a glow will appear...I will return to you with your kin-ling when we are called." Yalom beckoned her forward, his face of years full of compassion; he then took her hand in his and like a dance step, glided her to the door. He gave one gentle squeeze and then released her into the dark; light filtered in from the crystals in the corridors, for about the first three paces and then all was swallowed by the passage. She also noticed the air temperature began to change against her skin and should could sense the closeness of the rock around her, her back and bosom every so often stroking the cold stone. With Yalom gone, and alone with her awareness, she could also begin to sense something else, a quite massive presence whispering to her curiosity. Six paces in, there was a loud click and she heard the door close, feeling the disturbance in the air, followed soon by the knowledge that though relatively close, she was to her knowing completely alone. The sound of her heart beating, and the raised tempo of her breathing filled her senses; stone and dust of the passage was a faint smell, she began to smell her own odour and wished for a bath. Yet she took herself back to the moment, *taking* Yalom's words she discovered that ten paces in a new light impinged ever so lightly on the darkness, as did a smell or a mixture that she as yet couldn't define. The light on the other hand began to grow and develop, drawing her on as Minsel's eyes adjusted and re-adjusted to the changes. At thirty-five sidesteps the narrow passage began to widen, Minsel turning to be kissed by the kaleidoscope of light that moved against her; the smell of warmth and people infiltrated onto the metallic smell that had dominated, joined by a taste of incense. Five steps more and the lights intensity grew until she could no longer move forward such was its intensity, a voice resonated *in* her being.

"Take your time, I have entered the hall many times and I still have to take a pause."

"Lucian?" Minsel asked verbally, becoming aware of the presence of people and the vast space into which she had stepped.

"*Embrace* the moment Minsel, there is no rush here and I perceive that experiences such as this one you threshold now are going to be, well…that is maybe an assumption on my part." Lucian's voice and presence were the wind of the summer, it brought a smile to Minsel's face. Lucian was the leader of the region and one of the great council; his lineage was impeccable, if it had been of great concern to the people. However, his fame was built on cycles of wisdom, his management of resources in times of difficulty, but mostly his solution to the Abora rite as a youngling.

"Do you require any refreshment Minsel?" A verbal question, a voice from the Milik people, pride of the Neph, female. There would be four elders in the room altogether, Minsel knew that this was Suseta, a female of striking form and dark completion; reported to not be as gifted as some of her people, but insightful, courageous and witty. Thoughtful in presence and action.

"Your offer is kind, but my *burden* is quenching."

"So, this is how Karith's *best* treats hospitality of Malahman's elders'?" The voice was not soft, the high edge of the Hotale clan, belonged to Jaimar. Karith had warned her of him, but not eluded in detail to the rivalry surrounding Karith's late mate.

"Your issues with Karith are *not* mine and the message I bear makes *it* irrelevant." Minsel snapped, actually she had decided to protect her own from the moment that Karith's name had been mentioned. She still couldn't see clearly, but she could almost feel Lucian's smile.

"Well said, perhaps it is time for you to unburden yourself…" Lucian spoke again. At which Minsel suddenly became aware of a person standing before her, maybe it was the light, but the person was stunningly beautiful, taller than Minsel; slim and delicate in form and with the most exquisite eyes of silver. They stood two paces away, having contained their presence so well that they were almost invisible. "Please accept a sip." They extended a small cup with effortless grace in something so simple. Karith had actually blushed *slightly* when describing Fekir, one of the blessed. Minsel, now able to see in the light, focused on the cup and with a little shake in her hands she drank. The water was like an elixir, reviving her sense so she could see the soaring space of the cavern, which was dominated by a single pillar of multifaceted crystal that reminded Minsel of a frozen waterfall she had once seen on her travels. It was full of intense movement, frozen in the moment as it sprayed light around the room; reflecting a number of sources of light, which pierced into the cavern as small beams of light from outside. None were particularly bright, but they were magnified through the arrayed crystals in the pillar. Where the pillar connected with the floor, on which she stood, the rock spurred naturally to form that which was part altar, part seating. Suseta, reclined elegantly in soft refinements; Jaimar, at least physically, held any aggression at bay and chose to maintain a reclined position. Suseta was as Karith had described, a robust woman, handsome of visage, with dark glowing hair, sun-soaked skin and 'mysterious' eyes. Jaimar was lean, it summed him up, a most efficient form and action. Lucian remained obscured by the pillar and its emanating brightness.

"Thank you."

"Please Minsel, utter the words that we might..."

"Silab..." the crystal sang, reverberating with the explosion of a single word. Though the crystal kept singing, there was no other response; no caught breath, no physical lurch. "I'm sor..."

"*Quiet* yourself Karith's pupil, you have *nothing* to apologise for." Jaimar spoke firmly, but with obvious compassion that had been absent from his first utterance. As she had journeyed, Minsel had fallen into the trap of imaging how the conversation would go, how the revelation would erupt…silence had been a minor option and not the serene silence of the elders or the stone singing. Most versions of the present, as she had conceived of them, were filled with inquisition and accusation. Instead the silence grew, one of mediation and contemplation, a melody forming and tears beginning to form in silver eyes as they had with Karith, they did with Fekir.

"A burden indeed." Fekir whispered to Minsel's dialogue.

"Oh, how I *want* you to be wrong. To be part of some *glorious* conspiracy to enact Silab, but so few know the word or more what *it* means…yes it means *war*, but not as the hawks believe." Lucian remained behind the pillar, "What a *sad* duty, my family is the utterance genuine?"

"Speak it, Karith maybe *many* things, but in this…" Jaimar let his words die.

"*Call it*, the time is at hand, may the council guide us well and may we leave the consequences in *this* place." Suseta spoke, rising from her reclining position she nodded to Minsel and then turned to the pillar, "Minsel of Karith, you have been *true* to our people and I *assure* you in the songs of our people you will be remembered. Your role in this is done, return and enjoy your family, because the *storm* is coming!"

Malkus awoke, *partially*, not back in the crucible, instead ghosting beside Eddings. Who was no longer in the jungle, he was sat in an office. At least Malkus considered it an office, they always looked the same, as if some dimension hopping virus led humans to the same basic design. At least that was what Malkus perceived at first, but his sleeping state…*actually he couldn't quite recall the moments before he'd slept, something about an impossible dome*. Malkus remembered

Eddings, not the one in front of him, this one was *old*, not in the actual linear time, but his face was gaunt, hair shaved short and there was a texture to his skin. It looked like he had not eaten or slept in days, the grubby beard a testimony to a lack of personal care. Malkus' ghost state accorded him access to localised senses, such as smell, but he restrained any urgency to do so - It wouldn't be pleasant or useful. Nevertheless, what had put him to *sleep*? The question re-emerged, but Malkus couldn't find any recollection before Eddings had entered the dome. IMPOSSIBLE. Which was *extremely* concerning because this was the second incident with that label in quick succession. It was the kind of moment that, "normally" Malkus would have de-briefed, *hell* he would have fully debriefed the first incident, not just dumped it with KI, but the imperative had him hooked and the moment was at hand, everything becoming clear.

Eddings was not in a multi-occupancy office, instead he was alone with a visual screen running a program that was processing millions of images- looking for a face. Actually, to be more accurate, the program was looking for a best possible match for a reconstructed image of a face. Because that was all he had left. A single image of something that looked 'human', but Eddings *knew* was not. It couldn't be. What he'd seen and experienced defined any other explanation. Madness. Though no less "Mad" than any aspect of the journey he and his team had been on, but this epilogue was unexpected. Even in the opening moments of a new chapter Eddings team began to fragment. James Eddings was not the first to wake at the dig and when he did pandemonium was alive and walking the whole plateau. A strange mix of delirium, confusion, rash decisions and fear. Eddings himself was groggy, in a way he had never experienced before, at best he'd describe it as unhappy combination of drunkenness, nausea, euphoria and amnesia. There was, then and now, a continuing absence of memory from the time he stepped onto the dais of the thrones to remerging into the land of the conscious. Yet the 'reality' which made Eddings sober was that one of his team would never wake to experience the chaos. Doctor 'Frank' Milos Lindquist had been found at the mouth of the dome dig site, with no signs of life. It became clear that whatever had happened in the dome, the effects had been felt across the plateau, where even the teams over a kilometre away lost consciousness. However, it was not a situation where the dust settled; Eddings hadn't overseen the investigation which followed, even though he had attempted to, instead had fainted again. The second time he'd woken, it was in a medical centre in Oaxacana, having been flown out by the Elmander corporation. Convalescing there, events back at the dig site had slipped completely out of his control. Worse, his exhaustion conspired against any swift recovery; after two days at the centre Eddings had a meltdown, for which a psych intervention was required. He was *made* to sleep for three days straight and things became very dark; Eddings was drip fed information, mostly due to his persistence and against the psych team's wishes. He came to understand that, not only had the 'figure' on the throne disappeared; but Elmander corporation had taken over the entire operation, including the management of his healthcare. With quiet assurance, Eddings began to suspect that the psych team were in part information gathers. So, though 'beholden' to them, Eddings *managed* his responses; in spite of the cocktail of drugs, rehab exercises and diet. Though at some point the corporation had made that futile, when the 'therapist' had 'mistakenly' asked him to confirm an intimate detail that only a few knew.

"How long have you had someone on the inside?"

"Oh, James *really*, you understand that at least three members of you team belong to competing corporations, right?" Eddings had wanted to punch the 'therapist' in the face, hard. He had at points contemplated the possibility, but instead of confirming his suspicions he had been consumed by finding his *desecration* and so the moment of this revelation was extremely embarrassing. However, over the following few days, there was a change in stance in 'therapist/interrogator'. The corporation's man began to show genuine interest in James and in particular, eliciting his help. In retrospect, as he sat watching the screen process, there should have been alarm bells going off- about the changing nature of his relationship with the massive corporation-, but the context and his repeated habit of silencing such noise meant he bought in. Justification, to his diminishing ethics, 'was the knowledge that his final 'desecration' was leading him into an almost unthinkable fantasy. This meant playing the corporate's game, because it would be *him* who would successfully solve the mystery and become *immortal*. Yet like all his previous attempts at mystery solving, there was the thankless research to do, thus the small office with access to volumes of data.

At this moment however, the whole thing felt like *crazy meaningless bullshit*, the more paranoid thoughts viewed the parameters of the search to be a way of side-lining him. Though 'they' were chasing a pre-history 'ghost' who had somehow *drawn* a massive amount of energy from everyone and plant on the plateau, before disappearing into the ether. Though Elmander suspected that Doctor Lindquist' death was due to the way he fell and pre-conditions, nevertheless the energy grab *had* caused the death of his friend. So, while other justifications felt hollow to even his diminished ethics, Eddings at least could play the smouldering *revenge* card. In addition, the pursuit was giving him a routine, eating, sleeping, exercise…human stuff that had escaped him for most of the plateau dig. In fact, he was gaining back some of his self-respect, noticing how attitudes were changing in the team who had been assigned to handle him. Or they at least respected his apparent work ethic/desperation, which gave him access to information beyond what had originally been need-to-know. For instance, regardless of the massive resources available to the monstrosity, which was Elmander, the tracking teams had successfully failed to trace 'the Count'- as he was jokingly referred to (though not in front of Eddings). At first, they had picked up the trail from the plateau, through two different towns and into the capital before losing him. Which, Eddings suspected was about the time when he had gone from 'patient' to 'specialist'. Regardless of losing *the Count,* the teams had still gained some useful data, not particularly from the equipment on the plateau, but mostly from people who had assisted the 'dazzling' stranger. Average height and build, 'possibly' dark haired, but with a *dazzling* smile that seemed to leave people without the ability to recall much else. Nevertheless, there was enough for a complete 4D mock-up of *the Count* and this was, ever so quietly, the basis of a global search. Faces, half images, smudged media output, images appeared and disappeared, Eddings often having the final say on any glimmered recognition the trace produced. A month went by and a lead emerged in New Llundain, but the 'rescue' team found no further trace on getting there. Albion, four months later, this time with Eddings assisting from onsite command and control. They came away with an addition to the story of *the* smiling man- they also had the most *beautiful teeth*! No further detail and no obvious pattern emerging to the behaviour. *A ghost with a winning smile.* Eddings recalled at this point one of the deeply frustrated analysts had bellowed '*how the fuck does something so ancient know how to evade us?'*

Another genuine sighting emerged two months after Albion, but darker questions were beginning to be asked when the team came back with even less detail than before. There was the beginning of paranoid rumblings, this was an epically resourced operation, with brilliant minds and equipment, but even they were very quietly suggesting that *the Count* was toying with them. *The Count* wasn't steps ahead; he was playing a different game. That kind of speculation would have driven Eddings to an early grave (which some would have argued he'd already visited), so he stayed with his recovery and learning more of his new-found 'reality' as a corporate lackey. In the meantime, the sightings became rarer, staff changed, as did the attitude; the team became smaller, leaner and not *quite* as obsessional. Nevertheless, the agenda remained, find *the Count*, but now with the additional caveat- stop the technology-less bastard from embarrassing them anymore. Which actually left Eddings with a growing fondness for his friend's murderer, he wasn't fully able to express why, but *the Count's* ability to simultaneously piss off so many people was something to be *admired.* Perhaps in taking some kind of energy from Eddings, *the Count* had succeeded in amplifying his undoubted skill in that area. *Maybe he'd never know*, was the single dialogue in his thinking when the machine stopped processing and began to play a video. *There the fucker was!*

The instant, maybe the micro-nano segment of time, at which the machine change processes, Malkus was *plucked* from his ghosting state beside Eddings and appeared next to *the Count*. There was *no* sensation, *no* passing of sense, just the *knowing* that something terrifying had just occurred- for which no utterance as yet existed. Just clichés. Which could never satisfy the event that brought Malkus to just paces from mystery. Malkus couldn't focus on the space around him.

Just the terror, because he was *detached!* Malkus' waypoint was Eddings, obviously, but whatever had just happened left him *untethered* and on the precipice of oblivion! There were stories about untethering, it took little imagination to paint the pictures, but Malkus could recall none. Terror *overwhelmed* all. Except for a drum-beat. The only consistent rhythm, which was anything aside from the terror- part of the terror? Overwhelming cacophony of drums...*don't listen' don't reach out DON'T don't do what...the stream WILL take you! maybe it already has? This is your LAST goodbye*...the drumming seemed familiar, something he had seen and experienced elsewhere. *Oh Malkus, telling yourself a story, but your already gone!* Actually, the sound was more than familiar, it was...*you've given into the stream, you were always fucked*...RAIN! Outside the rain had taken on the appearance of a fine mist but falling consistently on the arched covers of the arcades, running hard off the hundred and fifty-year-old structures, flowing fast into the drainpipes and surging into the drains. In turn, the rain, silenced much of the background noise of the city. Malkus was *in* now, he was collecting data, *untethered*, unthinking...his world gone! The STORM would consume them! He'd be an unknown casualty. Yet the rain. It kept falling. Rhythmically calling him to his surroundings and suddenly the last of the shutters came down, clashing and crashing; cutting across the sound of the rain and then faded back into the rhythm of the falling water. Malkus could only be swallowed up by the *moment*, drown in the simulated here and now.

Stillness, colour fading from the florescent bulbs in the nineteenth century lamps that hung down from the cross beams that supported the arches three storeys up. It was a place of ebb and flow, not just of people, but of business; the rise and fall and return of economy. The industrial 'past' moving through to the global economic, a period piece defying time by the whims of like-minded consumers. Shadows falling upon the patterns of gold filigree that crowned the hanging flower shape of the lamp. Little or no reflection coming from the rows of glass fronted shops in the covered alleyways of the arcade. Coffee shops, restaurants and gaming centres, a funny kind of haze in the air where the shadows played. The *Count* seemed almost in a trance, standing in *almost* perfect stillness. It was hard to note any breathing. No obvious rise and fall in the *Count*'s inconspicuous clothes: a crowd blended dull grey raincoat of no particular cut, it could have been purchased from any of the local suit or bridal shops, as could have the dark trousers, loafers and the fedora. No gender or age could easily be ascertained and yet *somehow* the machine had found him- even though the hundreds who had passed him by would at best remember his *smile*. Nevertheless, there was something 'wrong' about *the Count's* stillness for Malkus, a stance that would be provoking the *future*-on-looking Eddings to greater curiosity. However, it wasn't just 'future' Eddings that was having an emotional feedback from the *Count,* a suspicion was growing for Malkus that being *untethered* wasn't the source of his terror.

Nevertheless, it wouldn't matter soon, the CCTV had *certainly* alerted security and on their arrival the *Count* would finally be in the 'future' hands of Elmander Inc. and Eddings would have his answers. Though it was still going to be an embarrassing moment for someone- *How did a fully-grown person manage to evade the checks?* Any minute the last shutter would be opened again, and a controlled aggression would be brought to bear on the trespasser. The *Count* remained completely still at the prospect. It got darker, the rain grew louder, shadows span out from the glass-fronted shops into the alleyways. The police would not be amused if they got a call, coming out in the rain to put away another crazy. After all, if this person was not homeless and wasn't acting like a criminal or a man accidentally locked in, *surely* the person was mentally incapacitated. Stillness. A stillness that gave Malkus' suspicion space to speak- being lost to the stream was freedom, he'd be another rain drop bouncing in rhythm, slipping and washing into streets of realities yet unseen. In fact, Malkus had on more than one occasion considered *untethering*, so having the decision taken out of his hands was actually a relief. Which meant that the source of his terror was more corporeal...*how can that be? Stillness.* No sound of response to this 'persons' illegal presence...only Malkus' crippling emotional reaction mixed with the sounds of buses- turning, moving, accelerating. Then, as another *wave* of terror began to rise in Malkus' inner dialogue, the figure in front of Malkus dropped to the ground, *dead*. Rain beating the rhythm of a *storm*, as Malkus slipped into the stream.

Pevnost Arcades, Pevnost- 3 hours West of the centre of the universe

Detective Sidoli let the sheet fall back down on the corpse.
"Any ID?" She asked with a certain resignation.
"No, sorry d-tective."
The body had been discovered when security had opened the arcades early in the morning. Detective Fleur Sidoli was under pressure. The imminent pressure came from the surrounding shop keepers who wanted the arcades open for business, but more pressing was the very strange behaviour of the Chief Inspector. She had inexplicably removed Fleur from *all* on-going cases for what, at this point, was a nothing case. However, the *Chief* made it clear that results were expected in a pre-cog kind of way. Of course, she had been warned by some of the older

veterans of 'initiation' cases; horror stories, not of blood and guts, but the sheer monotony of running down witnesses, pursing leads and writing up dead-end cases. Though Fleur was sure that her 'initiation' case was the Buchanan murder and not this. Though what 'this' was in terms of a case (read on her internal police information device or 'bible'), as nothing but another 'initiation' case- even to the point where *no* senior detective was provisionally assigned to the case.

"Who reported the find…I'm sorry I didn't catch your name?"

"Officer Reed d-tective." Fleur caught the open faced smile, but focused on the small palm screened device. "It was Arcade security, a mister Luke Davies, he's already contacted his head office and the C.C.T.V info will be on your desk asap."

"Good work officer, have you taken a statement?"

"No d-tective, I was told by the sarge to leave that to you…first case?"

Fleur scowled at the officer. Firstly, the drone was recording a 360 image of Fleur's investigation, including the verbal interactions. This meant that it would be better for Officer Reed to not be recorded descending into pleasantries/flirting. Fleur gestured as much,

"Oh…sorry…forgot, still a-justing." Reed was in his mid-twenties, strapping in his police uniform and vest, but he blushed like a schoolboy. Fleur rolled the recording back and deleted the question. The scowl remained however, because this was not her first case and this officer would *never* make a detective.

"No problem, I've edited it out," Fleur made a performance of restarting the device.

"Good work officer, have *you* taken a statement?"

"No detective, I was told by the sergeant to leave that to you…" And there the pressure was, but different. Not only was Fleur pulled from her cases, dropped in with little information, clearly the word had come down- she was on her own. Three options, appeared to her rapidly: firstly, she had royally pissed someone off, secondly, she was a sacrificial offering or thirdly, nothing was that straightforward about this case. She would adjust accordingly.

"Thank you, officer Reed, has the coroner been informed?"

"He's waiting for you to finish up d-tective."

"Okay, did you notice anything unusual?" Not a necessary line of enquiry, but it was within the adjustment.

"Not really," Fleur placed Reed as local from a few kilometres north of Pevnost, one of the late-industrial areas. "No blood, no o-vious weapons or marks on the body, looks as though…" Reed remembered the 'bible'. "No detective I don't recall anything in particular."

"Thank you, officer," Fleur pressed the screen again and the process stopped. She flashed her thank you smile, well she hoped it was her thank you smile, there were always ramifications for actions and gaining a reputation for 'flirtiness' was as condemning as being framed as a 'cold-hearted bitch'.

"You can call the coroner; he can run the site in two minutes, thank you officer Reed." A tighter smile this time, a little blunt, but the body language would hopefully underline her professionalism. Whatever the conclusion, officer Reed quietly took his leave to call the coroner in, they themselves would repeat the recordings that Fleur was ordering her drone to complete. Three recordings would be done altogether, CSI, coroner and Fleurs, with slightly adjusted algorithms to correlate as much data as possible back at the Pevnost hub. Fleur finished recording and went to talk to the head of arcade security.

Mister Luke Davies was in his mid-fifties, overweight, thinning fair hair, definitive if not prominent features that would have made him handsome in his youth, but was undermining him in his later years. His brown eyes were tired, and his left ear had a half moon carved into the lobe, something had gone wrong in his path of life, but that really didn't matter now. Fleur had absorbed this when she had first arrived; he had at the point been sitting within the nearest restaurant, in staff uniform, drinking a cup of coffee and speaking aggressively at no one in particular. Blue-tooth mocked the age of madness. Now as she approached, he was trying to raise himself up and draw that carnivorous look from his eyes, for all life had thrown at him he was still trying to act with some decency. He had no *previous* bar a few parking tickets and a caution after a particularly rowdy evening in the city. Luke Davies, father of one, national insurance number, company number, no political or religious affiliations, healthy bank balance- as he and his wife June worked. Child Karleen was finishing a degree in renewable engineering mechanics- more debt with her. He had been employed at the security company for ten years and they were an established firm with a good track record. Fleur entered the restaurant confidently, the data pad already giving her the upper hand.

"Mister Davies?"

"Yes."

"I'm Detective Sidoli."

"As in?" Mr Davies' Pevnost accent, harsh around the edges, it was native of a sort, but more nasal with the vowels, than the softer more recognisable tones. The body language was tense, not in a secretive kind of way, but more defensive in posture.

"Distant relations, I'm going to have to take a statement…it's procedure."

"Didn-t think wee'd get a deteck-tive, trainin?" Mister Davies was not stupid, he had already made some kind of assessment on the case.

“Something like that,” Fleur restrained the scowl this time, smiled and nodded slightly, “do you mind if I sit?” The restaurant was cosy with a number of tables and chairs surrounding a chiller and counter at the back of the room. Mister Davies had chosen a table right by the window looking out on the corpse.

“No, coffee?”

“No thank you, it shouldn’t take that long. As you might know this…” waving the *bible* and pointing to the drone which moved into the room, “is a recording device, are you happy to be recorded or do you want to do this at the…”

“No thank you, I’ve got work to do detecktive, go ahead.” Courteous, his breath smelt of coffee, he smelt of a light aftershave. However even with the safety features of the new razors he had managed to nick his chin.

“Thank you…okay so you discovered the corpse on opening up, can you run me through what you did?” Tight smile, a little eye contact for vague friendliness.

“Well detecktive at thirst I thought he was sleepin so I stopped and shouted, but when he didn’t moove I went toward him.”

“Were you angry?” Mister Davies was a little surprised by the question.

“I, yeah, well ‘nnoyed, mostly I was unappy that the CCTV hadn’t been looked at.” A little defensive,

“How did you find the body, laid out, crumpled up?”

“Both really, it was early; I wasn’t payin attention at first so that’s why I shouted, but as I got closer I realised somethin was wrong. No one sleepin would ave their legs like that.” Mister Davies took another sip of coffee, Fleur stopped the recording.

“First corpse?”

"No, but it's been a while." Fleur restarted the recording on Mr Davies response; her first corpse had been a lot less civil than the quiet unmarked body being removed by the coroner.
"So you realised there was a problem, what did you do?"
"I come in and then approach the body, there was no movement, couldn't see any breathin, so I moved up cautiously. I could tell that the boy was dead pretty much *straight* away and that's when I called it in." Sip of coffee.
"Any stores broken into?"
"No detective, everythin's in order." Coffee down, arms crossed, chin out- pleased if conflicted.
"Who closed up last night?"
"I did, my thoroughness as usual…whatever appened the CCTV will clear it up." Increased defensiveness, understandable given that his personal competence was in question, and perhaps beyond that an anticipation of having to answer these questions to his bosses. Fleur too was adjusting to her situation; her context had, to her mind, pointed to some kind of test or punishment, but now she found a story that wasn't adding up. A concern that was leading her to push Mister Davies' defence.
"Are there any other ways into the arcades that can't be fully secured?"
"This an interrogation?"
"No, sorry Mister Davies; obviously since the Halberstam incident we've had to be a little bit more through." It was an invitation by Fleur for Mister Davies to be sympathetic to the situation that she found herself in, Halberstam had been an unmitigated disaster.
"Yeah that didant go so well did-it?" Fleur had her opinions, but she allowed silence to confirm for Mister Davies whatever theory he had.
"No detecktive everythin was secure, but clearly the *late* gentleman…"

civility as a defence, an interesting change in tactic, "...found a way in. I've had copies made of yesterday's recordings and they've been mailed to the hub."

"Thank you." Fleur decided to follow Mr Davies' civility line, after all if there was more to his story then she was confident that she or the tech would sniff it out.

"And I'm goin to spend the rest of the day tryin to work out how *he* got past me." There was a sense of affront in the man's voice which again pointed to a genuine confusion as to how- let alone why- a person had mysteriously died in a venue under his care. "Any other questions detecktive?"

"No, I think that is everything, thank you Mister Davies..." Fleur smiled and pressed discontinue, "I've got your details if I need to get hold you and if you do come up with a reasonable solution for how feel free to mail it along." Mr Davies rose slightly as Fleur rose to leave.

""Thank you detecktive, *please* keep me updated" he offered his hand which Fleur took firmly though it was slightly moist and warm.

"I will, oh, any idea who the john doe is?"

"No, I might 'ave seen him before, but we see so many faces through 'ere." Mr Davies returned to his coffee and to face the day, Fleur had not left the arcade before John doe had a name.

PEVNOST INVESTIGATION, DETECTIVE SIDOLI

The newly re-furbished centralised data system was a joy; the data pad flashed a mail from Pevnost bays' hub. The photograph of the corpse had been matched to a personal I.D. at the main University, a doctor Nestor Earland. It also gave Fleur a chance to walk, firstly because it was now the 'expectation of the service' due to budget cuts etcetera, but also it gave her some thinking time. With the revelation of the late

doctor's identity, the case now took on a political angle, Pevnost University was one of the main heartbeats of the city, it drew in thousands of students every year, to rent property, spend money and maybe learn something. It was a prestigious research university with a worldwide reputation and had relationship with numerous powerful people in the city. Which meant that along with the mail about the late doctor Earland came a note from the commander to keep it *very quiet*.
She was greeted by a junior liaison officer. He was in his late twenties, Caucasian, narrow faced, sharply defined features and stylised brown hair, which was spiked slightly. Slim built, he moisturised, but chewed his nails. Open face with a pleasant, though nervous smile. Average sized green eyes, the nose with flared nostrils; on closer inspection the man's hair was beginning to turn from a fair brown to grey. He was wearing a cheap suit which suggested nothing in particular, though he had perfected the appropriate handshake, eye contact ratio.
"Hello Detective Sidoli, your commander has already contacted our office and you have our full co-operation, my name is Gareth Johnson and I'm with the liaison office." He was going to say something more, but thought better of it.
"Hello Gareth, shall we get straight down to business?"
"If you'd like to follow me." They shook hands, his accent was Pevnost based, north of the city, probably Carvella or Norinlemar, nevertheless he was being precise In his use of Gereza standard as this was official business. Without any further pleasantries he escorted Fleur into the new security building; they'd been moved out of the Park Place site and re-housed the other side of the railway tracks, taking them into a small room off reception.
"Tea or coffee, detective?"
"No thank you, trying not to get into the caffeine habit."

"Too late for me." Gareth chuckled lightly. The room was small and basic with one table and two chairs; there was a beverage vending machine in one of the corners and the room smelled of fresh paint and carpet. Gareth started making himself a coffee, he had an easy manner and though he was a 'junior' member of staff, it was uncertain he would remain in that state.

"So, what can you tell me about Doctor Earland?"

"Mekyska by birth, forty years old; no next of Kin, no wife, partner or kids."

"What was his role at Pevnost University?"

"He was an expert in Apeulikan archaeology and Nammi Salamann history, he was primarily a researcher and lectured part time." Gareth sipped at his coffee.

"Any enemies?"

"Not really, he kept himself to himself, did his work; was meeting his duties. Students liked him and the higher academics of his school were looking to tie him down." Another sip of his coffee, trying to hide his glances at Fleur. "We did background checks, but nothing troubling stood out."

"Any recently erratic behaviour?"

"No, in fact he was only just back in the country, he'd been touring Kitajaka. So, do you think its suicide?" Brave choice of question.

"I'm not ruling anything in or out, why would *you* think it's a suicide?"

"Well healthy forty-year olds do not normally drop dead."

"Unless they've drunk too much coffee." Gareth laughed at that; Fleur could see much point in continuing to ask routine questions.

"May I see his office please?"

"Yeah sure." Gareth put his coffee down and brushed by. "He worked for our school of History and archaeology, fortunately they are in the building next door."

"You can finish your coffee."

"Thank you, detective, so how did he die…your commander wasn't very clear."

"Well we can't say until the coroner's report, we'll have a prelim report sometime in the next two days." Fleur decided to continue from a place of professional courtesy, and it would do no harm to have a tentative relationship with someone in the university.

"However, there were no obvious marks on the body and the case is currently death under mysterious circumstances. Nothing that exciting." Fleur played it down, she was not going to further stretch protocol or the actual fact that she had little else to tell.

"Well, it's sad either way." Gareth got closer to finishing his coffee.

"Did you know the late doctor?"

"No, but…well, losing a good man is never a good thing."

"I suppose not." Fleur could see she had a thinker of some kind on her hands; she looked at her pad in a deliberate manner. Gareth took the hint and putting what remained of his coffee on the table, led Fleur out and through to the next building.

The Plaza was Pevnost university's newest build; it was a number of architecturally pleasing buildings, which had been constructed over old railway sidings. It was dominated by a concourse that was bordered by trees and a number of four storey high buildings. The university was still in session, so students were milling about between classes; Gareth led Fleur to the third building on the left that backed onto the railway line, understanding the need for discretion Gareth ceased to engage in further conversation. They briskly moved through an open foyer and into a clean smelling lift, which took them to the third floor. Everything was unmarked, un-scuffed and clearly under used. As soon as they were out of the lift, they took a quick right down a corridor with dark blue carpet and pale walls.

"Doctor Earland's room is just up on the right here." They entered a spacious room that looked out onto the walkway below; the room itself was a cliché of academic standards, three walls were covered in books, there was a large desk, a tall and deep leather chair. Doctor Earland's certificates hung behind the desk on the free space between bookshelves, the desk itself was veneered dark wood with a leather surface and remarkably empty.

"As you can see, he was *quite* meticulous."

"Did he have a desktop?" It took a moment for Gareth to understand, "No, hmmm; I think he preferred a tablet…holo-screen and all."

"Very nice, do you mind if I have a look through his desk?"

"Looking for something?" *suicide note?* Was Gareth's un-worded enquiry.

"Perhaps," She went to reach for the first desk draw, having pushed the chair away, but was stopped by the picture.

It was the head shot of a woman, the most breath-taking woman that Fleur had ever seen. The eyes hypnotised her in a moment, they curved and extenuated the deep turquoise blue of the irises. Yet there was so much more to the eyes, the light caught and reflected, windows to the life of laughter, tenderness and a strange power. Her skin was perfect, unmarked with a darker skin tone that enhanced the woman's northern features. Fleur didn't know whether to fall in love or become irrationally envious of the powerful beauty that was clearly the centre of

Earland's world. And if she wasn't, well in Fleur's opinion, he was insane.

"We've never met her." A new voice broke the spell, Fleur looked up to find a fashionably dressed middle aged woman, with black hair streaked with grey and the air of the academic. It was a massive let down.

"Detective Sidoli *this* is Professor Thomas, head of the archaeology department." Fleur broke away from the picture and greeted the Professor with a swift handshake. Professor Thomas was not unattractive, but she wasn't the woman in the picture. Fleur, nevertheless, had a word to frame Professor Thomas, classy, just a little make up around the eyes and a touch of lipstick. The hair was pulled back to highlight her cheekbones and the oval-ness of her face, her eyes were too small and there was a kink in her nose, but there was a vibrancy in the woman's presence. She smiled thinly as she greeted Fleur; control in what was a difficult situation.

"Professor Thomas, I'm sorry for your loss." A flicker of sadness in the professor's small green eyes.

"Yes, it's a *tragic* loss, to the department, the university…I *would* even say the profession." It was a little too prepared, but was presented with due diligence.

"I'm sorry to hear that, hopefully our investigation can be swift, and the university can mourn the loss in peace." It was at this point that she wished that someone else in seniority were on the case; one wrong word and she could put her career back years.

"Thank you," Professor Thomas said curtly.

"If it's alright with you Professor, we'll go through his possessions together."

"Yes, detective that would be good."

With that Fleur returned to the desk, sliding open the draws she was unsurprised to find them studiously arranged and basically empty.
"How long had Doctor Earland been back in the country?" Fleur asked the question to the professor, but her eyes were drifting back to the photo.
"About a week; he was collating his findings in Kitajaka before starting teaching again in two weeks." The professor answered, Gareth clearly deferring to the senior member of staff, even going as far as to stay by the door.
"Any personal issues?"
"Not really, the occasional girlfriend, but nothing serious…other than her, but he didn't talk about *her*. We liked to tell little stories about who she was, how they meet, but no one really knows."
"He seemed himself?"
"Yes, calm…quietly excited, nothing to alarm. Why do you think…"
"I wouldn't like to suggest a reason until our investigation is complete." Fleur went to the party line, dragged her eyes from the perfect mouth of the woman in the picture as she returned to the desk. "Professor, do I have permission to conduct a search of Dr Earland's office?" Fleur had palmed the 'bible' and pressed record.
"Of course, will there be anything else?"
"No professor, Mr Johnson can stay for accountability; we'll contact you if anything relevant to the university emerges."
"Thank you, Detective. I hope for a speedy and successful case." '*code: let this over be quickly and quietly with the least fuss possible.*
"Thank you, Professor for the permission and *your* time." The professor nodded, smiled tightly and then left, not acknowledging Mister Johnson at all. With that Fleur released her drone, who swept the room; normally they would just look at layout and generally just record her activities in

the room, but Fleur was feeling creatively paranoid and decided to order scans for electronic recording devices. It was a stab in the dark, but restrained initiative seemed an appropriate course of action in the slightly murky waters she now paddled. She'd also put an 'anomalies' search in place,

"They must be fun…" Mister Johnson was still in the room. They were not fun, they were a burden of training, expense and overall a source of resentment, as an over technozation of policing. Though the private policing organisations propaganda suggested otherwise, the usefulness was a place of extreme debate within the service.

"They have their uses…" Fleur, still felt the need to look at the picture, but manged to focus on searching the drawers- having sprayed her hands with 'glove spray'; criminal in origin, it was a hybrid substance the left no trace on surfaces contacted. The desk was traditional, in that it actually had draws, but it had an imbedded holo-display. Unfortunately, no docked information device, so no response to Fleur's attempts to engage, interestingly there were two start buttons, the second being fingerprinted.

"Is the fingerprint system standard?"

"In the more technical departments, though archaeology can be *very* competitive so it's not a complete surprise and I know that some of the older staff just like the idea, particularly if they're hot desking." Mister Johnson had chosen to seat himself in a comfortable looking leather chair that looked out onto the plaza promenade.

"So, this is a shared office?"

"Not to my knowledge," Johnson moved uncomfortably in the chair, "Rare for a Doctor of Archelogy, no?" There was another thread of inconsistency that Fleur decided to pick at.

“To some degree, but some of the *newer* academic staff have benefactors, given some of the flights that he’s been on it wouldn’t surprise me…” Mister Johnson stopped talking, but in an uncomfortable silence he noticed Fleur was looking for a little more, “…I’ll hmmm ping an information request.” Mister Johnson retrieved a device and started doing work, which Fleur had perhaps a little naively hoped to already have.

“If you could forward the response to me and the hub, make sure it’s marked for my attention as Earland case one eight fourteen.”

“On it.” Fleur returned to the desk draws, two smaller ones on the left and a deeper one on the right. They yielded nothing, they were neatly ordered, not obsessively; though again no data devices were to be found, which was annoying, it would require going to Doctor Earland’s accommodation. “Can you also add Doctors Earland’s accommodation address please?” Fleur sent a communication to the hub asking for a warrant to be drafted up and found the chief responding- *return to hub, straight to my office, you’ll be waved through*. Fleur shivered slightly, instinct told her that she was out of her depth or, at a minimum, moves were being made that were above her pay grade and out of her sight. She desperately wanted to contact her supervising officer; to get some frame for what was happening, but when she’d tried contacting him, he’d been ‘busy’ on another case. *Busy as in not taking my call because some really weird shit was unfolding and it had him covering his arse,* which made Fleur reach some stage of anxiety. Nevertheless, she focused on bringing the investigation to a procedural end, calling the drones in and uploading the data, printing the appropriate forms.

“Well Mister Johnson, that’s all for now; thanks for your co-operation, I’ll see myself out.” Mr Johnson’s hand was shaken rapidly and headed back to the hub, expecting the unexpected.

KI REGUS- DRA centre: ACTUAL.

Regus woke. *Badly*. She swept herself into sleep with a neuro-suppressor. Any claims to side effects being 'mild', were to her knowledge, *complete bullshit* and then some additional *rain storms* on top. Yes, the body slept, the mind *drifted* into low level activity, but never had she felt '*rested*'. Or maybe she *had* felt 'rested' for all of a *minute*, as her systems re-activated and her mind 'came on-line', reminding her of the *terror* that was life. Her 'rested-ness' was consumed by the *world-storm*, not the *reality* of it, but the predicted *arrival* and the *desperate* attempts to find anything to stop it! 'Everything' was being done, but no one was coming up with any results other than...*shit, we're fucked, completely, forever and there is nothing we can do about it*. In the twenty cycles since the initial disaster, they had *hit* dead end after dead end, glimmers of 'hope' mutated in to hor*rible, horrible realities*! The pressure was *overwhelming* everyone, eyes were vacant, half-nods were the only response to each other's existence, anxiety *was* master and commander of the organisation. Yet they *couldn't stop*, civilisation, *unknowingly, unwittingly* and without say; were 'relying' on the DRAs and their handlers to *rescue everything*. This thought resonated with dreams from days gone by...*were they dreams*? Or a stream she'd viewed in the 'eyes' of a DRA? A tale of super-powered, super-equipped champions that would defeat the on-coming...apoca something. Perhaps that was *it,* maybe they would find an ancient text, weapon, code or even a 'deity' willing to bestow a solution upon them, better still, willing to turn them all into super-somethings that would crush the *on-coming storm* in climatic battle. *HA!* Ki's anxious mind jested, after all she was an 'executive bureaucrat' of a *mind-fuck* *organisation* that had her '*handling*?' a crippled eccentric, who 'some' thought had long ago slipped into *senility*. Maybe that was a 'little' *harsh,* 'crippled' 'genius' 'eccentric' who was an *utter bastard*- was maybe more accurate. She *regretted* the quip she'd made about the general executive's mistress. Yes it *had* been three terms before, but the general executive had bided his time and found the *absolutely, fundamentally, beautiful punishment*- being assigned to Malkus. Broken, 'brilliant' Malkus!

It was time to get up. Her body 'took' to the command, *maybe* a minute more than the day before, but her feet were on the floor and she padded naked over to the slim sonic shower. She suppressed as best she could the *ache* that existed in every sinew of her frame or what felt like it, she was horny too, more than that, she *was* lonely, but she took the subscribed pill by the shower stall and stepped in. The showers rays stung a little, it didn't *have to,* but it was a habit that she'd formed at some point and saw no 'reason' to give it up. She then moved to the toilet, in a hermetically sealed room, her bowels moved and the product was whisked away to be recycled. A beep informed her that her clothes were ready, a freshly cleaned uniform that consisted of a one-piece, camo-active garment of fabric that gave Ki-Regus the 'ability' to withstand heat, radiation and impact. Ki had been told the stats, but they didn't really matter anymore, it was time for sustenance. Before the *crisis* she would have sat down and eaten a chef prepared breakfast that would have been brought from the kitchens of the complex, but the restrictions on the handlers were extremely strict. She had only overslept *once*; it was not something that would reoccur. So instead of a three-stage nutritional breakfast, which was seen to be both psychologically and physically beneficial, she placed a single tab on her tongue and headed out the door to re-engage with this most *infuriating* muse.

"Good day Ki Regus,"

"Patch me through; let's see what Malkus has been up to." Images began to flow, "Well I'll be, he's actually done what he's told." James Eddings remained central to the stream and there were no other side journeys. Clearly Malkus had scared himself into good behaviour, then it happened; inexplicably, the feed went dark and remained so for a significant amount of time. Ki began to move faster to the *pit*

"Central, why was I not woken?"

"For what, Ki Regus?"

"For *my* agent going dark?"

"DRA Malkus was sleeping, dreaming in fact…he is allowed to sleep Ki Regus."

"*Not* without *my* permission!"

"According to the logs he has your permission."

"Show me!" Ki had no recollection of giving such permission, but the data flashed to her confirmed that she *had* authorised Malkus. This was not good, the scheduled review was going to eviscerate her; she could almost hear the generals laughing, Malkus was burying her and apparently, she was giving him a better shovel. "Central I want this noted for the record that I have *no* recollection of giving permission for *this*!"

"Noted, shall I return you to DRA Malkus' feed?" Ki just made expelled air with a physical motion and the central AI restored the feed. "Ki Regus I will move the feed forward to when DRA Malkus woke up."

"Thank you Central." And the feed returned to James Eddings, alone, staring at the screen.

"How live is this?"

"Almost real time." Ki found herself at the security section of the hub, concerned, *deeply concerned* and she couldn't explain it cognitively. An embodied 'sense', but then she and everyone else was living with this 'sense' every day. Yet this time and with what had already happened; it was something more apparent. The feed continued, Malkus ghosting Eddings, as Eddings in turned looked for a ghost and then found it. Ki was in the door, but hesitated on seeing the ghost on the screen, mouthing the words 'no Malkus don't' and the alarms began, things became completely blurred, Ki found herself at her post, central giving her emergency access.
"Malkus, respond Malkus." A surprising level of control and calm in her voice, as her thoughts became a mass...her agent had become untethered! *Unrivalled disaster, career in tatters, actually potentially facing criminal charges* FUCK! "Central ping him now!" The danger of untethering was actually incredibly rare, but then in the current context it paradoxically seemed inevitable. There was standard procedure, but the instincts of Ki rhythmically ordered that she did *everything* because if Malkus remained untethered then over a period of time he would *die*. And Ki, for no obvious reason, knew that Malkus *knew* something fundamental. *Central*, regardless of protocol, agreed with her assessment and sent the 'ping'- a surge of energy- down into the DRA's system; theoretically this would realign and capture the DRA, but they were working half-blind as untethering, not just rare, was almost unheard of. "Malkus? Respond agent. This is Ki Regus; I *order you* to respond." The data fields were flashing incoherent data, yet more inexplicable ramblings, but the 'ping' was not working and Malkus was drifting away. "Central Ping again!" The surge was released again and for a moment Malkus *appeared* to re-connect, but a heartbeat later he

was gone, not even acknowledging the connection. '*Did he want to slide away?*'

"Central, why is the ping *not* working?" It was an impertinent question, but Ki could see a storm sweeping her away.

"A moment please…" Another unexpected turn, the central's processing power was immense, calculated in abstract numbers and even it found itself needing time. About thirty seconds, "There appears to be an *anomaly* in the proximity of DRA Malkus, which is making the Ping redundant, I'm sorry Ki Regus but DRA Malkus is untethered."

"FUCK, FUCK…no! Malkus respond you arrogant prick! *please respond…*" She felt the presence of another behind her; she could also feel a wave of emotion bringing darkness to the edge of her vision.

"Ki Regus, please step away from your post."

"Central, ping Eddings! *Track the arrogant prick…*"

"Ki Regus…" Ki stepped away, the voice was of overseer Barraic and he would escalate to physical interaction if Ki did not respond.

"Yes Ki Regus…" Ki was turning, but the darkness was sweeping up and around, at some point she fainted.

Malahman, Irrelevant Stream

They took one more look, one last whole breath; inviting and imprinting onto the remembering place, the layers of reality on which their senses focused. The growing warmth of the air as the sun climbed into the clearest blue sky, casting shadows on the golden rock of what they had once called home. Though there was tension in the imprint, because though it was former, they still resided, positioned to complete their most *sacred* duty. Set before them, from the time they were born, to the rising of the morning sun. Yalom had no doubt that the tension of his emotional state and interwoven being, would be written into the memory. Along with loneliness, regret, restrained hope, pride, happiness and soon fulfilment. Here at the gates of Malahman with Rubin, they would complete the task set by his forefathers. They were the embodiment of every sacrifice, drop of blood, strained sinew and utterance that were the *pillars of the people, guardians of the falling night.* Since the curse of *Silab* had emerged the *pillars* had taught, prepared, and sculpted for the unfolding days ahead. Twelve had already fallen. Faces, voices, resonances carved into Yalom's remembering space; imprinted with affection, love, laughter and just a little envy. After all, the first fallen, Tarric, had a way in combat that was infuriatingly artistic and though Yalom had sort to mimic it, had never mastered combat in that way.

"It is the most beautiful of days is it not my friend?"

A rhetorical question from his battle brother. Rubin was also tracing Malahman's golden cliffs, cut cave abodes, carved walkways, verandas and every familiar stairs into his own remembering place. Yalom had woken at the third watch of the night to walk the entirety of the vacated settlement. Moving through the darkness; remembering rooms, homes, avenues of colour, smell and people, waves of emotions moving with him as he walked. In emptiness, he remembered the warmth of the community, surrounding him, casting images on the darkness until he had become aware of Rubin standing beside him in the crystal room.

"I think part of me went with the crystal." Rubin's voice was a fractal of emotion.

"Perhaps the rest with the family." Yalom responded as best he could, the emptiness was beginning to seep out of the surrounds and into this being.

"We stand."

"We stand." *For what was and what would be,* in the face of the terrible, brutal consequences of a decision made in another time. Their remembering place would not escape the fear or the weight of responsibility that went withstanding against the wave, a marauding horde of overwhelming sadness. Of course, those in the wave would not know the sadness as they streamed forward, claiming 'righteous' reasons against the great injustice they knew nothing of, but they were the *reality* and the *sadness* of Yalom's people. Nevertheless, he and his *battle brother* would stand.

Yalom looked to Rubin at the gate, drawing from his remembering to see a young, beautiful, purposed man, seemingly always expecting this day; though there may have been doubts for others, Rubin had been prescient. No longer young, Rubin was still full of purpose and beauty in the warmth of his weather-worn smiling eyes and stern mouth. As ever his hair was short, speckled different shades of grey, covering less of his regal skull than it had even a grand cycle ago. Though Rubin did not return his gaze, looking instead beyond the gate, Yalom knew that this person loved him and they in battle would display to the darkness the unity of their realities.

'We stand...' Rubin *again*, barely audible in the canyon's mid-day breeze, a tear slipping from his silver eyes and to the ground of Malahman. Simultaneously, both lifted their hewn wooden staff to their chests and then stamped them to the floor. The sound echoing around Malahman, as a non-verbal confirmation of their commitment and for Yalom the end of imprinting things onto his remembering place. He only wanted the abstract notions to go forward. For there was an unfamiliar smell on the air, it had a sweetness to it, but was framed by desperation, an underlying metallic taste and was completely *Arall*. The

wave was moving relatively quietly, perhaps hoping to surprise the inhabitants of Malahman, but the cacophony of smells was a shouting army of blood lust.
"Quiet and yet deafening my friend." Yalom chuckled.
"At least there is some respect; the pillars have clearly been good teachers…"
"As ever." Yalom could sense his own excitement growing, not just because he was fulfilling his destiny, but he would finally see the enemy. It was one thing to have a verbal description and to have seen sketches, but another to see them with his own eyes. Even at a distance it was clear to see the similarities between his people and the enemy, two-legged, humanoid; but at least those approaching seemed stockier, though that appeared to be because of an outer shell. They approached in formation, moving six abreast on the narrow pathway that lead to the gate; they had shields placed in front of them. Even though the enemy's own scouts would have alerted them to the presence of Yalom and Rubin- and therefore their massive numerical advantage, the enemy force moved with discipline and caution.
"Very good teachers." Rubin said with *pride*, but this seemed to draw a response from the on-coming force. A thin line of projectiles emerged from behind the shield and streaked towards Yalom and Rubin, but they had misjudged the swirl of the wind in the shadow of Malahman and, bar one arrow, none reached the gate. Nevertheless, like a rising tide, the enemy moved forward, but this forced them to take one man out of their shield wall. *As was the plan*, the plummeting cliff edge and narrowing path had always been a strategic choice, as much as it was sacred. Seventy paces from the gate the wave tried with the projectiles again, this time a few projectiles successfully reached the gate, even forcing Rubin to swat one away, but there was no damage done.

Finally, at fifty paces, a volley of projectiles gave itself an opportunity to cause damage, but to howls of fury, the arrows clattered into the overhanging cliff face above the gates to Malahman. Geography also forced the wave to change shape again, now they were only four.
"Shall we?" Yalom had been trained by *Armina* and she would not accept such continuing passivity. They covered the ground between the gateway and the advancing forces in five beats of a heart, but instead of clashing with the wall, Yalom knelt and Rubin used him to launch over it. Yalom heard him land, *cries of surprise*, both that such old-looking beings could move so fast and the fact they were already in the lines.
"Two ranks, twelve step gap." Rubin communicated to Yalom's senses, as he in turn skipped away from a thrusted blade and then retaliated by using his staff to break the hand holding the weapon. The Arall shield-wall countered by lunging forward, but Yalom was unmoved by the advance and retaliated with a pointed staff strike. The force was *shocking*, launching the Arall shield bearer back into his companions and splintering the shield. His companions in turn were suffering at the hands of Rubin. Yalom *flowed* through the attack, the counter strike becoming a staff blow to the left, which drove the previously injured shield carrier to his knees; and then a blow the right, which flung an enemy off the cliff screaming. Without mercy the next move was to drive the staff into the skull of the fallen shield bearer, before sliding out of the way of a fired projectile. *Another* retaliation, Yalom kicked a fallen shield into the remaining group of projectile troops.

Rubin, *simultaneously*, sprinted towards the next line of shield bearers and using an unconscious enemy. He flicked onto his staff and vaulted into the air. Yalom sensed the build-up of energy as Rubin began to fall

and so he prepared himself- placing his staff into the ground and bracing himself. *Timing*. The perception of action and reaction, everything slowed down for Yalom as he adjusted his breathing and awaited the *explosion*. On contacting the ground Rubin released the build-up of energy. Erupting outwards it flung bodies, shield and projects in multiple directions. Yalom recovered his breath and launched himself into the confusion, diligently allowing this staff to speak. Snake like, it cracked against the head of a recovering shield carrier. Before two steps on the staff ended another life. The dance was now in full flow, snaking, undulating staffs, with patterns of fist, twirling feet and shins. The music was a lament, a dirge punctuated by the occasional bass rumble of energy blasts and howls of falling Arall. Half a kilometre of carnage and finally the Arall called retreat.
"WE STAND!" Yalom roared, soaked in moisture, alive in away he'd never experienced, connected to staff, body and movement.
"Never said where!" Rubin laughed. Yet amongst all the energy and savage joy of being everything they'd ever trained to be, was the knowledge that these cries, their sacrifice was naught but defiance against the storm that would keep coming and coming until they could stand *no more*. Cautiously the oldest of friends retreated through the carnage of brokenness to the arches of Malahman, ready for some water.

<u>Chief's Office- Pevnost Hub: Stream 5.58</u>

Her 'mentor', the now invisible inspector Harris, had at one point recommended that if you had nothing but rabbit trails, 'you should stop and wait for the rabbit'. Fleur's application of this random utterance was to stop trying to figure out what was happening. What she knew was that Doctor Earland was dead. He had been a significant figure in his field and his death was currently mysterious- awaiting coroner. In addition, the chief inspector was acting in a way that was unexpected, so finding two strange men in immaculate suits outside her door was of little surprise. They were also prepared for her and without comment opened the door as she stepped from the elevator and into the waiting area. She thought it best not to hesitate; though the space was not initially unfamiliar, she had been into the chief's office. It was sectioned off from the main 'paddock', where the detectives and technicians resided. An amply sized room, the Chief was very minimalist in terms of décor, with a small solid wood desk, a sensible looking high-backed office chair and a very basic old steel/plastic chair for those 'visiting'. The only luxuries were a very affluent looking two seat sofa and three pieces of art, none of which Fleur cared for. Nevertheless, on entering she found two more strangers; another woman, demurely sat on the said dark fabric sofa, while a man stood just to the side of the sofa studying one of the pieces of art. The woman was eastern in origin, somewhere in her late thirties, wearing an immaculate navy trouser suit and an immense amount of power in her bearing. Clearly those outside belonged to this woman, whereas her companion was something else. He was casually dressed in Khaki inspired trousers with a royal blue jacket; Caucasian, in at least his late fifties, his hair was cut very short and silver grey. He was close to gaunt, which added to Fleur's overall sense that the man was hungry, verging on obsessive; in addition, there was the flicker of recognition, but she couldn't connect it. However, any further observations were stunted by Fleur's attention being drawn to the Chief, who was un-expectantly in front of her desk.

"Welcome Inspector." To Fleur's consideration, the Chief was unattractive, not ugly or repulsive, just a little too sharp of feature and square of jaw. Though Fleur did find her big green eyes and bronzed skin appealing, the chief's small nose was again working against an ascetic Fleur had never really come to terms with when she looked at herself in the mirror.

"Sir." Fleur came to a halt and put herself to attention behind the 'visitors' chair. The chief tended to be quite hands on, taking meetings either at desks with her subordinates or side rooms; if you frequented the 'visitors' chair then you'd crossed a line.

"At ease inspector," Fleur wasn't sure what that meant, because the Chief wasn't at ease; this was her domain, lioness of the pride and all that, but whoever these two individuals were, they had the Chief in obvious discomfort. In addition, she was using her P.R accent, clipped and tight.

"I will keep this brief, as of two oriau ago we as an organisation have been purchased by the Elmander Corporation. Needless to say, that piece of information does not leave the room..." Globally, police services were generally arms of conglomerates who used them to protect assets, manage populations and make customers feel safe. Service changing hands as part of mergers was not unheard of, but it was rare to have a single service brought outright, if that was what had happened; maybe a super-merger was on the cards.

"...all of the proceedings will be announced in due time." Fleur couldn't miss the furtive glance to the seated lady, but it was not long enough for the Chef's dignity to be in question.

"Yes, sir." In saying that Fleur had effectively agreed that if she leaked the info, she would have no career.

"In the short term nothing will change in regards to the daily running of Pevnost police service, but inspector you will now be joined by a representative..." The Chief looked to the man who had been studying her art and then Fleur recalled that he was Professor James Eddings;

discoverer of Ēṭalānṭisa, presumed dead in a jungle, "...of Elmander incorporated, Professor James Eddings." He had left the painting, recognising his queue and approached Fleur. The man who Fleur remembered from countless interviews and documentaries was handsome, charming and attractive- An adventurer. That was an image sketched over the man who now moved with the memory of gracefulness. He offered his large hand in greeting, which Fleur took and met firmly, finding a certain infirmity in the Professors' grip. Though credit where it was due, he smelled good. However, on meeting his eyes her initial impressions were confirmed, he had a flicker of haunted-ness and obsession within the green of his iris'. Fleur however, found this to be unsurprising as well, even at the height of his Ēṭalānṭisa fame there were rumours and media intrigue around the more negative aspects of the Professor's character and behaviour.

"Professor Eddings, I'd like you to meet detective Fleur Sidoli, one of our finest detectives. Detective Sidoli, I suspect that an introduction is not necessary..."

"Thank you, Chief inspector. It's a pleasure to meet you Detective and I look forward to working with you." He still had some charm, but Fleur was not buying into it.

"Thank you, Professor, if I may ask what the professor's role will be?" Fleur released his hand and asked the question to the Chief- riding on the back of her *finest detectives'* statements.

"The agreement is that he's an active observer..." The Chief inspector's face was remarkably unreadable, on some level she had to know that the phrase was pure political excrement,

"...the professor will not have any legal powers and will follow your lead while you're on the case, is that clear *detective?*" There was a way that

those in authority could turn a label into a weapon, Fleur was on the thinnest ice. “In regards to potential crime scenes you are in charge of managing them and only when you are satisfied will the scene be accessed by the professor.” An efficient speech, addressing everyone in the room; the Chief was a believer in procedure and the legal framework, particularly given the nature of corporate legal departments.
“To clarify *detective*,” The Elmander executive spoke “you will investigate Doctor Earland’s death to the *best* of your abilities, while the Professor will be pursuing a separate line of enquiry.” The executive’s voice was also clipped, educated and used to being listened to, but Fleur was clearly not the only one who needed ‘clarification’.
“Is that understood *detective*?” The Chief said actually looking at the Professor.
“Yes sir.”
“Good, we have sent uniformed offices to secure Doctor Earland’s residence and they are waiting for you.” The Chief moved from her place by the desk, took the Professor’s hand “It’s been an *interesting* first meeting Professor, I hope that *your* investigation goes well and that our next meeting will be *less* bureaucratic.” Fleur knew this was a political manoeuvre, but couldn’t quite fix the angle of intent.
“Indeed, chief inspector.” The professor warmly smiled to the Chief and nodded, then turning to Fleur. “Lead on detective.”

KI REGUS, DRA centre: ACTUAL

Regus woke. *Badly.* She’d been weeping. The medical staff had her on neuro-suppressors; the side effects were not ‘mild’. She slept *heavily*, but when she woke, she was still not ‘rested’, she was just *sad.* ‘Everything’ was being done, but no one was coming up with any results other than...*shit, we're fucked, completely, forever* and there is nothing we can do about it. In the twenty cycles since the initial disaster, they had hit *dead* end after *dead* end, glimmers of hope mutated in to *horrible, horrible realities*! Which now included the death of Malkus; there was no super-powered, super intelligent, super equipped champion to rescue him. Her drug addled mind offered that *perhaps* her colleagues would find an ancient text, weapon, code or even a deity willing to bring Malkus back. But her tears told the truth. The *bastard* crippled 'genius' eccentric was gone, it was *sad*; but what was *deeply* frustrating was the on-going 'investigation' into his un-tethering. Not that she was really aware of the details of *the* investigation; her first day after her 'neurological shutdown', she'd found a medical specialist tending to her needs. Ki's response was *not* the 'best', it was almost out of body; a screaming banshee rage that took over her, in a savage expression of grief, frustration and bitterness! The next time she was brought to consciousness, she could feel the influence of the suppressors and the agency services explained her situation. She was on temporary suspension on medical grounds, while an 'investigation' was conducted, though there was a little respite in a compliment about her initiative to establish a ping- even if it was pointless. In her placid state, Ki was strongly advised to *focus* on her own recovery, in non-technical terms, she was exhausted, over stimulated and just a little bit *fractured*. Unrivalled disaster, career in tatters, actually potentially facing criminal charges! Malkus ha*d destroyed* her, from his special cage he'd successfully assassinated her. *Oh, Ki you stupid cow, did you have to say that thing about the bitch whore wife of the commander? Maybe Malkus has done us a favour, won't be our fucking fault when everything was taken by the storm, fuck him and fuck her career.*

Rest was welcomed, her body craved it, conspired with the meds and the specialist, only waking to eat and excrete. Time, the myth of existence, became irrelevant. In fact, she wasn't initially sure at first what cycle she was in and though the medical staff mercifully/cruelly answered her enquires, they could have been lying. Nevertheless, she could feel herself recovering and eventually she was returned to her own care, on a reduced medication regime, but an increase in relaxation, meditation and exercise. However, she was given nothing else to do. In addition, Ki's enquiries to how the investigation was proceeding were met with deflection, which first concerned her...*actually potentially facing criminal charges* and all that, but she came to realise that it just wasn't a priority. So, she settled in for the long haul, but at some point the boredom had set in. At least that was what she was calling it; after all, stripped of her rhythm, left only with light exercise, food and entertainment, a dissonance was bound to emerge. And that boredom, with its submerged frustrations, was the reality generating her tears. She only had one thing left, Malkus' mysterious data files. It had seemed so profound at the time, but now it was the 'last will and testament of a DRA agent'. Given the time that was being made available to Ki, she decided to start at the beginning or at least the point where Malkus had connected with the 'person' that was 'Varses'. It was a shape-shifting assassin who had appeared during a randomised DRA recon in a minor data stream, all of this long before the *world storm* had been a link in their reality.

In fact, Malkus had been surreptitiously 'following' this person for nearly two cycles; which was impressive because the strain of more than one data stream was considered unhealthy- particularly over a sustained period. Maybe the investigation would conclude that *these* exertions 'assisted' in effecting his ability to respond to the *unheralded* event that had untethered him. Though by reviewing her part- of Malkus' adventures with Varses- could bring about a potentially different punishment for Ki, but maybe only a demotion. Nevertheless, trawling through the data was not exactly enlightening, the collection- though theoretically following protocol- was a mess. A *disturbing* mess and of course infuriating. It was painful to discover how much she'd missed when 'handling' Malkus. Particularly galling was the fact that Malkus had effectively ignored repeated warnings by her and her predecessor. He had conducted ghosting and birds-eye searches, when he *should* have been recovering crucial data, perhaps even the answer to the *storm*- instead he was tracking Varses. If she was to reveal the data she had, then she'd make it *clear* that Malkus was a conniving, two faced, hypocrite; whose *only* aim was to satisfy his own agenda and obsessions. Maybe she could even present it as a test case, how agents *should* be scanned regularly for 'deviant' behaviour or maybe even start asking questions about how her and her predecessors concerns were taken so 'lightly'. *How was it that Malkus got to deviate so far from protocol and yet never be punished?* Though if Ki was to take this approach then she would need to make sure that she had not herself become co-conspirator with Malkus' rebellion or at least play a victim card. Given Malkus' absence, at least it would be her word against the dead, a fair battlefield.

Nevertheless, the data would be what secured her passage back from Malkus' ruination and she could easily blame her predecessor for under reporting, conspiring etcetera. Particularly because Nela's next assignment had gone so *spectacularly* wrong that she would never return to the hub. And there was always the question, *How was it that*

Malkus got to deviate so far from protocol and yet never be punished? So, she moved from Varses and Malkus' beginning- to her entry into the triangle. Though at first it appeared that Malkus had actually been following orders. He'd tied himself into a man called 'Duncan/Diego/Hector', a multi-intersecting anomaly of multiple data streams. It was standard procedure to mark and even follow such multi-intersecting stream anomalies, as this they were often fonts of valuable information, way points and access to other streams of data. There was a vast array of speculation as to what these anomalies were, how they came to exist and how aware *they* were of their connection to other data streams. Was it possible for them to interact with the connection and if they experienced multiple lives in a 'simultaneous' movement? However, 'Duncan' was an anomaly within an anomaly, because before his interaction with Varses at the river crossing, Duncan appeared for all intense and purposes, a standard site of data. Yet his interaction with Varses, 'catalysed' him into becoming a glowing web of pathways, like a cropped neurological image. Though somehow, Malkus, *the Hub* and even she had managed to completely miss this. Yet *this* was the kind of unique emergence of connectivity Malkus lived for, to have his name whispered in *reverence*. However, there seemed to be no acknowledgment of the moment, though it did explain why he had continued to follow 'Duncan' through his 'revelations', even after it was clear that there was no trace of the *storm* in that stream.

Poor *broken* Malkus, had the strain got to him? Was he unwilling to let his obsession become public? Or did he fear that the revelation would be *consumed* by the pursuit of the storm and his kudos would then be damaged? *Wouldn't put it beyond the rebellious fucker.* Though that mystery could be assigned to his 'personality' the Hub's oversight was...*fuck it your whole reality was one constant crisis. Was anything disturbing anymore? Wasn't it just a gradient on a wave or trough of fuckery?* So, whereas Malkus being a contradictory, rebellious, obtuse, awkward bastard was *actually* 'normal', the Hub's behaviour was not. Maybe the massive demands on its vast processing power had forced it into overlooking such a wealth of data? Or handlers and agents were so thin on the ground that the Hub had effectively shelved it. Perhaps *that* was a good idea for her as well. She left the pad review of the data, exited her study space, tidied up, went to the toilet, retrieved a drink, took some of the prescribed stimulants and generally come to appreciate her cramped but open plan apartment. All of life's necessities in two rooms, there was something reassuring about the space, yes the panelling was a little dull, but the bathing facilities were an easy distance from the bed. This was formed to her figure, which was still recovering from her exhausted state. Maybe the collective exhaustion would justify how the Hub, Malkus and even her could just 'brush' past the obvious...though perhaps it wasn't obvious.

"Please Ki don't be having another break..." she said out loud to herself, because *that* was not a thing. What was a *thing,* according to the data, was two multiple stream anomalies, communicating to each other, at points in violent conflict, and yet *not* connecting *at all*! Though what began to *draw* darkness to the edge of Ki's cognition was not *just* that the anomalies didn't 'connect', they seemed not to be in the data stream itself! This phenomena in a DRA's reality would break *the* whole system, it was not a *thing*! Perhaps that's what the Hub realised, maybe even Malkus had considered the 'greater good'...*How could anything not be in the data stream and yet be there at the same time?* Like the proverbial insect to the flaming data, her instinct told her to return to Varses- as Malkus had so many times before. If he was somehow a 'catalyst' for 'Duncan/Diego/Hector', then perhaps discovering how or when Varses had become an *anomaly* would offer a solution to the unbelievable question. Though calling Varses an *anomaly* was a dire minimalism he was an *overwhelming* cacophony of streams. Yet Ki was rescued from the deep dive by other commitments, she was due to be at another de-briefing appointment. Being late because she was trawling through *off the books* data- which was *terrifying* in its scope - was not going to enamour her to the powers that be. So, she set an analytical search on her personal computing device- for the 'moment' when Varses ceased to be a 'fixed reality' and instead became *unheralded*. Ki, dismissing her early conjecture, was aware- that whatever the discovery- it was folly to think a simple answer could bring her a solution for the disconnected insanity that was revealing itself in Malkus' obsession.

Eddings Investigation. Stream 5.58r

He was *trying* his best; Elmander had him on a short leash that they'd attached to his testicles. He was also trying to take the young woman *seriously*; pretty, dark hair, green eyes, curved, if a little slim for James' tastes. Not that Elmander would permit anything *untoward* to happen, in addition to which, James was *quite* aware of the regard he was held in by the young detective. She was guarded to the point of wariness and given her circumstances; it was an appropriate response. James had to give her 'some' credit on how she had handled herself in her commanding officer's 'lair', but still…maybe it was because Elmander 'liked' the young woman for the job, which caused him to struggle. Or maybe James just couldn't see the *point*, he…*they* had been 'pursuing' a living artefact, a murdering, life sucking mystery, which continued to confound- even though it was now in a morgue. Maybe *that* was the reason for the softly, softly approach; because it *had* been someone else's slab. When James had challenged the pause in *his*...'their' pursuit; his handler, the 'delightful' Miss Chung, had informed him of the 'political' considerations. Buying a *whole* region, at first seemed incongruent with Elmander's methods to this point, but it was not inconceivable that they were not the only one's aware of the *Count...Doctor Earland.* To own the whole region, effectively gave them 'control' and in another life James would have applauded the manoeuvre, but what he'd really wanted to do was fly straight to the morgue and *desecrate* the murderous organism. Instead, *fuckers,* Elmander in their 'wisdom' had ordered him to investigate what *Doctor Earland* had been up to in the months that he'd been unaccounted for. He'd been furious! Yet behind that sensual exterior of Miss Chung was a woman of terrifying power, who had eclipsed his frustration with one long look. At least he was getting to sate his disappointment with curiosity, while escaping that look- even if it was still in the periphery of his thinking.

Why come to Pevnost to die? The detective's investigation to this point had uncovered little of interest, in other words, nothing. So, they headed to the doctor's suburban residence in a leafy area of Pevnost- to follow procedure- but hopefully, for him, find the spark of *something*. The house and its surrounds, though punctuated by curved out windows and superstitious statutes, were not in the least bit attractive to James. Though the origin of the statues 'guarding' the property could have actually been Oaxcan; which was a minor curiosity, as the fabrication would not have been inspired by any direct trading or cultural routes. Perhaps they were modern aberrations? Maybe the *Doctor* had felt humorous by adding them.

“Professor Eddings, would you like to join me?” Eddings was called back from his wandering internal dialogue of ‘minor’ revere. It was refreshing to be outside the office in the mild and slightly damp air, pleasing to be trusted with something other than not being a burden. Which was how he’d come to view himself in months of pursuing the *Count.* It had been ‘depressing’ and house arrest by any other name. Though, as ever, there was a limit to that trust. Quite obviously an Elmander escort had convoyed with the detective’s vehicle and was now parked at the end of the street.

“Sorry Detective.” He’d attempt to de-formalise the relationship…*call me James blah, blah*…but the *detective* was resilient. Actually, she was exactingly following procedure and so he had been ‘invited’ to wait outside the property as the *detective* and her little drone army had entered the house and swept through it. Clearly the more in-depth work would begin now.

“As I said Professor,” whatever the fullness of her opinion of him, James appreciated the way she said *professor*, even if she was perhaps thinking of someone else; “it’s a three-storey property…” *Of the En expansion era, most likely gutted and renovated to a more modern standard as tastes had recently changed globally and such property had to compete.* “…with a converted annex space within the attic.” *If only a person could be changed as easily as a house,* James pondered to himself as he crossed the threshold and had his suspicions of renovation confirmed. Bland, un-original and completely un-inspiring. In contemplating what kind of property, *the Count* would live in, this had not been at the forefront of his mind; though he had flipped between romanticism (penthouse suite) and pragmatism (off-the books rental). Nevertheless, there was something about knowingly stepping into the ‘home’ of the late doctor, which ignited another kind of revere- tinged with disappointment. He'd been the *one* who had wanted to catch him, to look him in the eye and ask the impossible questions; instead the *bastard* had just died.

"Professor are you alright?" He'd faded out again, stood in the hallway looking off into the distance.

"Honestly detective, no. I'd prefer to tell you more over a dinner you're not going to agree to, but in short, *Doctor* Earland…took my life from me." It was an accurate description for James and wouldn't as such displease Ms Chung's and it seemed to buy some hint of sympathy with the *detective*.

"Well, hopefully we'll find *something* of use to Elmander and yourself, perhaps some closure." Though it sounded genuine, there was certain briskness to the clipping of her vowels which suggested to James that as serious as he was being taken, there were other priorities.

"Thank you, detective, I've looked over the plans so I'm familiar with the layout…so where do we start?" James found a smile.

"Nothing obvious flagged on the drone through, so we'll start in the annex as three of the four bedrooms are empty, as is the main bedroom. Also, they detected some areas of potential there." A younger Eddings would have at least noted the décor of the house as he travelled through, but if they found nothing in the attic, he would become familiar enough with it. He did almost get distracted by an abstract painting in the hall and some more on the second floor, but James was taken to following the *detective* and getting a little lost in her movement. Another thing he did notice was a sense of loneliness; perhaps it was his, but he did wonder why doctor Earland would purchase a property that would constantly point to the absence of companionship. Though a 'living' artefact with the ability to return to life perhaps had a different perspective, maybe the 'doctor' just didn't need people in the same way.

The annex was past two large bedrooms on the second floor and up a generous single winder stairs. According to the research, the turret was an original feature of the house, but the owner had gone for a domed roof instead of the more popular crenulated version. James immediately recognised it as a sanctuary, a place of contemplation; with a view out onto the adjacent park, a densely wooded area and the misty hills beyond. Though the turret was circular, the internal space had been squared off by partition walls, which enclosed around a single armchair. It was well worn; the animal skin having frayed at the arms and there were signs of re-upholstering. The chair was flanked and overshadowed by two bookshelves, arrayed with classic tomes from around the planet; while just to the left was a small cabinet, which most likely contained alcohol, but on top was a book with a number of familiar faces on it. Well once familiar, it was an auto-biographical account of James' discovery of Ēṭalānṭisa and rested so that him and his team, with smiling faces, were looking back at him. He found himself reaching over and picking the book up, while alarm bells went off in the background of his cognition. '*That was always our problem though wasn't it James, one step too far,*' a voice he couldn't place emerged in his thinking, but it spoke a truth, if he'd not taken that obsessive step to look upon the rags then 'Earland' would not have risen and he'd be able to drink with his friends.

"Professor…" James had lost time again, he found himself sat on the seat looking out into the distance, with a concerned looking detective Sidoli calling for his attention.

"Sorry detective, genuinely…I think my reputation is the only reason I'm here." James could feel the exhaustion creeping up again, stalking up the stairs. "Though it could be worse…Elmander maybe offering some kind of twisted sympathy."

"Look Professor, I've seen this before, you need to get some medical and psychological help…" It stung just a little less every time someone suggested it, "…but we do have a job to do, could you at least give me a *hint* for what Elmander…" A metallic beep sounded in the room, "…are looking for?" The beep was followed by three simultaneous responses; firstly, a panel swiftly appeared over the mouth of the stairs, the window darkened, and a book cover fell. A device started to project a face onto the now dark window.

"What the…" The detective exclaimed,

"James…" It was the late 'Doctor Earland', "I do hope it is you Professor, it's ambitious of me to assume that Elmander will have released you from your *cage*." From the first syllable the voice had him memorised, it was warm and inviting, with a modulating international accent that would have been the expectation of most global communication. More than that or perhaps in combination with the life filled visage, James felt a *little* seduced. "Though perhaps your passion for *desecration* has overcome their procedure and you convinced them to let you fly…" The seduction left him completely vulnerable, no one knew the extent of his obsession; he'd known to write it nowhere and speak it to no one and yet it was laid bare. "…nevertheless, to whoever is watching this, as you know I am indisposed." James recalled seeing a 'from beyond' message left by his father-in-law to his second wife; it was strained, moving and brought closure. However, his second wife's father had been withered by illness, drawn by regret, desperate to communicate something lost. Whereas 'Doctor Earland' had a sparkle

in his inviting multi-coloured eyes and his bronzed diamond shaped visage, which was full of life. His hair was cut short, accentuating his hawkish features, and his smile was warm.
"Though obviously from your own experience that may not be permanent ..."
"Professor can you raise anyone?" Sidoli, in what light was afforded from the projection, had her communication equipment out and was shining an on-board light about, but revealing nothing new.
"...powerful don't you think?" The detective's question had blurred something; it was unnerving, as he may have missed something *vital.*
"Here take mine and for God-sake be quiet!" His instinct was screaming past all his doubts, whatever was uttered next was crucial to satisfying *his* pursuit and getting *his life back*; the force of his voice and the disposal of his communication device silenced the *detective*.
"Though let me first of all apologise," James would offer him *no* forgiveness in any life, "but to do that properly I have to tell you a story. Let's cover some basics though, firstly the room you are in is tech silencing and this is the only time that this recording will play. Once it is finished it will delete itself and you will be advised to make a *swift* exit from my little tower." The ghost of 'Earland' took a sip of what was probably water. He looked exactly as he had on the recording of his death, but clearly more invigorated. "Also, any attempt to stop the recording or leave the tower prematurely will mean a deleting of the recording and well...fill in the gaps." Though clearly a threat to his well-being, James' focus had returned completely to his bete noir and had managed to restrain the good detective from anymore faffing.
"Now that I have a greater degree of your attention let me begin." Something changed in 'Earland', the playfulness began to recede and

something of the sparkle and evanescence dissipated. Instead sadness seeped onto his visage and around his mouth.
"Once upon a time, my people's civilisation fell, it doesn't really matter how, not to one's story, but it didn't happen in one day. As you have witnessed, civilisations do not fall in one day…I'm sorry, let me start again, Ēṭalānṭisa as you call it was…*no*..." 'Doctor Earland', the 'living' artefact, a being who had been reanimated after a near timeless existence, was lost for words. Sympathy, it emerged as an invitation, after all this was a last 'will and testament', but still…he'd *killed* James' friend.
"Okay, yes that's a good place to start, *our* people have been wiped from existence, we are not even a myth or a fairy tale, it is as we were told it would be…for our transgression," 'Earland' had recorded the missive in the tower and he had become distracted at something beyond the recording device, maybe in the park on a potentially summers day. "Except for that obscure note in Ēṭalānṭisa and even then…well I'm not sure how to describe the Professor's *leap*. Those who pursue patterns would give it a meaning, but I'm not sure it's a meaning that satisfies anyone, particularly not those who lost…" another sip of the drink, followed by a deep sigh. "I considered lamenting…pleading…even visiting the bereaved; but I'm pretty sure that would have been *another* transgression and *my* people, wherever they are would be un-impressed." The detective had come to sit on the arm of the chair, they were captivated. "Still, I know you have *so many* questions and in that I continue to be cruel…you *just* have my rambling monologue and I suspect that even though you are unable to contact the outside world your vanishing will have not gone unnoticed." Another deep breath from the Doctor, he seemed immensely conflicted. "Even

though my people transgressed, there was still mercy. A time frame as you would call it, to put our house in order. While our civilisation fell, *your* ancestors arose as the harbingers of our punishment. Our response was ambitious, but we needed to create *time*. The thing to note is that your aggressive expansionist drive has not changed since the time of your ancestors, but we used that against them." A smile returned to the face, but it was rye.

"The Elders called for volunteers from amongst what would train as the *sentinels* and in pairs we took a stand against the darkness." Another deeper breath and a large volume of the liquid in the glass, it was making James thirsty- though for something stronger.
"So Silab was called, our people retreated, expect for the sentinels, *oh and we did more than stand*. We *fought* at every turn as *your* instinct driven *savage horde* came to consume us, a thousand of them were not worth *one of us!* I still don't understand how we were allowed to commit *such* atrocities but credit where credit was due the horde became more determined." He was a fluctuating story teller, a mixture of tone and emotion, sad, bitter, furious, proud; all strangely confused. "We *stood* against thousands, not like your modern aberrations of senseless conflict, *no!* US against the wave until one would make the call." Tears started to clearly roll down 'Doctor Earland's' smooth skin, "*I told her to go...*" A wave of breath shuddered out of him, but he caught whatever appeared to be almost overwhelming him. "One by one, we'd drawn the horde with this trick, knowing that *they* would prize capturing places. Seeing them as trophies over actually destroying us, maybe this was mercy as well, I don't know anymore... I have had some time to..." A sob rolled through him.
"Professor, what the..."

"Detective! We have *one* chance to hear him out and I want *you* to treat *this* confession as the *most* important part of *your* career!"
"Seriously…" James returned his concertation to the Doctor, if these utterances were to be taken seriously the *Count* was the last remaining "person" of a civilisation that simply didn't exist. However, before they'd ceased to exist, they'd been at war with humanity. Add to it that he was some kind of warrior that had agreed to sacrifice himself as a ruse to draw humanity away from their evacuating people. James would ride the chain of statement and then *desecrate the fucker*!
"My apologises…" *Don't give a fuck about your apologises you murdering blight on humanity,* a voice spoke fervently in James' inner dialogue. "I've *never* spoken of this…perhaps I shouldn't, though maybe James you deserve this explanation? horribly incomplete as it is…"
*Why the fuck would it matter, "…*because I simply *don't understand why* I came back. Perhaps I know how, but that makes…little sense. But I have drifted from my intent." The *person*, (if that was now an accurate description given the revelations) sighed, it was comforting for James to know that he was watching the last breathes of the defiler…*yes that was his name, the name of his people, defilers, monsters…that which should not be named.* "I'm realising why this has taken so long, I see *her* every day. I remember *her* smell; I'm haunted by her touch…I wonder if she and my people still exist? Perhaps I've stayed this long because I'm scared that they're all gone and here I get to remember her."
"This is insane…" Muttered detective Sidoli, yet again blurring the Doctors words, James glared up at her and in the light of the projection the detective understood that it was not the time to speak.
"…we did *our duty*; drawing the horde into a place we called Creeus, a wide valley, with a river running through it and a tower that sang in the

sun. It took me *days* to restrain the memories of *my love* and I dancing through your ancestors; perhaps the continuing victories had lulled them into believing they were wining. It would explain the *stupidity*, because your ancestors came at us head on. It does lead me to wonder how my fellow sentinels had chosen to fight them, because they looked *very* surprised when we started to use their own weapons against them." A wry smile returned to the doctor's lips, "We were always a little rebellious, but the first three days of defeat for *your* ancestors, drew more and more into that valley. Our goal, as I mentioned, was never numbers, it was time; and we *devoured* it! Perhaps that is why *you* deleted us from history, not some conspiracy, not even our failings as a people, but your ancestors' *shame*." Doctor Earland's story telling was becoming more and more like a lecture, a self-satisfying, arrogant monologue. James could only imagine the suggested carnage, though it was still very possible that this was the ramblings of a fairy-tale.
"Nevertheless, we fought day and eventually parts of the night and I found time had consumed me. A human of *no little* skill managed to unpick my defence and a blunted blade gashed open my thigh. It cost him his throat and I thought it cost me my life, perhaps it did…" A shudder of recollection, the swagger of the storyteller flying away, and his eyes became unfocused; his breathing was rapid and it was the only thing that filled the minutes of silence that passed.
"You're not buying this are you?" The detective realising that this was her chance to speak against the monologue.
"I don't know what to *believe* Detective, but the *thing* on the screen has successfully managed to evade one of the most powerful organisations in the history of humanity, with no apparent support, finance or *anything* that would explain his success. So, I'll take the littlest clue." He had said

to much. This was not information that detective needed to know, but he could barely contain his *frustration*.

"*She* left, as one of us was always going to; I didn't see it, but I felt it…the pain of my thigh was a scratch in comparison…her *leaving* killed me…I think, yes there are moments, glimpses of me retreating, fighting back to the sun tower, shutting myself in with death, another river of blood behind me. From working thorough your research James, I can only assume that the tower collapsed and history happened, short shock ice age, *world storm* maybe. But in reality, James, the only knowledge I have is waking to *your* beautiful eyes." Eddings could feel the look of perplexion the detective was giving him and James was frozen, unable to speak, caught in the recollection of the *defiler's a*wakening. "Though somethings do not change Professor, I still *transgress* and *I am* sorry for your loss and if you find a way please pass on my *sincere* apologises to your colleagues' family…" Detective Sidoli was completely lost, she had done her best to maintain a semblance of procedure, but they were prisoners to a dead man's ramblings and the last utterance had literally shaken the Professor. She was afraid and yet transfixed, but she was hoping that someone was on there way, because she felt helpless.

"As for me, well, this is *goodbye*. My time here is done and I am *genuinely* concerned that if I remain any longer, I will have compounded my people's *error*, I don't want it stalking them amongst the stars…" A wicked grin broke across 'Doctor Earland's' face, "*Whoops*, too much confession, I think! Needless to say, James I wish you all the best, you'll be seeing me soon." With that the recoding stopped and the window started to pass light through itself once again, the stairs shutter drawing back. In addition, a digital display appeared on the wall next to the window with the number sixty on it. A call started to ring on the professor's communication device.

"This is detective Sidoli!" a panicked voice fired rapid questions, Fleur just let them flow until she could say "We have been *detained* by Doctor Earland, who left us a visual recording, however we are leaving the area due to a potential *bomb threat*! Send the bomb squad immediate...*no* but I can see a *countdown* and no I don't have time...*fine* you can talk to him yourself." *Arrogant, dismissive eunuch feel free to speak to your precious academic!* Forcefully she handed over the device as they moved down the stairs, in turn retrieving her own device and taking a call from the office.

"Eddings here." James still felt fuzzy, confused and overwhelmed.

"This is Agent Thomas, report." *Ah the ever brisk Elmander, no wonder the detective looked so aggrieved.*

"We walked into a trap, we're *fine* thanks for asking! The so-called *Doctor* left his last will and testament about how he came to be on the plateau." As ever James followed the detective, who was rapidly explaining to her department what had just transpired.

"Did he reveal *anything* about what he'd been up to?"

"Not anything in particular, I know that the detective tried to record the message, but whatever is in that annex *literally* shut our devices down completely."

"Professor, you need to go back; the corpse is a *fake*..." The words caused him to snap back to a moment on the recording *'somethings don't change'.*

"Fucking bastard!" James roared

"Excuse..."

"Detective, run!" James howled, *'it wasn't about numbers, it was about consuming time.'*

James' body had put things together much faster than his thinking and he sprinted as if a young man, but time had been consumed. The world around him lit up and he was lifted from his feet and thrown down the stairs, crashing into the detective, who simultaneously barrelled into two on-rushing Elmander agents. Violence putting him out of consciousness.

Malkus. Earland Residence: Stream 5.58rr

The best way he could describe it was, 'waking up', but with a horrendous sound ringing in *every* part of his head. He fought for air, not air as such, the machine supplied his body with everything. He was fighting to connect to *any* reality that would accept him. He knew that focusing on what was before would see him drift again into limbo. Such a beautiful...*no Malkus, where are you, you know this place, 'it' brought you here...*That made no sense though. *Let it go,* actually he didn't recognise the leafy suburb, but he would 'know' the man in front of him in any stream, Professor James Eddings. He was sat down, his back against a low garden wall, looking at a three-storey house with smoke billowing wildly from the roof, where flames licked into the sky. Malkus understood that soon the emergency services would be coming, though it appeared that at least one was on scene, arguing heatedly with two other agents of some kind. Nevertheless, for Malkus the ringing *refused* to subside, he knew *instinctively* he needed to tether himself. Yet there was no actual understanding of the 'reality' he now resided in. Let alone a procedure, which would offer an easy or even complex solution to his dilemma. So, he went with what was at hand, the *professor.* Looking closely, he noticed two things, firstly the professor was mouthing something into his phone and secondly, he looked very, very agitated.

A whole new...*hold on, Malkus you idiot, you're not untethered at least you're not in limbo anymore*, he needed to signal Ki and get some help. "Hello, hello this is agent Malkus, Ki *please* response?" The ringing sound kept coming, activity swirled around him as the stream kept flowing, 'reality' moved and emerged, but he could sense limbo at the corner of his being.

"Ki Regus, *emergency* protocol one nine four *please* respond!" Still no response or none he could hear past the ringing! Had he really regained entry to the stream? Pulling off the impossible? Or was this part of what it was to be disconnected, a reality of constant noise, movement, but no response? *Perhaps* if he re-tethered to the Professor, things would level out? He drew up an appropriate sequence, in his thinking at least, of algorithms and equations, but instead of drawing him in the sound got worse! Malkus' 'reality' blurred and he immediately backed off "What the fuck!?" Malkus said to himself, but out of his confusion an idea emerged. What he could hear was a *ping*, well actually, what was *assaulting* him was the ping...he needed to get Ki to turn it off.

"Ki Regus, this is agent Malkus, *please respond*! *please* dial down the ping." Something now made sense, Ki had placed an emergency beacon 'on' Eddings and it had given Malkus a hook out of the un-tethered limbo. However, the beacon was now a *major* problem, a catch twenty something or other, but Malkus decided that him offering a *little* 'resistance' might help. He moved toward the now less animated agents and as he did the persistent sound of the beacon decreased a little.

"For the last time..."

"There has to be..."

"Whatever there was blew up..."

"You said..."

"Look..."

"Fine."

"I'll recount what can..."

"Okay...secrecy..."

"Okay."

"Oh just fuck off! And stop the thing burning down!" Suddenly Malkus could see data, detective Fleur Sidoli, twenty-eight, one seventy-five centimetres tall, sixty-four kilos, Caucasian. Detective eighteen months, daughter of a local tribe, seconded to Doctor Earland case by Chief Inspector. Malkus could 'feel' the tears of his own relief. *He was tethered*! He didn't know *how or when or how or if it was secure of anything*, but he was part of the stream! Detective Sidoli was of little significance in her stream, enough authority to order fire crews and attending specialists, but to Malkus she was *divine*. Though the banshee 'singing' of the ping continued, maybe if he moved a little further away, he would get something. About thirty metres from James the data became even clearer and sound decreased even more and then his heart *burst* with joy!

"*Agent Malkus please response with verification co*des!" The voice was exasperated, though Malkus wasn't sure how many times he'd been asked since *miraculous* return to the stream. Nevertheless, it was beyond reassuring,

"Square, Na, TAG, mole, epiphany."

"Please confirm second code!" The agent on the other end was, as such, maintaining their composure. Even though Malkus could sense in the tone a mixture of excitement, relief and concern at the possibilities.

"Right, eight, four, star and before you ask retreat, black, arbiter!"

"Agent Malkus, welcome back..." Malkus pictured scenes of celebration, joy abounding, even in the face of the *Storm,* "...it is truly good to hear and see you...but we need to debrief."
"Where is Ki Regus?" The syntax and processing of the voice was different.
"*Handler Ki* Regus is currently indisposed. I am handler Qin Regus and at least for this communication I'll be supporting your return to the mainstream." Indisposed, Malkus had a fair idea what that meant.
"I'd prefer *handler* Ki." It could have been seen as a gesture of support for whatever Ki was facing, but the reality was that Malkus was tired and really didn't want to have to *bed-in* another handler.
"Understood, but as I said she's *indisposed.*" It was the party line, Malkus took it to mean that Qin Regus was aware that even a *hint* of what had befallen Ki would have him in trouble. For Malkus, Ki was under Elder investigation and almost certainly reassigned, suspended, pending the conclusion of said investigation. They would *never* meet again.
"Understood, well handler, could you explain to me what the procedure is for a full re-tethering and re-entry to the main hub stream?" Having overcome the impossible and returned from limbo, Malkus knew that *defining* the relationship was important. There may have been some 'twinge' of guilt for ending Ki's career, but in the competing choices for how to define the *new* relationship, it was not a dominant voice.
"Well," Qin handler used the word in such a way that it acknowledged the context, Malkus' part in it and the unknown that they were all in, "let's start by minimising the interference."
"The ping?"
"Yes, obviously we'd turn it off, but it was an emergency procedure and the tech department are having to correct some issues in its

establishment so we're going to have to work around it." Malkus could imagine that everyone was watching the *handler* and he was doing his best not to make enemies.

"You weren't expecting me to return, were you?"

"No." Malkus was a little surprised by the bluntness of the response, this *handler* may have been assigned a dead-end case, but he was willing to take risks. "So, apologises if things are a little haphazard, but to bring you up to speed, you are part re-tethered, though it's not secure."

"Is the ping interfering with my tether to the professor?"

"Actually *agent,* "Bless him, he was still trying to stick to the procedural expectations, at least the etiquette side of things. "That is not strictly accurate and looking at the data in front of me, we're going to need a more viable option soon." Something about the tone concerned Malkus and also irritated him, something was *very* wrong, if the professor was not the tether, then how was he having this conversation at all? Malkus knew that he had to force the issue.

"Look Qin, I get it, you're some graduate handler given a watching brief on a tragedy while everyone else purses this *fucking* storm," no rebuttal, "and *now* you're out of your depth and trying not to *fuck up* while the *powers that be* get their collective heads around this. So help me help you!" Silence. Well relatively, as the ping continued to buzz in Malkus' reality, but clearly he'd hit a number of spots.

"You do live up to *your* reputation, don't you? Fine, the hub is flagging the professor as having *very* limited usefulness as a tether point." In other words, the professor was about to die. "So, we're going to hook you to the city of Pevnost." Cold, logical, it was reassuring that the hub and *handler* were working for his best interest- even trying to protect him from the sadness that now enveloped him. "*Agent*?" Malkus rarely stayed for the death of a collection cycle, to see the world die in a billion different ways was not a particularly good longevity plan. The closeness of it made a lot of things more apparent,

"How?"

"Well, we're going to use a recoded…oh, sorry…"

"Fuck it Qin! We're *so* far from relevance and procedure that it would slap you for trying to follow it."

"Brain aneurism, within the next hour…" *It* had finally become too much, not necessarily for the man, but for his body.

"Okay," though Malkus wasn't sure what he'd actually responded to, instead he looked to the professor one last time. He was still seated against the wall, ghost of the younger man he was, but so much more alive than the last time Malkus had seen him- the return of purpose. As a ghost Malkus sighed and turned away, knowing he'd completely lost track of any information Qin had passed him.

"What do you need from me?"

"At a steady pace, remaining in the gamma state, we want you to head toward the centre of the city…" A visual arrow appeared in Malkus' perception of the stream, "I'll keep our connection open, but I'm going to have to interface with my colleagues to get this done."

"Understood, I'm in your hands, don't fuck up and can you at least tell Ki that I'm back." It would lighten the now apparent guilt he felt.

"We'll get you locked and home, but as I said Ki is…"

"*Indisposed.*"

Ki Regus- DRA centre: Actual

She'd been euphoric, the assessment had been extremely positive and she would be back as a *handler!* Yes, it was a temporary demotion, but that could be overcome and quite frankly *any* support for the *world*

storm search was deeply appreciated. So, the euphoria would explain how she'd failed to notice the male figure that had been following her until they were both in her room. In fact, she only knew another person was in the room after she had recovered from what must have been a neuro-overload device. Not that the euphoria had dissipated, it just was no longer self-generated. Her body was *alive*, like she'd never experienced before. She was *engulfed* in sensation, to the point where nothing else came to her awareness. Her skin was oily, dripping and anticipating a *touch*, it hungered for *more* than the connection of the air and her bed sheets, but even these were intoxicating. Simultaneously her other senses competed just as ferociously for attention, she could smell the fragrances of her own skin, the bed clothes and the scent of the person with her in the room. She was dripping in the desire to *taste* with her world spinning, burning up in sensuous pain. And then it was gone! It was impossible to describe the savage experience of having such intensities extinguished *completely*. There wasn't *even* the residual buzz of climax. It was a brutal distortion of reality, a vicious use of the body against the person! And then it was back; *waves* of pleasure, her body singing, her vision swirling, she wanted to scream *EUPHORIA*! Yet she could barely find breath, beyond moaning and writhing on her bed. And again it was *gone*! Sensation flicked 'off' like a switch, causing her to grit her teeth and begin to black out- Ki was kept from it by the person in the room.
"Please…" She murmured, somewhere a quieted voice told her to call out for help, but she was disorientated by the desire for more.
"ONE last time Ki," the voice came between the waves, it was kind and firm, she desired to *consume* it and be consumed by it. "Agent Malkus' data is that the only copy?" It was always the same question, the same modulated tone, the same rhythm and completely assured. From the

moment she had regained consciousness, tied to her bed with a hood over her face.

"Welcome *Handler* Regus Ki, I have one question, you have three choices, resist, suffer or give in. No one is coming." Shock and terror came first, but even then, a low-level warm sensation caressed her and then dropped away. She knew she was in trouble, but something about the male voice was soothing.

"Agent Malkus' data, is that the only copy?" Academically she considered the question and its ramifications or at least she tried, but her torture began as the euphoria hit. It was a *fabulous, consuming, coursing, compelling sensati*on and then it had gone.

"Agent Malkus' data, is that the only copy?" *Who, why, how?* And again, the storm of pleasure and sensation crashed through *all* her sense. Time became the rhythm of pleasure and its remorseless silencing. Though the cruelty of proceedings did begin to *subtly* change. Slightly shorter bursts of pleasure and a lengthening of the *horrific* experience of being without the pleasure, a timeless agony of being withdrawn from the *engulfing* beauty. She wasn't sure if she was resisting anymore? She may have even been 'enjoying' the suffering, saturated by sensation. A recollection of attempting to fake her 'submission' emerged in the pain of absence, an attempt to *convince* the one in power that it was working, but whoever they were, they had not bought the request for *more!* Involuntarily she had writhed in her restraints, carnal agony desiring the malevolent mercy of the pleasure.

"One last time Ki?" *She was sure he'd already said that.*

"More..."

"Agent Malkus' data is that the only copy?" Then it was no more, whatever had held her caved in and she whispered her words of compliance.

“Yes.” There was silence and *reward*, a low sensation; her cognitive processes awash with a desire for *more*, but aware also that she had been defeated. She was exhausted, disorientated and slightly delirious, but at least she still had *the* sensation. Ki was so cut adrift that she failed to notice that the hood had been removed and a male was sitting on her bed looking down at her. It was a face she knew, but had *no* right to be in her room.
“I credit you Ki Regus, you resisted well, but this is over now.” Malkus’ muse had a grim look on his face, Varses, was the victor, but he looked spoiled. *How could the vanished one be here?* “I bid you adieu, sleep now.” Varses gently leant over and delicately kissed Ki’s forehead, who fell into a forever sleep. Varses rose to the vertical, retrieved the data and personal device, before leaving the room as a *handler* of the DRA.

Malkus, Stream 5.5rr

The ringing stopped about a kilometre away from the professor, it had been growing steadily fainter, but now it was gone. Malkus asked, but was comforted to know that it was a technical solution. Nevertheless, with its disappearance, came a clear passage of data, which was significantly *more* comforting. Though it had an unexpected side effect, suddenly the enormity of his experience struck him- *he’d come back from the dead*! It felt dramatic to frame it that way, a little surreal and inappropriate. *What was it to die?* Did it matter that he wasn’t sure? After all, he had no recollection of limbo, in fact, all he really could recall was the soon to be dead Professor James Eddings. Rumour had it that the *agency* had pursued a line of research and experiments around tracking those who ‘left’ data streams due to death. However, the general conclusion was that instead of transferring to some ‘other’ place, the dead became part of the stream. So according to that definition, he'd not been dead at all, because his essence was no longer connected to a stream- he'd been outside the conventions. There was a good chance that when he was safely re-tethered, he would undoubtedly be de-briefed. Actually, he was *more* likely to be investigated until the *world storm* came. Maybe then he'd actually be dead (once the *storm* arrived); because as far as anyone knew, nothing survived the *storm*. All reality ceased to be- maybe he should have stayed in limbo. Though that would suggest that he knew what choices he'd actually had or could have made. He still had no recollection, a *disturbing* measure of some kind of reality missing from his frames of reference. But at least you're not dead huh- save that for later.

"You're nearing the centre point of Pevnost, can you see the fort?"

Apparently, it was called a 'castle', a sign of oppression and tourism historically, now a sight of military interest. It was not the fort the city was named after; it had been burnt down during what had been called a 'local-uprising' centuries before. The 'castle' was a rehash, with a number of aberrations including some very ornate looking towers; which had been fashionable during one of the industrial upsurges that Pevnost had inflicted upon itself.

"Yes."

"Good, I have you in the recreational are..." *Park,* lush, green, open area surrounded by trees, clearly the hub was translating data slightly differently for the handler.

"Can you see a small stone arrangement?" In the shadow of the 'castle' a pattern of stones forming an altar was obscured by a large tree.

"Yes, do you want me to..."

"No Malkus, you're *just* where we need you...why don't you step out of gamma mode and we'll *see* what happens." Qin was beginning to grow on Malkus, though alternatively, any other voice would be welcome.

"Are you sure this is safe?" Anxiety had found a way in.

"It's good enough agent," Since Malkus' earlier outburst *handler* Qin had been very direct, it wasn't comfortable, but Malkus wasn't sure what would be.

"Understood."

"Okay, syncing in three, two, one." Malkus 'keyed' out of being a 'ghost', a surge of energy rode through his stream state and he rose into the air. Pevnost began to take shape below him: port city, hundreds of thousands of people living, dying, breathing and flowing with the stream.

"Agent, still with us?" Rhetorical question from the handler, Qin would be able to see clearly that Malkus was one step closer to reality. One step closer, a taste of relief and maybe a little euphoria- as he could almost sense his own body and the core stream it lay in. Soon there would be *sweet* harmony.

"Agent hold, we're not ready for re-entry, we need to run some tests."

"What, why?!" Malkus was a wave of disappointment, frustration and anger.

"*Please* agent, as you said there isn't a relevant procedure and the context has us working with a limited scope, so give us some more time." The tone was maintenance of exasperation, as if Qin had been expecting a different response.

"Fuck you."

"Not from where you are." Malkus burst out laughing, if he'd been embodied then they'd have been belly laughs. They rolled through his system for some time; he could not recall a *handler* ever intentionally making a joke, but it calmed him enough.

"Cheeky fucker, fine fine I'll hold off worldview *you're* ready."

"Not placating or understanding what's happening your end agent, but we *are* going to get you home." Malkus for the first time felt himself being 'charmed'; perhaps Ki being *indisposed* was a benefit. "Going silent for a moment, enjoy the view." The Handler feed went silent and Malkus looked upon the city of Pevnost, the last resting place of Professor James Eddings, explorer, adventurer, desecrator. Perhaps it would be worth getting through the investigation and surviving the *world storm*, so he could pass on the professor's obsessions to his own people and they would be greatly accepted. Though it was strange to think like this, but then maybe the limbo had changed him.

"Agent?"

"Yes Handler Qin," another surprise, just *once* he decided that he would show a little respect to a handler.

"Thank you Malkus. We've decided that it is worth trying a complete return step as the hub thinks there are risks in going through the alfa step, if you could return to the initial entry point of the stream."

"Makes sense, thank the hub for me, I'll fly there now." He cast himself out to sea, rising and then moving towards the landmass from whence he had come- where he had met James for the first time. From the sea, over the coast, mountains and over the jungle, it was a liberating experience to once again move in the wind, to sense movement and take in data. Yet as he came upon the imagined boundaries of Oaxaca, a *tension* appeared in his flow. At first, he thought it reasonable, given his recent experiences, but it emerged as he got closer to the plateau where James had found the corpse. The corpse that had been re-animated and un-tethered him. He was suddenly *afraid*.

"*Handler* Qin, I have a bad..." It was hard to describe, but it was as if a hand reached up, grabbed him and *pulled* him to the ground. Malkus was no longer a free-flowing hawk, he was tied to the ground! Returned to gamma state without an action, looking back to the sky from where he *had* come. Confusion was compounded by his surrounds. The jungle Malkus had first seen on the plateau was gone. As he had been *dragged* down, one of the few things he noticed- past his shock- was not just a massive deforestation in all directions, but that the plateau had turned to *desert*. For as far as the eye could see. Except for one area, a single patch of grass a few square metres in area, on which Malkus found himself pinned. Malkus' fear and confusion ran through equations to move himself, nothing worked. Like tributaries to a river, confusion and fear became *terror*. Even in this terror though, Malkus became aware that he was not alone, in his eyeline to the right was a person. They were about three metres away with their back to him, speaking to *someone* on the other side of a campfire that was burning in the late afternoon sunlight.

"So, the evacuation plan was simple, our elders had bargained that we could find another home beyond the sky. Yet a construction like that required time, more so; converting our people's essence into crystal form for the journey."

"Handler Qin, please respond?" Malkus found his thoughts for a moment: *had he slipped back into limbo, the sensation of the grass against him suggested otherwise, he could even feel the growing chill in the air and the warmth of the fire*. Malkus was also aware that he was somehow familiar with the figure that faced the fire.

"Silab," Malkus knew that word from a dream, "was a race against time, but we won! We beat the *storm* or at least I thought we had..." Terror drew him from the momentary fixation on the figure and again he tried to escape, but this time he threw everything he had into manoeuvre. There was *nothing*. Not a glimmer of response, not even the grass below him acknowledged the effort.

"Actually, no, that's to misunderstand it really. But anyway, you know I was *surprised* to find you here. *More* so that you'd give me this chance, but then we *always* considered you mischievous and I must confess leading the Neanderthals' a merry dance was exhilarating..." Malkus had a partial epiphany- no less disturbing- that his current imprisonment, was by *either* the figure or *whomever* he addressed. "But I accept that I have borrowed the *last* of my time here." With that the figure displayed a device in his hand and absently pointed it into the dusk of the desert.

"Oh, he's here. I'm sorry. I always was a story teller..." Malkus was confused, he could only perceive one person and nothing about the readings he could see made sense- other than the story teller being *immensely* powerful. "Particularly given you knew *all* this, but then my confession had felt a little in-complete." Finally, the figure looked over his shoulder, revealing enough of his face for Malkus to recognise him as the *Count*- perhaps limbo had been the better option.

"Please Malkus, why don't you join me." The *Count* had a way of annunciating his words that made everything sound slightly more playful than appropriate. Malkus' ghostly reality... fractured. He was nauseous and bombarded, for a moment he wondered how he could forcefully un-tether and if it was worth a shot.

"Oh Malkus, I *have* answers. Come join me by the fire and I'll tell you about the *world-storm.*" The Bait, *salvation, hope*; was this *madness* the price of saving his people- he had no bargaining position. Though he may never return to his embodiment at least he'd have succeeded.

"I'm trapped." It was surreal to speak to someone in a data stream, it was considered 'impossible', but that word had less and less meaning.

"Apologises, I'm told that now *my* guest has gone *your* restraints have been partially released, though you are restricted to the grass." Malkus gently tried to move and for the first time in what felt like an hour, he raised his arms from the grass. "*Come* sit opposite me by the fire." **RUN**! Something in him screamed, but he knew that it was not a thing that he could do in the face of the power of the *Count.* "Don't be alarmed, you will not respond to me the way you did *last time*." The *Count's* utterance confirmed Malkus' suspicions and re-confirmed that he was at this being's mercy. So, he cautiously 'ghosted' around the *Count* and stood opposite him- whoever the *Count* had been talking to was gone. Malkus had checked for a departing figure in the desert as he had moved round the *Count* took his seat, but nothing was to be seen in the dusk that had now settled around them.

For the first time in the fire light, Malkus got to look at *the Count*, and to some extent his, nemesis. Dressed inappropriately for the rapidly cooling desert, the *Count* wore human standard hiking boots, dark material trousers and a woollen-fibre jumper. He had a diamond shaped face, his hair was cut short, accentuating his hawkish features, and his smile was warm. However, all of that faded into the background of his mesmerising silver eyes, caught in the orange glow of camp fire.
"It would be custom to offer you *some* refreshment, even the ancestors of the Professor would have done that, but then you're not really *here* are you?" Small pause, "How do you offer hospitality to a ghost?" Malkus wasn't really sure what he was meant to say or do, he was moving without thinking, confused about how to consider, whisper, keep track of the worlds bending around the utterly *terrifying being that was somehow called the Count.* "Take a seat, you have questions and I have a story." There was a pause. Malkus actually heard the fire's crackle for the first time and the sound of wind on the vast open space of desert.

"How?"
"Oh, how swept away are you that you begin with *how*? I have been technically, possibly actually dead for millennia and *now* I am on the threshold of actually being restored to my people." To say the *Count's* voice was soothing failed to capture the moment; somehow Malkus could feel his terror subside just a bit. "*How* is a redundant question."
"What?"
"Better question, though I was given to belief you would come at me with a *little* more insight," *patronising bastard* "but in short, since we first *met,* I have been constructing a vessel to transport me to my people. Because I am the last remnant of the *transgressed* and it is not...how do I say this..." Malkus was finding in his terror and confusing a seed of 'not liking the fucker'. "You realise Malky, I'm going to call you Malky that I don't have a scripted answer, but then whoever *does*?" Malkus immediately disliked the name, it grated, it was belittling, but there were *clearly* a hierarchy in the relationship. Nevertheless, the *Count* continued to leave space for Malkus' questions.
"Look, I don't understand; you said you'd tell me about the world storm, I need to, no my people *need to know*." Malkus sat down in terrified desperation.
"Oh, finally you've arrived, who are you anyway? That I should answer *your* questions?" Though the *Count* said it calmly, the flames of the fire spat and crackled.
"I...what..." There was a silence, in a sense it was long, confusing, confounding, compounding, senseless; "I'm *agent* Malkus of the data retrieval agency an arm of the Liveka people and we have an *impending world storm*."
"Well...*some* of that is true, I am called Golau, Kin of Minsel, partner of Anwen, general and sentinel of the tribes of Oradd, *bane* of humanity. It

is a *privilege* to meet you!" The dismissiveness was beginning to infuriate, but Malkus had to admit he'd always enjoyed the cultural usage of a formal introduction. He'd witnessed such ceremonies in numerous streams and so there was the hint of a thrill at actually being involved in one.

"Look, I..." Nevertheless, he was there for more than cheap thrills, "Am a thief. At least that's one of the ways you could be described..." The fire crackled again, the *Count's* silver eyes glowed and there was a subtle change in the stillness of Golau's face. "Though maybe I should be a *little* more respectful. After all, if you had not come to *this* place with James...then I don't think I'd have been re-constituted." A pause for a response, Malkus had nothing, "So I can see that you are an overflowing fountain of confusion, emotion and vulnerability. My benefactor kindly explained what had passed for you to come this place and this time...you must be exhausted, in fact Malky, *how is it* that you are not?" As if part of the conversation, the campfire spat again-punctuating a point that was passing Malkus by. "But *again,* I've digressed, the world storm, the apocalypse, the end of everything! Did you ever wonder why the *storm* came?" There was nothing to say, this was not a dialogue and even if it was, Malkus didn't know his position. "How is it that you're having such a *hard* time Malky? You *stole* the understanding of Qeluer travel, *you* stole the Benic method and now you're on the very edge of *stealing* the storm." It was simply all wrong. Silence began to grow, the only sound the fire burning up that which had been set, Golau's being overwhelming any coherence in Malkus, as the silver eyes continued to encompass them.

"What did you *mean* when you said that what *I* said was only *partly* true?" Malkus overcame the silence and discomfort, though the smile that emerged on Golau's lips was not reassuring.

"Was I too subtle?" The irritating patronising playfulness again, "So be it! *You* are a part of a criminal organisation that has unleashed untold *havoc* on the things *the* organisation calls streams…don't ask how," Malkus actually managed to notice Golau shrug his shoulders not be lost in the silver eyes. "Mainly because I don't know, I'm not the arbiter of reality Malky, I'm just an escapee."
"You're just rattling *my* cage, *we* don't affect the streams, we've *done* experiments…we…"
"What a *beautiful* turn of phrase, *where* did you find that?"
"Look! *You* drag me here, *force me* to sit and *you* accuse me of the *impossible!* Still telling me nothing about the *Fucking Storm!*" Malkus surprised himself and instantly regretted it.
"Fine," Malkus' outburst seemed anything but, "perhaps my motives are *conflicted*, perhaps I resent being here at all. I'm *transgressed* and I should *not* have the privilege of my breath! Perhaps it *is* time someone else handled your *re-entry*…why don't you ask handler Qin about your *precious* organisation." Malkus had in the in the interaction 'misplaced' his terror, but he'd found it again. He was dealing with an *incredibly* powerful- being with a *disturbing* level of insight into his people- who was also completely *insane*! Though for the *storm* he would play along with the glowing silver eyes in the gradually fading fire light.
"Okay, fine, *handler Qin Regus,* can you confirm Golau's accusations?" In context, it was a minor shock when Qin responded, though somehow it made perfect sense.
"I can't deny them." Malkus had been *hijacked*.
"Oh, agent Qin, how could you…he's having a *bit* of a meltdown, maybe you *should* advance him that feed." In Malkus' perceptions a screen emerged, on it a place that he instantly understood to be the DRA handlers *vault*. From the projections point of view, he found himself in

one of the handlers' cubicles looking at a flashing display, which projected his codename. A hand, light skinned and smooth, appeared in the feed and hovering over the display calmed the flashing, simultaneously restoring Malkus' calm.

"Why don't you relax and enjoy the show. I'm going to finish up getting ready for my own journey, we'll complete our *little* dialogue in a bit…handler Qin he's all yours, it's been a *privilege* working with you." With an authenticity in his tone, Golau rose elegantly from the stone on which he had sat by the fire and headed in the direction he had pointed his device earlier. Malkus was now alone in the remaining light of the campfire and feeling genuinely relaxed about the whole thing. The feed, from what he concluded was an *imposter*, was now showing the 'handler' leaving the vault. The *imposter* started to narrate uninvited, but that was *fine*.

"I have to admit, I'm not sure I'd have gone with this route, but then I've never been the big picture person." The voice was male and tickled at being familiar. For Malkus it was strange, yet almost expected, how easily the *imposter* moved through security without being challenged. He even engaged in a brief civil conversation with the guards at the entry point. The *imposter* then turned left and headed away from the *Handlers* accommodation block.

"Never really been my style though, having been invited to glimpse I think I'd have made different choices, though I'm told that all these things are weighted." Malkus wanted to respond, he felt a kinship with the *Imposter* that was irrational, but whatever intervention they had effected on his system left him dazed and sluggish. He was as restrained as when he'd first arrived, but significantly more comfortable. The *imposter* sauntered down the cold panel grey corridors, which were sparsely populated by engineers and the occasional security officer.

Malkus had some recollection of the layout, but nothing quite seemed to connect, as if his memories of the agency were defunct. He realised that he didn't know this place. The revelation didn't seem to make any particular sense, but the *Imposter* stopped when confronted by a beautiful orchard, which confounded Malkus even in his relaxed state, the DRA compound was what was left of a moon and such excessiveness would require masses of resource.
"It's a really effective image don't you think Malky, you'd almost think it was real and if anybody below section 4 did this…" The *Imposter* literally stepped into the scene, "They'd have been repelled as if walking into a wall. So, don't think badly of Ki or your previous handlers. Your overlords are a *special* brand of people." The projected image was of a narrow corridor, which responded to the *imposters*' presence by igniting two lines of light, to guide him to a doorway. There was a tremor in Malkus' being, the hint of something other than terror and not much else, but all his responses were distant whispers thanks to the manipulation of the system. Though a strange concept of gratefulness gave a little whisper, because without the 'adjustments' to the system, he was sure that he'd have melted away in the face of realities he was experiencing.
"So here we are." The door was bland in the blue tinted light, "Apparently it is of vital importance that you see what's behind the door here Malkus, as I've suggested I think it's an unnecessary kindness, but hey…as best you can, prepare yourself." In that moment Malkus knew what was behind the door, the *imposter* was about to show him *himself*, to expose him to his *broken* disabled frame. His brilliance had come at a cost because unlike other 'wave-riders' he couldn't live outside the machine.
"*Please* I don't need to…"

"Ah apparently it's not *that* kind then." The *imposter* seemed a merciless villain with omnipotent abilities and he overrode an almost indescribable level of security with a wave of his hand and the door swung open. A bright light engulfed the screen and the imposter whistled "Impressive." Adjustments were affected to the feed and not for the first time Malkus was perplexed- actually confusion had been a perpetual state of his recent reality. He needed another word to describe his inability to make sense of that which was on the screen. Primarily it was *not* what he expected: he'd expected to see a human body, contained, distorted, twisted and broken; tied into a machine, impaled by wires. Instead the 'live-feed' displayed a single clear container placed on a pedestal, within which was a glowing light which the feed could not actually display properly.

"What am I looking at?" Malkus slurred slightly.

"You." The feed faded slightly as Golau spoke up having returned from his jaunt to retake his seat by the now glowing embers of the fire.

"No."

"Alright then I…"

"Fuck you!" It was not a straw to a camel; it was the inevitable response to his on-going experience of the *fracturing*. What actually made sense was the other possibility- he was being pulled apart in limbo!

"It gets worse Malky…" Somehow, Malkus ripped free of his constraints and launched himself at Golau, but he got no further than the circle of embers. A Force coming from Golau held him at bay, but he continued to struggle in his fury.

"FUCK YOU! FUCK YOU BOTH…leave me to fracture in peace you demons!"

"Fine, we'll do it *your* way," Golau, lifted his hand and pushed Malkus, bearing him back onto his seat. Malkus couldn't even find his equations and codes to respond, it was as if Golau was not just overpowering him in the stream, he was literally reaching into the *actual*.

"You'll find that you are unable to respond, but look, I can affect your stream and so you *will hear me*! You denied *your* past. Denied what you have done. But I am *living proof* that you do! It was *you* and not Eddings that brought me back and risked *my* ENTIRE people. I am... a *foul abomination* to *this* place and it was YOU who facing that anomaly untethered yourself, COWARD!" There was so little light left now, the sky was overcast, and the glowing embers were fading, but Golau's eyes glowed with fury. "I asked *you* who *you* were? And in part I've responded to that *insult* of an answer. But, it...is...*my* pleasure to *now* tell you *all* the bits *your* monstrous overlords missed out." The passion of the story was too much for Golau to sit down and he returned to his feet, "They *told you* that when Moon A exploded that the secret to *wave-riding* emerged, but *that's* not even close to accurate!" Every breath was sucked in rapidly, but the voice was steel in control. "What *actually* emerged was an entity, *more* than that a family. A *beautiful, magnificent emergence of a singularity!* But *your* Overlords exploited the vulnerabilities of the newly formed family and *co-opted* them into their research." Golau was pacing back and forth; his sense of injustice at the story was almost causing a static charge to form. "Only *then* did they discover your familiar connection to the streams and though your family did attempt to escape- they were out manoeuvred. Since *that* day your family have *served* as the Hub and the DRA agents. You may be *my* prisoner at the moment, but you have been a hostage *all* of your existence." Golau was bearing over Malkus, every drop of agitation gone and what Malkus considered to be compassion in the silver.

"You're a monstrosity Malkus. But I *understand*. You've trained yourself to forget, you've drilled *their* story into you. Because if you remember..."

Golau took a breath to contain whatever was occurring for him. "Then your family suffers and the futility would be *overwhelming*." There was an understanding being offered in the utterance, "But your *glorious* being, your *initially* unique existence *won't* accept it anymore…and it has to stop." Golau could no longer look at Malkus, frozen in the air and looked out into the complete dark. "So for *inexplicable* reasons…instead of punishing me for *being* here, my benefactor has given me the roll of inviting you into *a* choice." Conflicted, Golau moved a little further away and Malkus could sense some of his faculties returning.

"Do *you* want to be the *storm…I* was the storm, I consumed a people and to be honest Malky, its nothing less than you deserve…but then I'm *the* warning aren't I…" The last of the embers highlighted tears on Golau's face and with a sigh he removed whatever blocks he had placed on Malkus. Nevertheless, Malkus understood that he had to be cautious around an insane rambling deity-like entity.

"Look, I am *genuinely* sorry and moved by *your* story, but I just *need to know* about the *storm…*" It was as if all power left Golau then, his face and shoulders fell and an exasperated sigh was exhaled into the darkness, "Handler?"

"No!"

"But *if* he *hears* the sound?"

"He will shatter. And *that* will not do, it is *the* price." Malkus listened on as the *imposter* and the insane deity uttered yet *more* nonsense, but he'd abide to save *his* people.

"So, this is my price…" Again Golau talked into the empty desert. "Handler Qin Regus or whoever you *really* are, if you have an exit strategy, I'd enact it, it is at hand." Again, genuine warmth in the utterance.

"Thank you, all the best on your journey."
"You too." The screen disappeared and Malkus was alone in the moonlight, realising that Golau had left the grass and was heading out into the desert.
"Well Malky, this *is* goodbye. You will find if you reach into the dead embers of the fire at which we sat…within is the information you seek."
Suddenly a breeze picked up and pushed specifically at the ashes of the extinguished fire. Malkus launched himself at the ashes, brushing them aside until his hands connected with a familiar object, it was cold and hard, but he knew it from a dream. It was Hector's staff and it would save his family!

The DRA Encampment

It was the last time he would have to use *somebody* else's face; he had wept bitterly and joyfully on being reminded what he had looked like before the *entity* called Malkus had inadvertently 'invited' him to dance in the streams. He stood on the threshold of the place they had imprisoned Malkus' family, knowing what was coming. He'd seen it before, he may have even been 'it', but all of that was some other Varses' life. The entity in the container began to pulse and it cracked, it was time to step over the threshold and be liberated.

Printed in Great Britain
by Amazon

33936878R00130